SECRETS
at the
IRISH ADOPTION HOUSE

BOOKS BY MICHELLE VERNAL

THE LITTLE IRISH VILLAGE SERIES
Christmas in the Little Irish Village
New Beginnings in the Little Irish Village
A Christmas Miracle in the Little Irish Village
Secrets in the Little Irish Village
Saving Christmas in the Little Irish Village

BRIDES OF BOLD STREET SERIES
The Dressmaker's Secret
The Dressmaker's Past
The Dressmaker's War
The Dressmaker's Chance

THE IRISH ADOPTION HOUSE SERIES
The Irish Adoption House

The Little Irish Farm

LOVE ON THE ISLE OF WIGHT SERIES
The Promise
The Letter

THE IRISH GUESTHOUSE ON THE GREEN SERIES
O'Mara's
Moira-Lisa Smile
What Goes on Tour

Rosi's Regrets

Christmas at O'Mara's

A Wedding at O'Mara's

Maureen's Song

The O'Maras in LaLa Land

Due in March

A Baby at O'Mara's

The Housewarming

Rainbows over O'Mara's

O'Mara's Reunion

The O'Maras Go Greek

Mat Magic at O'Mara's

Matchmaking at O'Mara's

Cruising with the O'Mara's

When We Say Goodbye

Staying at Eleni's

The Traveller's Daughter

Sweet Home Summer

SECRETS
at the
IRISH ADOPTION HOUSE

MICHELLE VERNAL

Bookouture

Published by Bookouture in 2025

An imprint of Storyfire Ltd.
Carmelite House
50 Victoria Embankment
London EC4Y 0DZ

www.bookouture.com

The authorised representative in the EEA is Hachette Ireland
8 Castlecourt Centre
Dublin 15 D15 XTP3
Ireland
(email: info@hbgi.ie)

ISBN: 978-1-80550-009-4
eBook ISBN: 978-1-80550-010-0

For my wonderful readers

PROLOGUE

The Irish sea was angry today, and the ferry rose up to teeter on the crest of the frothing waves, only to smash back down before bracing for the next one. Rain lashed the windows in the smoky saloon lounge on the upper deck of the boat where Cecelia, huddled against Lizzie, was trying not to let the stink of wet wool, bodies and tobacco suffocate her. Stewards skated past, managing to stay on their feet as they doled out basins and offered saltine crackers and hot lemon tea to those groaning that they were 'dying'.

It was too warm in here, Cecelia thought, fanning herself, her other hand rested on her small mound of belly. She'd grown used to bouts of nausea over these last months, but they were swift to pass, unlike the rising and falling queasiness she felt now. There'd be no respite either until the ferry butted up against the North Quay harbour wall in Dublin. 'How much longer, Lizzie?'

'Another half an hour CeeCee. Hang in there.'

Half an hour! It felt like a lifetime. This crossing had to be punishment for what she'd done in London. She closed her eyes and saw Hogan's cold, unflinching gaze. His parting threat echoed in her ears.

A word of advice, girl. Forget you were ever in London. If you've any sense, you'll disappear when you get back to Ireland. The arrangement we had means you don't get to decide when to leave the army, and if you so much as breathe a word about what you've been doing for the cause, then we'll find out, and there'll be consequences. It won't be the Brits you'll have to worry about either. It will be our boys at home. So if I were you, Lady Cecelia, I'd watch my back.

The Irish chauffeur employed by her uncle had, under duress, helped her and Lizzie flee London for Holyhead in the middle of the night. He'd only agreed to drive them when Cecelia had threatened to tell her uncle what else he got up to other than driving the Cathcart family about. Hogan didn't need to worry though. She was used to keeping secrets.

As the boat lurched violently, a low moan escaped her lips, and she rested her head on Lizzie's shoulder. She might have been employed by her mother as a lady's maid, but Lizzie had proved herself to be a dear friend. A friend who had the constitution of an ox and wasn't suffering from seasickness in the slightest.

Dear, dear Lizzie. If it wasn't for her, Cecelia knew she'd be making this terrifying journey into the unknown alone.

'I'm sorry it's come to this, Lizzie,' she murmured.

'Sure, don't be. I've no qualms leaving London. It wasn't for the likes of me, and I'll be glad to set my feet back down on Irish soil where I belong.'

She might belong, but Cecelia was no longer sure *she* did. That was her last coherent thought because she must have drifted off to sleep, waking to Lizzie nudging her.

'We're here, CeeCee. We're home.'

Cecelia roused herself, eager to get off this wretched boat. After picking up their suitcases, she and Lizzie joined the queue of equally desperate passengers waiting for the gang-plank to go down.

Her fear over what lay ahead must have shown in her face because Lizzie linked her arm through hers. 'We'll be all right you know, whatever happens. We've just got to stick to the plan.'

The best laid plans of mice and men, ran through Cecelia's mind because theirs was a rough plan at best with Lizzie having heard through a cousin about a home for unwed mothers in Dublin. St Patrick's was a place where girls in Cecelia's predicament could find refuge. She'd be safe there from not just Hogan and his lot but her mother too, given she was Anglo Irish and not Catholic like the sisters who ran it. No one would think of looking for her in such a place. So their plan, such as it was, had Cecelia throwing herself on the mercy of the nuns until she'd borne the babe.

As the line shuffled forward, she set her jaw determinedly, making a vow to her unborn child. *No matter what, I won't let anyone hurt you, and I won't let my mother find you and take you away.* Yet even as she formed the promise, Cecelia could feel Lady Kildurran's long arm reaching out across the Irish sea toward her.

PART ONE

1

———————

DUBLIN, IRELAND, 1985

Cecelia sometimes felt as though she'd lived nine lives in her eighty-something years. She'd been an unloved daughter, a debutante and a spy, a blackmailer and a fallen woman, a mother then a wife too, a granny and now a great-grandma. She'd been lost and alone, heartbroken, happy and loved. Her life had not been an easy one, but there were those who'd had it harder, and no one could ever say her journey had been dull.

She likened the years that had passed in the blink of an eye to a patchwork quilt not quite finished. Some squares were colourful, others grey. There was more colour than not, she thought, grateful for that as she gazed out the car window, watching the sea of tightly packed brick houses spooling past. They all had net curtains hanging in their front windows and handkerchief-sized front gardens.

'Heavens to Betsy! These roads are so narrow.'

Cecelia jumped. She'd been lost in her thoughts and looked to where the sides of the road were lined with cars.

'I remember a time when it was ponies and traps ambling down these streets,' she mused.

'Give me a horse any day over this tin can of a car the hire company loaned us. I feel off-kilter driving on the left-hand side too,' came a further lament from behind the steering wheel.

Cecelia tuned out the rest of the mutterings. She could still hardly believe she was here. Ireland was somewhere she'd never thought she'd return to, and especially not at this time of life, but if not now, then when? Or so the argument had gone when she'd first got wind that St Patrick's Mother and Baby Home was to be demolished. The site where there'd been so much sorrow would be developed, though the home wouldn't close but rather relocate.

There wouldn't be another time to go back and see it, she'd been told, to which she'd retorted she'd no desire to revisit her past.

'It's not just your past though, is it?' had been lobbed back at her, and there hadn't been much Cecelia could say to that. It was true.

'Stare down your demons,' she'd been advised.

Cecelia could never say no to a challenge.

And so with a little more gentle persuasion and a promise that the horses back home at the equestrian centre she still liked to keep a finger in would be fine in her absence, she'd agreed to come on this journey. No, not a journey. This was a pilgrimage. There would be graves to visits and flowers to lay, goodbyes to be said, but first they were to return to the building with its echoing corridors that still haunted her dreams from time to time.

Soon, the road had opened up and they were passing by the high stone wall surrounding Phoenix Park. There was greenery rising above it, overseen by a stone-coloured sky. Cecelia wasn't sure where she'd heard there were deer roaming freely in the park. Perhaps it was the chatty girl on the front desk of the hotel where they were staying. She'd have liked to have visited, but there was no time for that today. They might manage an hour or two to explore before they flew home in a few days.

Home.

Strange to think this country had once been hers. Her life in America, with its wide-open skies, was vastly different. Everything was bigger, cars included for one! Home wasn't a place, in Cecelia's opinion, but another word for family, and she knew she could live anywhere so long as she had hers with her. Although her children did drive her batty with their fretting and fussing these days. Getting old wasn't for the faint-hearted, she thought, not for the first time.

The vista quickly grew more industrial, with smatterings of open farmland in between housing estates, until there it was. Tucked away from the eyes of the world by imposing walls, just as she and all the other girls and their babies who'd resided there had been.

They pulled up outside the main gates, open today, and Cecelia eased herself out of the car, using her walking stick to right herself. Her leg ached terribly in the damp weather Dublin had showered on them, although it had cleared for now. She forgot about that, however, as she breathed the familiar but foreign scent of drifting turf-fire smoke and stepped toward the gates.

Ahead, near the entrance at the end of a long sweep of drive, she could see her friend, so she waved. It was time for her to sew the last pieces of her quilt. What colour for closure? Cecelia wondered, no longer a forgotten or fallen woman, as she held her head high and made her way through the gates and into a mineshaft of memories.

2

IRELAND, 1920

The tang of salt was sharp in eighteen-year-old Cecelia's nostrils, but so was the stench of poverty as she walked through a neighbourhood she'd never imagined stepping foot in. She was making her way down a soot-stained street near the North Wall docks, where warehouses were jammed in beside houses, and railway lines ferried coal and goods unloaded by the dock workers who lived here.

The church she was standing outside was like this pocket, worn down by the hardships of life. Cecelia, christened an Anglican, hesitated with her hand resting on the heavy oak door of this Catholic house of God. She was aware that once she pushed it open and stepped over the threshold, there would be no going back.

Taking a deep breath in, the air of the church cool and clear, she steadied herself and went to see the priest, Father Brophy, in his cluttered and rather dirty sacristy. He flapped his hand toward a chair, and she sat down while he stood over her, asking if she wished to join the one true faith. To which she replied she did.

'For love, for land or to save your immortal soul?'

'To save my immortal soul.' Cecelia refused to blush with shame about her condition, which was becoming more obvious by the day, and she'd already confessed why she wished to convert and needed his help. Still he ran through the patter with her answering as and when required until he gave a satisfied grunt. 'You'll need to confess now, Cecily, so repeat after me: "Forgive me, Father, for I have sinned. This is my first confession."'

'Cecelia.'

'God knows who ye are. Now repeat and confess.' He looked at her expectantly.

Cecelia decided that she couldn't risk saying everything that had happened this year. Even before this man of God. Lying to the priest was hardly the worst thing she'd done, after all.

If he didn't believe her, Father Brophy said nothing, until it was time for him to mutter something unintelligible in Latin and make the sign of the cross over her head. Then he indicated she should stand. She watched warily as he took two steps toward the lopsided font near the door and ladled up the holy water.

'Bow your head, child.'

Cecelia did so, bracing herself for what she guessed was coming next.

'*Ego te baptizo in nomine Patris, et Filii, et Spiritus Sancti,*' Father Brophy muttered before dumping the water over her head.

'Oh!' The cold water was still a shock as it trickled down her neck and traced a route down her spine.

'There. That's you. All done, child. You're one of us now, Cecelia Shanahan.'

The good father returned to his desk and opened a drawer, fetching a worn rosary which he passed to her, so he didn't notice her delayed reaction to her assumed name.

'I'll be able to deliver you to the St Patrick's Mother and

Baby Home without the sisters asking too many questions now, as requested.' He cleared his throat, looking at the envelope she'd placed on his desk – half of what they had agreed while arranging her baptism. The other half would come when he collected her tonight. 'And your donation will help fund new hymn books for the congregation.'

The thirsty gleam in his eyes and the whisky fumes on his breath hadn't convinced her the mouldy old books would be replaced any time soon, and wondering if it would go on drink or at the bookies, she closed the door on his inner sanctum. She'd wondered how she might feel once she'd become a Catholic, but upon stepping outside the church found nothing had changed. Her chin lifted skyward, though she was unsure what she expected to see. An angel perched on a cloud applauding her perhaps? Of course, there were only clouds scudding past.

As she'd known they would, the hours until she was to make her way back through the priest's stomping ground to the agreed pick-up spot near the church had crawled by. At last, though, here she was, keeping her head down and doing her best to ignore her jitteriness because it didn't pay to show weakness, and as such, Cecelia summoned her most haughty glare, fixing it on a man with cheeks blackened by coal dust. He was leering at her, and she was gratified when he looked away first.

The unsavoury neighbourhood wasn't what had her nerves jangling though; rather, she was worried that the drunkard priest would have forgotten their arrangement. If he wasn't waiting for her this evening as arranged, she didn't know what she'd do. There was no other plan.

Rounding the corner, she felt the knot between her shoulder blades loosen just a notch because through a gap in the heads weaving down the pavement ahead of her, she caught sight of Father Brophy's thin form.

As she drew closer, she saw his cassock was as creased as
he was.

He clambered up onto the bench seat of a trap with a
brown-and-white pony attached and picked up the reins. Terrified he'd leave without her, Cecelia raised one hand, then
swapped the suitcase she was carrying to that hand, held her
belly with the other and started to run. Whether he'd seen her
or not, she was clambering onto the bench seat next to him
within a matter of seconds, commenting on how pretty the pony
attached to the trap was in between catching her breath.

'She's on loan from an obliging parishioner,' the priest said,
blasting her with whisky fumes. His eyes were bloodshot and
his jowly jaw stubbled.

'Grand. I wasn't sure how we'd get there.'

'I said I'd have things in hand, child.'

'You did. I should have more faith, Father. I've brought the
remainder of your donation as a thank you.'

She pulled out the envelope, and it disappeared in amongst
the pleats of his cassock.

'Bless you, child. That will help fill the parish coffers.'

Father Brophy flicked the reins and asked as they set off,
'How'd you get that limp? Polio, was it?'

'Yes.' She examined her hands, surprised he was only asking
her now. Her limp was a permanent hangover from a childhood
fight with the disease, but she refused to let it slow her down.
The moment the brace had been removed when she was four
years old, she'd made her mind up it wouldn't hold her back.
And nor would the opinions of those around her. As such, she'd
developed a style of movement whereby she swung her hip a
certain way, enabling her to move swiftly when need be. Her
unusual gait caused people to stare on occasion, but she didn't
care. For her mother, however, this had been an intense source
of embarrassment.

Father Brophy began humming a tune, and Cecelia's mind

retraced the footsteps that had brought her to the working-class enclave by the docks exactly one month to the day since she and Lizzie had arrived back in Dublin with Cecelia's ill-gotten gains – funds acquired by illicit means. The stash of money was being eked out for lodgings at Lizzie's aunt's house and to grease the palm of the priest Lizzie's cousin had said would help Cecelia with the predicament she was in.

A tidy sum would be left over and tucked away for when she needed it to make a fresh start after the baby was born. She'd made her mind up not to keep it, given how impossible her situation was. She couldn't spend the rest of her life in Ireland watching their backs, and trying to leave the country with a baby would make her vulnerable when she'd need to be strong. So she'd ensure the little one went to a good and loving home, then she'd leave Ireland for America and put all that had happened here and in London behind her.

A particularly violent bump as the trap rattled over the heaving cobbled streets saw her grasp the bench seat as her anxiety quickly returned. The good father's humming was now a full-blown, boisterous hymn, and it had become apparent she was at the mercy of an inebriated priest who had no business being in charge of a pony and trap. To keep him alert, she peppered him with questions as to what the home he was taking her to was like, but he was intent on finishing his ode to God, much to the amusement of the pedestrians they clattered past.

So intent was she on being ready to take the reins if Father Brophy's head began to loll and ensure they stayed on the road, she barely registered any of the unfolding scenes around them and was unprepared when the pony was brought to a standstill outside an imposing set of gates.

3

———

ST PATRICK'S MOTHER AND BABY HOME, 1920

'This is it, child – St Patrick's Mother and Baby Home. You can open those gates for me and don't bother closing them behind me. I won't be here long enough for that.'

Cecelia clambered down before wrestling with the catch and pushing the gates aside. She glanced toward the sea of brick at the end of the drive. The rambling buildings were foreboding, with windows she imagined full of disapproving nuns peering out to see who the new arrivals were. It was a far cry from the likes of London's swanky Claridge's or The Savoy, which she'd frequented once upon a time.

'It looks like a prison.'

She didn't realise she'd spoken her thoughts out loud until Father Brophy cheerily replied.

'It started out as a workhouse until the Sisters of Bon Secours moved in.'

Once she was seated next to him again, he geed the pony, and as they drew closer, trepidation at what lay ahead for her was heightened by a lonely crow cawing their arrival. It felt like an omen.

Cecelia thought of Lizzie, wishing she were here with her.

As it was, her dire need of help, given her condition, had seen her drag her mother's lady's maid and her loyal friend away from London's bright lights and back here, to Ireland.

Lizzie had told her she was prideful and selfish once; childish had been in the mix too. Cecelia had protested at the time. She'd spent her life rallying against the privileged house she'd been born into, and as Lizzie knew, she'd not had an easy time of it growing up with the intense dislike of her mother hanging over her. But when she'd asked her to flee London with her, she'd wondered if perhaps she had a point after all. Lizzie had been happy in her new role in a posh London house as a lady's maid, and now, presumably, she was back with her mam in a tumbledown cottage in the tiny village of Kildurran, betrothed to a man she didn't love.

A spell in a mother and baby home was the only option the two of them had been able to come up with for Cecelia's immediate future, but now, staring at the building where she would spend the next four and a half months, she feared coming here was a mistake.

You must stay positive, Cecelia, she told herself. While the adoption house, as she and Lizzie referred to it, appeared grim, she had to hold on to the fact that inside she'd receive food, shelter and help birthing the baby. And no one would know her, or whom and what she was running from.

'C'mon on down with you, child.'

She took Father Brophy's outstretched hand then hauled her own case off the back of the trap, holding it tightly as she followed him to a door. The crow cawed a second time as the priest raised the knocker and rapped twice. Despite everything she'd just told herself, Cecelia felt her knees begin to knock uncontrollably. She had a bad feeling. Inside, approaching footsteps sounded, and the prickling at the back of her neck screamed at her to leave now while she still could.

She heard the bolt sliding across the door and tugged at

Father Brophy's cassock sleeve. 'Father, perhaps I could come and live with you as a housekeeper until the baby's born. You must know a good family the child could go to, and I'm a hard worker.'

She'd never worked a day in her life, and her only experience of running a household was trailing after Lizzie as she went about her duties at her family home, Foxbourne House. She was also dubious as to what sort of home Father Brophy would find the baby. She'd seen his parish, after all. Still, right then she didn't care. It was survival of the fittest, and it wasn't damned well fair she'd been left to bear the brunt of a tryst, while the man she thought loved her got to walk away scot-free.

Father Brophy shook her off. 'This is where you belong, child. You'll repent and atone for your fall. It's for the best now.'

'But I've changed my mind. I don't want to stay here after all.' She stumbled backward, panic swelling as Father Brophy hissed at her not to be causing a scene.

The heavy door inched open, and Cecelia froze agog at the sight of a petite nun with a white headdress unlike anything she'd seen. It made her look like a seagull in flight. She also registered how sweet and innocent her face was. She was quite beautiful.

'Yes?'

'Good evening, Sister.' Father Brophy sounded surprisingly sober. 'This is Cecelia Shanahan. She's confessed her sins and comes to do penance under your care. I entrust her into your capable hands.' He produced a piece of paper from his person and pressed it on the sister, who wrinkled her nose – presumably at the boozy whiff he was giving off.

Cecelia might have been marginally comforted that an ogre hadn't been on the other side of that door, but she still felt trepidation. 'But, Father, I told you I've changed my mind. I'm sorry to have wasted your time, Sister.'

'You should have thought of that before you offended against chastity.' There was a flintiness in the priest's whisky-addled eyes as, his job done, he turned his back on her and weaved back to the pony and trap.

'Get inside, child.' The nun, whose voice was as melodic as she was pretty, lunged forward, grabbed Cecelia by the arm and half dragged her in through the door.

It threw Cecelia off-kilter because her cadence and angelic face were at odds with her actions, and she was surprisingly strong.

As the door clanged shut, the nun selected a key from the large bunch she was holding. Hearing the lock click before the door was bolted, Cecelia knew her first impression had been correct. She'd entered a prison, and she had a four-and-a-half-month sentence to serve.

The stench of lye burned her nostrils as the nun affixed the bundle of keys to her belt.

'I'm Sister Agnes. Follow me.'

When Cecelia didn't move, transfixed by her surroundings, Sister Agnes grasped hold of her forearm so hard it hurt.

'You're hurting me.' Cecelia tried to wriggle free of her grip.

The sister's jaw tightened, and sneering that she wasn't helping herself, she yanked Cecelia toward an ajar door. Inside was a room that managed to be cramped, even though its only furnishings were a desk and two chairs, the white walls bare but for a crucifix. A connecting door was open just enough to reveal a storage space beyond, its shelves laden with neatly folded clothing and shoes. There were also a few worn carpet bags, several leather satchels and small battered cases, along with shawl knapsacks tied with twine. Alarm twinged at the thought of her belongings being taken from her.

The sister released her arm, and Cecelia rubbed at the spot where her fingers had dug in. How could the room feel so cold even though the waning sunlight of a summer's day still filtered through the single window? she wondered.

The unsmiling sister took her place behind the desk and gestured for Cecelia to sit down opposite her. She did so, feeling the sharp wooden edge of the seat digging into the back of her thighs through the fabric of her skirt. It only served to add to her discomfort.

The nun took her time smoothing out the crumpled paper Father Brophy had handed to her and read over it slowly. There was something about her that warned Cecelia not to cross her. She was beautiful, yes, but like Cecelia's mother, her beauty was marred by razor-sharp edges. When she'd finished with the paper, she slid the fat ledger in the corner of the desk over, opening it before she dipped the nib pen in the inkwell. She blotted it carefully before snapping, 'Name.'

'Cecelia Shanahan.' It was right there in front of her, written on the paper Father Brophy had supplied her with, but she didn't say this out loud. In the plan she'd hatched with Lizzie, they'd decided it would be better to pretend she was a widow, instead of a girl with no clue as to where the father of her baby might be. The name Shanahan had been chosen because it belonged to Tomas, who'd been a dear friend to her but whom she'd let down badly.

'And you're widowed, you say?'

'Yes, Sister.'

'What was your maiden name?'

Cecelia hesitated, almost giving her true family name. She couldn't be too careful where her mother especially was concerned, not after everything she'd done. 'Ayles— Aylesford.'

The nib scratched across the page, Sister Agnes pausing every now and again to dip the pen once more. Cecelia couldn't see what she was writing but assumed it was a record of her admittance here. The fact this arrangement was being formalised saw her clasp her hands tightly, and she fidgeted. Her bladder was uncomfortably full, a common occurrence these days.

'And how is it you became lame?'

Cecelia's head snapped up – it was only the second time she'd been asked that question in the space of an hour. 'I had polio as a young child, Sister. But I have never allowed the affliction to hold me back in any way.'

This was jotted down, and at last Sister Agnes closed the ledger. The thud of the weighty tome closing sent dust motes sailing up into the air. 'You're to address my fellow sisters here as "Sister" and the Reverend Mother as "Mother".'

'Yes, Sister.'

'The rules at St Patrick's are simple. Silence, obedience, prayer and work. You don't speak unless spoken to.'

'Yes, Sister,' Cecelia repeated.

'You're to hand over any personal items as well as your case. They'll be returned to you upon your departure from St Patrick's.'

'I've nothing on me, just this case. And I'd rather keep it with me, if you don't mind.' Cecelia picked up the leather case with its brass clasps and held it to her. Inside were some basic items of clothing and toiletries, easily replaceable. The remainder of all the money she had in the world, however, was not. Currently stashed inside a stocking and rolled up in a skirt, it was her ticket to freedom once the child was born.

Sister Agnes stood up, glowering over Cecelia. For a short woman, she seemed awfully tall.

'Hand it to me this minute.'

Cecelia hugged the case tighter to her. 'I'm sorry, Sister, but there are deeply personal items inside it. I wish to keep it with me. Surely that isn't an unreasonable request?'

The shove was so hard and fast, all Cecelia had time to

register was one minute she was seated in the chair, the next splayed on the ground in an undignified sprawl, still clutching her case. She'd smacked her head, but any pain or injury was masked by shock. A warm sensation spread slowly beneath her, and for a moment she wondered if she'd lost the baby. Then she realised she'd opened her bladder.

Sister Agnes came round from her desk and wrenched the case from Cecelia's grip, setting it aside before she bent over her with a curled lip and snarled, 'Look at you, wallowing in your own filth like an animal. Sure, for all your plummy vowels and fine clothes, you're no better than the rest of them. A dirty, filthy, disgusting girl and a liar too. I don't believe your story for a second. There'll be no special treatment for you here, and don't you go forgetting that. Now get up.'

Sister Agnes stepped through to the storage room with her case, leaving Cecelia alone. Somehow, she hauled herself to her feet. Her skirt clung wetly to her legs, and shame at being able to smell herself washed over her. She gently touched the back of her head, feeling an egg-sized lump there. Right then, she didn't care whether God was Anglican or Catholic, only that He listened while she sent up a prayer that the rest of the sisters weren't like Sister Agnes and that her money remained undiscovered.

The nun returned with a pile of clothes, a pair of well-worn boots balanced on top of them, then set them down on the chair. 'Put those on. Then I'll take you to the Reverend Mother.'

If Cecelia hoped for a little privacy as she stripped out of her wet things, then she didn't get it. Sister Agnes stood in the doorway watching her, and Cecelia sensed she was just waiting for another reason to strike. The foreign underwear and smock she slipped on felt scratchy against her skin, but at least they were dry, and she pulled the cardigan over the top, wondering how many other girls had worn these items before her.

'Hurry up,' Sister Agnes fumed as Cecelia fumbled with the

boot laces, but finally she stood up. They were clown boots, far too big and clumpy for her, but she wouldn't speak up because Cecelia was beginning to understand that was the point – to make her uncomfortable.

'Follow me.'

She was told to wait on a wooden bench outside the Reverend Mother's office as the nun knocked then waited.

A voice called back, 'Enter,' and Sister Agnes disappeared inside the office.

Cecelia's eyes lit upon a small statue of the Virgin Mary on a pedestal near the foot of a staircase, and the sight of her serene and sorrowful made her sad. The sadness evaporated when the door burst open, and she sat to attention.

'The Reverend Mother will see you now.'

Sister Agnes swept off, and Cecelia hesitated in the doorway of the office.

'Come in, child,' an impatient voice sounded.

Cecelia stepped inside and pulled the door to behind her. The Reverend Mother's room, although austere like the one she'd just left, was softened by a floor rug. It also had a filing cabinet near a larger window which let in considerably more light, and the room was warmer too. A portly woman with a selection of chins over the top of her wimple was seated in a high-back chair at a desk strewn with paperwork. Behind her, an image of Jesus, his hands outstretched, and a crucifix clung to the wall. She was sipping a cup of tea and peered over the top of her spectacles, sizing Cecelia up.

For her part, Cecelia sought a glimmer of kindness in the lined face, though the deep vertical grooves either side of thin wrinkled lips told her not to get her hopes up.

''Tis an unusual path that's brought you to us.'

'Yes, Mother.' Cecelia took her enquiring gaze to be her cue to explain. 'My family has an estate a mile or so from Rush.' She referenced the closest town. 'They didn't approve of my marrying a Catholic and disowned me. My husband was shot and killed recently fighting for Ireland, and I've nowhere else to go.'

'His family wouldn't take you in?'

'No, Mother. They didn't approve of his match.'

'Yet you don't wear a ring, and no marriage certificate has been supplied here with your paperwork. And if what you say is true, then you are certainly guilty of the sins of pride and disobedience.'

Cecelia trotted out her rehearsed lines. 'I pawned my wedding ring to pay for lodgings, Mother. I was desperate, and my marriage certificate was stolen from me along with other belongings.'

'Enough, child. I also think you sin against truth.'

'Mother, I—'

'Silence. I believe you're here because you chose to commit a grave offence against purity and now you must seek forgiveness through penance.'

Cecelia said nothing, digging her nails into her palms. To answer back was in her nature. A trait her mother had tried unsuccessfully to knock out of her. But she sensed the Mother Superior would have no qualms meting out punishment if she were to argue the point, and her head hurt. The memory of her wet underclothes was still raw too. It was better to remain silent.

'As such, you must forget the life you led outside these walls. Not only that but as a sign of your intention to repent and to seek a fresh start in the eyes of God, you will take a new name. From this day forth, you will be called Margaret. Your former name will no longer be used. Do you understand, Margaret?'

'Yes, Mother.' Another lie to keep track of. But if it kept her safe, it would be worth it surely.

Standing there, she resolved to keep her head down and stay out of bother. *Four and a half months, Cecelia, that's all,* she told herself. *Stick to your own company – which shouldn't be hard. And then you can become someone entirely different to Cecelia Shanahan, Cecelia Aylesford, Margaret... or even Cecelia Altringham.*

The lady, the lover... the spy and the blackmailer.

The one who'd got into this mess in the first place.

4

'Hello there. I'm Sister Louise. What's your name, child?'

How odd to be called 'child' by a woman who wasn't much older than herself, Cecelia thought, emerging from the Reverend Mother's office to find a different nun waiting for her. She was in complete contrast to Sister Agnes – plump with a warm smile for one thing, and her tone was kindly with a soft country lilt. Cecelia liked the woman instantly, relieved to see no bitter judgment in Sister Louise's brown button eyes.

'Cecelia – I mean Margaret.' She wondered where Sister Louise hailed from but didn't like to ask given the no-speaking-unless-spoken-to rule.

'Margaret. Sure now, that's a lovely name. Don't I have a younger sister called Margaret? I do miss her. Do you have a sister?'

Cecelia nodded, doing her best not to retort that it might be a lovely name, but it certainly wasn't hers. She didn't want to get offside with this nun who was trying to be welcoming. 'Just the one. Beatrice.'

'You sound like a young lady of breeding with that voice. It could cut crystal,' Sister Louise said, a note of surprise evident in her voice.

Cecelia didn't know how to reply. There was no point repeating a story dismissed as lies by Sister Agnes and the Reverend Mother. She worried how she was to hide where she'd come from – especially from the other girls – when her voice was clearly going to set her apart.

Sister Louise didn't press her, simply saying, 'Well, we're all God's children. Come with me now and I'll show you to St Mary's dormitory where you're to sleep. I'm afraid you've missed tea – it's served at five o'clock sharp – and I'd fetch you a plate, only I'd get my hand slapped if I was caught in the kitchen helping myself.'

She chattered on, slowing down halfway up the stairs when she noticed Cecelia's limp, though she didn't remark on it. 'The girls are just finishing their evening prayers. It's lights out at eight as you'll be up at the crack of dawn. But, sure, you'll soon settle into the routines here.'

It would still be light at eight, Cecelia thought, relieved that this nun was aware of what a shock arriving here must be for newcomers.

The kindly sister was puffing by the time they reached the top of the stairs and took a moment to catch her breath before leading Cecelia down the length of corridor. White paint flaked off walls, speckles of mould decorated the ceilings, and the linoleum floor had patches of old soap visible where it had been scrubbed. There were unidentifiable smells that made her feel ill too, and she remembered Father Brophy saying St Patrick's was a former workhouse. A shiver coursed through her as she imagined the poor souls who'd gone before her.

The sounds of the home seemed magnified in the silence. A door closed somewhere, followed by quick footsteps, then Cecelia became aware of the distant sound of communal prayer, but in the background she realised, listening hard, were the faint cries of babies. A trickle of foreboding dripped down her spine because how could babies be brought into a place like this where the building was decaying around them?

'The washroom is in there.' Sister Louise flapped her arm in the general direction of an open door with an even stronger stench of disinfectant than that which had first assailed Cecelia's nostrils when she'd arrived.

She caught a glimpse of a line of sinks and toilets with rust around the old iron taps. Rust was also making its mark in the chipped enamel of the sinks, while there were pools of yellow-brown beneath the pipes too. Her nose wrinkled at the thought of having to wash in here.

'Here we are, Margaret – this is you.'

Sister Louise pushed open the door to a dormitory, and Cecelia stretched her neck to see over her shoulder. There was row upon row of little iron beds all neatly made with a blanket folded at the end. The windows were high above the beds, and as she wandered between the lines of cots, she became aware of the lingering smell of bodies and night breath crammed together in close quarters.

'You'll be sleeping here.' Sister Louise came to a standstill nearer the far end of the dormitory in front of an unmade bed.

The mattress bore the stains of its previous occupant, and she felt utterly lost at the thought of sleeping in a communal space, certain, too, she'd be covered in flea bites within minutes of laying her head down. St Patrick's – and this dormitory she was to share with women from Lord only knew what sort of backgrounds – was not somewhere she belonged. Unease filled her.

The sister's innocent features turned furtive, then she glanced back toward the door before thrusting her hand into the pocket of her habit. She pulled out a chunk of bread. 'It's not much, but it will help stave off the hunger pangs until morning.'

Cecelia hadn't realised until then how famished she was, and she took it gratefully, heartened by the kindness. 'Thank you, Sister.'

She leaned toward her and whispered, 'That's to be our secret now.'

'Yes, Sister.'

What did she want in return? Cecelia wondered, unused to acts of kindness for the simple sake of being kind.

'You'll find your nightgown in that lot there.' Sister Louise pointed to the small pile on the bed and gave her an encouraging smile. 'Put everything in the basket under your bed – it's numbered – and I'll give you a hand to make it, then I'll leave you to settle in. Sure, you'll be grand. Just keep your head down and follow the other girls' lead.'

'Thank you, Sister Louise.' She dug out the basket and put everything in it, then with the flap of a sheet, she was shown how to tuck the corners before Sister Louise gave her a pleased smile and left her to it.

Cecelia bit into the bread, not wanting the nun who felt like an ally to leave her alone here. She ate quickly, mindful of the other girls' imminent return. The bread was dry, sticking in her throat and making her thirsty, but she didn't dare go in search of a cup of water. Instead, she sat on the bed, unsure what to do next, then a noise saw her straighten, putting her on high alert. It was a thudding sound, and it was drawing closer, she realised, then it dawned on her – what she was hearing was an army of marching footsteps.

She brushed the crumbs off her front and quickly changed into her nightgown, folding her clothes and placing them in the basket which she pushed back under the bed. As she clambered between threadbare sheets, she tried to put the stains she'd seen on the mattress from her mind, not wanting to think about how many bodies before hers had lain on its sagging straw. Her hand flapped about and grasped hold of the thin blanket before she pulled it over top of her. *Please let it not be lice ridden.*

She'd no wish to talk to any of the other girls who'd found themselves in this terrible place. Cecelia knew she'd have nothing in common with them, and she hadn't come here to make friends. One thing this past year had taught her was that she couldn't trust anybody, Lizzie being the exception. Besides, Cecelia wasn't one for friends. Her limp set her apart from others, and the distaste she'd glimpse in the eyes of her peers had put her on guard. She'd let her defences slip around Foxbourne's staff, however, and had been fond of Cyril, the gardener; Tomas, the stablehand, whose last name she'd borrowed; and Lizzie, the housemaid and her dear confidante of course.

She didn't much like people, preferring the company of her horse. It would not be hard to keep herself to herself while she was at St Patrick's, given she'd been doing so her whole life. So she squeezed her eyes shut and pretended to be asleep.

'No talking and modesty at all times,' an authoritative voice snapped from the far end of the dormitory, then Cecelia heard the clumping of ill-fitting boots on a creaking floor all around her.

She risked a peek, and the sight of a young girl barely old enough to have started her courses with an enormous rounded belly horrified her. What sort of people was she to be surrounded by?

It was worse than she'd thought. The girls, some women, were of varying ages, but they all had a common denominator. Hollow eyes and slumped shoulders. They looked defeated.

Across from her, a waif-like girl with dark hair caught her looking. She was different from the others, Cecelia saw, because a lively spark danced in her deep brown eyes when she caught her looking. Cecelia snapped her eyes closed once more.

There was a collective whisper and rustling of material, a

scraping of baskets being fetched out from under beds, and finally the groaning of iron bed frames as their occupants climbed in and curled up.

'Silence until morning. Remember God is all-seeing.' The stern words were followed by receding footsteps.

What did God think when he saw this place then? Cecelia thought, every muscle tensed as all around her, unfamiliar breathing sucked the air. Someone began to cry, trying to muffle the noise with their mattress but not succeeding, and it was distressing.

'Shush, Mol.'

'I want my mammy, Nessa.'

'Sure, you'll see her again soon. I'll look after you in the meantime.'

'You heard Sister – God's all-seeing. You'll both be for it in the morning,' another voice, further away from the other two, spoke up.

The sobs continued, and Cecelia covered her ears, but she could still hear them.

'What's your name?' a voice whispered.

Was she talking to her? Cecelia uncovered her ears and raised her head to see the girl with the dark hair and eyes propped up on one elbow, staring over at her.

'I'm Nessa, but the big bonnets call me Jillian.'

Cecelia lay back down, saying nothing, and eventually heard Nessa give a huff. All the while, the girl called Mol continued to sob. The odd cough and parp of breaking wind filled the passing minutes, and Cecelia rolled onto her back and stared up at the windows, willing darkness to hurry up and fall.

Mol's tears eased as she slipped into sleep, and gradually the crinkling of the straw mattresses ceased as the other girls' breathing became more even or turned into gentle snores. Still Cecelia lay awake, aware of a scratching and scurrying behind the walls that made her grimace. The mattress was lumpy and coarse, so far removed from her spacious and comfortable bed at home, but it wasn't wishing for her old material comforts that was keeping her up. Her mind was racing, taking her back to when she felt she could still trust people. To when she'd had friends – and more. To the thrill of the chase and stolen kisses at Foxbourne and to the man with the flashing dark eyes and hair she'd given her heart to.

5

FOXBOURNE HOUSE, IRELAND, 1919

The sound of hooves thundered in Cecelia's ears as she galloped through the winter fields beyond her home, Foxbourne House. Her father, Alastair Altringham, the Earl of Kildurran, and generations of the Altringham family had resided here for centuries.

She was uncaring that her hair – fair beneath her bowler hat – had come loose from the half-hearted bun she'd fashioned it into and refused to ride side-saddle, not giving two hoots that it was unladylike to straddle a horse. She had never been afraid to stand out. Not after years of ill treatment because of things over which she had no control, and that set her apart from those around her, like her limp.

Cecelia's cheeks were slapped red by both winter's icy hands and the adrenaline that surged upon hearing the hooves gaining on her. She risked a glance over her shoulder and saw the dark-haired figure hunched over the thoroughbred, driving his horse toward her. Her heart was pounding, her breath coming in white-hot bursts, as she shifted her weight forward in the saddle slightly, squeezing her calves to urge her horse, Camelot, on.

'Come on, boy! Don't let him catch us!' Her eyes watered against the wind as she squinted ahead to the dense woodland at the edge of the estate, growing ever closer. 'That's where we'll lose him, boy. You know where to go.'

Within seconds, she was ducking low to avoid the bare branches snaking out in readiness to snare her and tumble her onto the hard earth. The air was sharper in here. The woods dank and secretive. Cecelia knew the thick trunks of the ancient oaks and beech trees would render her and Camelot invisible as they slipped between them – if he dared come in here after her.

Camelot, sure of foot, led her deeper into the woods where there was no path to follow and the beefy branches almost blocked the sky overhead. Slowly, her horse's frantic pace eased to a canter, a trot and then a meandering walk, as did her racing heartbeat.

All she could hear now was her own breathing and Camelot's rhythmic clip-clopping. He hadn't followed them in here. He must have turned Raven around and headed back to the stables, which was disappointing because the chase had made her feel alive, and she could only imagine how she would feel if he were to catch her. The thought of being alone with the off-limits Finian Fahy was exciting and exhilarating.

She carried on a short distance, hearing a curlew's melancholy song, and she shivered despite her wool riding coat as she emerged into the clearing. It didn't matter that she rode here every morning; the sight of Lough Rae spread out before her, a mirror flanked by wavering reeds, never failed to take her breath away.

Lough Rae, the faerie lake rife with legend thanks to the small island in the middle, was made all the more mysterious this morning by the shroud of mist dancing over it. Nobody ever rowed out to the island because Irish folklore stated that to do so would anger the faeries. The village folk of nearby Kildurran believed the faeries guarded the ancient secrets contained within the lake from their water-logged island home.

Cecelia had believed the legend wholeheartedly ever since her brother, Julian, the Viscount of Rathlin, older than her by a year, had rowed out to the island just to disprove the story one long, dull summer. Closing her eyes for a moment, Cecelia conjured his sneering face as he told her the villagers were all simple-headed folk. That same afternoon he'd fallen off his horse and broken his leg in three places. It served him right, she'd thought. He'd angered the faeries.

There was no love lost between her and her brother. Or her fourteen-year-old sister, Beatrice, either for that matter. Cecelia was the odd one out. The cuckoo in the nest.

Her eyes flicked open, and she shooed Julian's irritating face away, preferring to track the dark waters instead, which were said to hold healing properties. This she wasn't so sure of because they'd not healed her. It was also why she was happiest with the wind on her face riding Camelot. Then she was as able-bodied as anyone.

Camelot's ears twitched, and Cecelia froze. The crunch of dead leaves and snap of a twig suggested there was no magic afoot. A deer perhaps?

Finian Fahy emerged into the clearing astride Lord Kildurran's pride and joy, the gleaming black thoroughbred aptly named Raven. Cecelia was aware her father had hung his hopes for the future of ailing Foxbourne House on both Finian and this racehorse. A triumphant glint shone in Finian's eyes, black to match the horse he ambled toward her on, and Cecelia had the feeling if she stared too long into those inky pools, she might lose herself for good.

'So this is where you disappear to when you ride off each morning like you're racing in the Irish Derby,' he said with the fast-paced vowels of a working-class Dubliner. 'You'll see Tomas out of a job riding like that.'

Finian's attention drifted past her to sweep over the body of water. 'I didn't know there was a lake here.'

'This was my secret place, but now you've found it.' Cecelia's tone was haughty as she tried to hide her skittering heartbeat and insecurity at being alone in his presence. He was a handsome man with his dark eyes and wild curls, but it was his roguish charm that appealed to her most. She couldn't seem to raise her gaze from his mouth. It had mesmerised her. What would it be like to kiss those shapely lips? How she managed to keep up the facade she'd donned to protect herself, chin jutting forth as she met his gaze with what she hoped was impervious-ness, she'd never know. If anything, his raised brow and twitching mouth hinted at him being amused rather than intimi-dated. Tomas was right, she decided, recalling his remark after first meeting Finian – that he struck him as a cocky so-and-so. The trouble was it only added to his appeal.

'A penny for them?' A curling lock of black hair had tumbled into Finian's eye, and Cecelia's gloved hand twitched with the urge to push it off his face as she realised she'd been staring at him.

What must he think of her behaving like a lovesick puppy? Her face flamed at the very idea of revealing her private thoughts to him. 'I wouldn't share them with you for a pound.'

She raised her head high then used the reins and her leg to turn Camelot back toward the woods, feeling Finian's eyes scorching her back as she gave a flick of her wrists. The trees swallowed her up, and she thought that if he'd tossed her a pound, she might have told him that Tomas didn't trust him... and she didn't trust herself around him.

The mist had turned to soft rain as Cecelia galloped toward Foxbourne. She hadn't heard hoofbeats behind her and assumed Finian had stayed on to explore the lakeside further. Ahead of her, the house rose splendidly through the haze, an other-worldly castle full of turrets and chimneys. Inside its thick stone walls were rooms that echoed of the past and the ghosts of relatives long since dead and buried who couldn't leave. They were trapped at Foxbourne like she was.

At that thought, she shivered. Her eyes strayed to the windows punctuating Foxbourne's grand facade, sensing she was being watched. Whoever was spying on her wouldn't be able to see from this distance, but she still poked her tongue out childishly. Then she rode around to the rear of the house to the low-slung brick cluster of stables where she'd be out of sight.

The rain was becoming steadier by the time she dismounted Camelot and handed the reins to Tomas. He'd heard her approach and abandoned his mucking out to greet her. A frown puckered his freckled brow, his face arranged in a scowl. Cecelia suspected she knew what had him in foul humour, and it wasn't the sudden downpour.

'I saw Finian chasing after you on Raven earlier.' A question flickered in his brown eyes.

Cecelia wasn't sure what he wanted her to say, and she didn't like the proprietary tone in his voice, so she shrugged the question away. 'Sure, he can chase all he wants. He won't catch me.'

'Stay away from him, CeeCee. I've heard rumours.'

Whatever Tomas had heard would have to wait because Beatrice – ringlets pinging about her face, no coat and wearing her indoor slippers – had appeared around the side of the house and was running toward them.

'What on earth...?' Had someone died? Cecelia kept this thought to herself but sensed Tomas was as wary as she was.

As Beatrice, slippers ruined and dress drenched, reached them, Cecelia made a quick inventory, preparing for the worst. However, instead of panic, she saw slyness in her sister's blue eyes. Her cheeks too were flushed with excitement, and she'd an aura of being hungry for drama. There was no family emergency then. Cecelia steeled her resolve not to give her the satisfaction of asking what she'd braved the rain to run outside and tell her.

'Mother and Father are having the most terrible row in the study, and it's all over what to do with you!' Beatrice, fed up with waiting for her cue, blurted, her finger jabbing in Cecelia's direction.

Cecelia merely blinked at her. 'You're getting awfully wet, Bea.' She'd been right – someone had been watching her as she'd ridden toward the house. Beatrice must have run straight from the drawing room, where, instead of practising the piano as she was supposed to be doing, she'd been spying out the window, waiting for her return. Her sister was making the most of her governess not being there to keep a watchful eye on her. The awful Miss Flemington had taken a short leave of absence while she sorted care for her ailing mother.

The younger girl huffed and flounced back around the house, taking the longer route to the front door, despite the downpour. She refused to use the more practical servants' entrance Cecelia preferred. Ridiculous really, Cecelia thought, given there were barely any servants left to care these days.

Tomas indicated the house with a dip of his head. 'Hadn't you best go and see what she's on about?'

'I suppose I had.' She had a sinking feeling her parents' heated discussion involved marrying her off because most girls her age were already betrothed. A fate she'd managed to avoid thus far by refusing to play the part of simpering young lady when potential suitors had been welcomed to the house.

'Do you mind seeing to Camelot for me, Tomas?'

'It's not a bother. Sure, it's my job, as I'm always after telling you. G'won with you.'

'Thank you.' Cecelia dimpled, pleased he seemed to have forgotten his pique over Finian, and after giving Camelot's forehead a gentle kiss, she hitched up her coat and hurried across the loose stones to the servants' entrance. In the kitchen garden, she could see Cyril, his back to her as he sprinkled poultry manure sparingly amongst the kale and cabbages.

Tomas's voice floated after her. 'CeeCee, remember what I said. Stay away from Finian Fahy. He's involved with people you want no part of. He's going to bring trouble to this house.'

But his words fell on deaf ears.

6

ST PATRICK'S MOTHER AND BABY HOME, 1920

Cecelia had barely slept lying on the rough mattress in the unfamiliar surroundings, wishing with all her heart she'd listened to Tomas's warning that day. If only she'd known it was a turning point, perhaps she'd have chosen a different path, one that didn't lead her here to St Patrick's. Black eyes and coal-black curls taunted her, and she wished she didn't long for him still.

The sudden shrill ringing of a bell saw the dormitory spring into life, and almost relieved it was time to get up, she shelved her memories and fell in with the other girls as they washed, then dressed in their grey smocks and clumpy boots before plodding silently to the chapel. She couldn't imagine ever carrying herself with such an air of defeat as these women and girls.

Head held high, shoulders back, spine straight, the imaginary voice of Cecelia's former dance tutor, Madame Vacani, trilled in her ear. She did as she was told, catching Nessa – the dark-haired girl who'd tried to talk to her last night – watching her, curiosity stamped on her elfin features.

Cecelia was the first to swivel her eyes away as she took in the space she now found herself in. She didn't want or need friends. Lizzie was the only person she trusted, the only one who hadn't betrayed her; had helped her no matter what.

The chapel, on the ground floor, had plain white walls, a high wooden altar and rows of pews in the same dark timber. It was the three nuns already kneeling that caught her attention though. The Mother Superior, Sister Agnes and another sister whom Cecelia was certain she'd encounter soon enough were praying in a separate area to where the girls ahead of her were silently taking their places. Quickly lowering her gaze, she shuffled along the pew and kneeled on the hard floor like the others. The pervasive lye smell she'd noticed last night hadn't drifted in here, and the candlewax and polish scents were a welcome respite.

For the next half hour, she didn't once look in the direction of Sister Agnes, whom she felt certain was scrutinising her every move. She'd marked her card with that one, so intent on not standing out, she clasped and unclasped her hands, standing and kneeling, taking her cues from the other girls, while her lips moved along to the unfamiliar prayers. Her knees ached from the hard floor, and it was a relief when it was over and they began to file out.

Somewhere in the orderly line, Cecelia heard a girl hiss, 'Don't push – you'll get us all in trouble.'

Then, after someone tapped her on the shoulder, she swung round to see Nessa's inquisitive face sandwiched between long plaits. Her brow creased in annoyance; she wished the other girl would leave her be.

'Where are you from?'

Cecelia turned away. She wouldn't give Sister Agnes, or any of the nuns for that matter, a reason to single her out.

'Are you dumb? Is that it? There was a lad a few cottages down from where I used to live who was. He used to get terribly angry at not being able to make himself understood.'

'Shush, Nessa,' urged the young girl Cecelia had noticed last night with the belly bigger than she was.

'I'm only trying to talk to her, Mol. Well, are you?'

Why wasn't this girl picking up that Cecelia had no wish to talk?

'No, I'm not,' Cecelia snapped as quietly as she could. 'I've no wish to break the rules, that's all, so please stop talking to me.'

Cecelia caught the surprise in the girl's eyes as she exited the chapel and heard her say, 'You're a toff. What on earth are you doing here? Are you even Catholic? And why do you walk so strange?'

'Silence!' The order echoed up and down the draughty corridor.

The girls began to disperse, and Cecelia hung back, not sure where she could go and wishing she could blend into the wall. She didn't want to get in bother for standing about.

'Your name, child?'

'Cec— Margaret,' Cecelia quickly corrected herself. She hadn't seen the nondescript nun holding a sheet of paper until she was nearly upon her.

The nun's eyes were the same grey as the hair visible around the edges of her wimple. She looked stern but not unkind, and held the paper almost at arm's length in order to read it.

'I'm House Sister Mary, and I'm in charge of chapel attendance and the chores roster. I've assigned you to kitchen duties. You, child.' She beckoned to a girl emerging through the chapel doorway. 'Show the new girl to the kitchen.'

'Yes, Sister.'

The girl didn't bother to ask Cecelia to follow her as she led her down a labyrinth of corridors. Nor did she ask what her name was. Then again, she probably didn't dare, Cecelia thought.

The absence of voices speaking to one another in the spaces that echoed only with footfall, doors closing and the distant cry of a small child set Cecelia's teeth on edge. She tried to pay attention to the direction the girl was taking her in, thinking she was like a timid mouse scuttling along. The only clue they were headed toward the kitchen was the smell of boiled cabbage growing stronger. She'd never liked cabbage.

Then the girl stopped abruptly and pointed to an open door at the end of the corridor. 'Down there.'

'Thank you.'

She was already hurrying away and Cecelia watched her go feeling like she'd been abandoned. Standing there in that empty corridor with its flaking painted walls and mould splattered ceiling, she'd never felt lonelier in her life. She pulled the cardigan together trying to ward off the sudden bout of shivering.

'Pull yourself together, Cecelia,' she admonished. Self-pity would not get her through her time at St Patrick's. This was merely a means to an end, and she would get through it best by keeping to herself. Remembering Madame Vacani's instructions, she breathed in deeply, held her head high then strode toward the door through which light glowed.

The sound of clattering pots and pans led her onward, but as she approached the kitchen, the confidence she was trying to keep hold of faltered. Should she knock on the door and announce her arrival or simply barrel in? Cecelia nipped at her bottom lip and threw caution to the wind, stepping inside what turned out to be another utilitarian space.

The kitchen was hot and smoky thanks to the large turf-burning range, and girls were knotting aprons behind their backs or already setting about their tasks in silence. Her heart sank as she saw the sister in charge. It was Sister Agnes.

'So you're to work here in the kitchen, Margaret?'

'Yes, Sister Agnes.' Cecelia's stomach fluttered fearfully, and she hated the nun for making her feel like that.

'Well, don't just stand there then. Fetch an apron, child, like the others.'

Cecelia looked about for the aprons and caught another girl's eye. She dipped her head toward the laden shelves on which everything from pots and pans to glass jars of preserves and sacks of potatoes, flour and tinned goods were kept. In her haste not to get the day off on the wrong foot with Sister Agnes, Cecelia hurried toward it – and thanks to the ill-fitting boots tripped over a bucket full of scraps.

Her hand flew to her mouth, her eyes wide with horror at the mess on the floor. 'I'm sorry!' She fell to her knees and braced for a blow of some sort as she frantically began scooping vegetable peels up.

'My but you are a lame duck,' Sister Agnes tutted. 'You can take that out to the pigs when you've finished, then set to scrubbing the dishes.'

'Yes, Sister.'

Cecelia silently cursed her leg for letting her down as she scooped up the last of the scraps and carried the heavy bucket out the back door where she gulped at the air greedily. The pigs squealed and grunted with anticipation, and not daring to dawdle, she tipped the bucket into their pen, watching them snuffle about on the ground for a split second before steeling herself for the day ahead.

The aprons were in a basket next to a stack of chipped enamel plates, and she quickly knotted one behind her back.

'Those dishes won't wash themselves,' Sister Agnes barked. 'Roll your sleeves up, child. There's no scullery maid waiting on you here.'

Cecelia felt a few curious eyes turn her way as she pushed the sleeves of her cardigan and smock up. She eyed the stack of dishes on the worktop next to the deep tin tub with a tap over it and recalled having seen Grainne, the scullery maid at

Foxbourne, scrubbing her family's dirty dishes. She'd never given the poor girl a thought before and felt badly as she put the plug in the tub and turned on the tap.

'Fill a pan and boil it on the range, you stupid girl.'

Cecelia stiffened, feeling Sister Agnes almost breathing on her and more stares from the other girls. If they could, she sensed they'd snigger at her ineptness.

She swiftly filled the largest pot on the shelf and was unsure what to do while she waited for it to come to the boil. Not daring to stand there twiddling her thumbs, she decided to help the lank-haired, heavily pregnant woman peeling a mound of potatoes by picking up a paring knife and copying what she was doing. It was a blessing the knife was so blunt or she'd have nicked herself more than once, but it made the job tricky, so she'd no qualms about abandoning the knife when the pot finally began to bubble.

The handles were hot as she picked the pot up, and water sloshed over the side. A splash scalded her leg, but she bit down on her lip to stop herself from crying out. There'd be no sympathy to be had here if she did. Then she poured the contents of the pot into the sink, added cold water and picked up the first of the bowls before sluicing it around and wiping it out with a cloth.

'You're to use this in the water.'

Cecelia, startled at the raspy sound of a voice that didn't belong to one of the sisters, took the proffered block of carbolic soap.

'And there's sand for scouring the pots.'

'Thank you,' she whispered back. Then, for the first time in her life, Cecelia Altringham began to scrub dishes.

As she set to her task, she felt the oddest sensation deep in her belly, like a tiny butterfly beating its wings. She was taken aback by yet another first. So much had changed for her recently. She wished Lizzie was here. But she was strong – she would pull through on her own. For the sake of the baby if nothing else.

7

FOXBOURNE HOUSE, IRELAND, 1919

Cecelia didn't break her stride down the servants' corridor as she returned alone to the house, past Lizzie's small quarters and the housekeeper Mrs Behan's larger room. Lastly, she passed the small office, where the housekeeper had the unenviable task of juggling the day-to-day running of Foxbourne House on a shoestring budget. Then she hauled herself up the narrow staircase, where she breathlessly flung open a door, sending Lizzie flying.

'Lizzie! Oh, I'm sorry! How clumsy of me. Are you hurt?' Cecelia made to help the flustered chambermaid, who was lying on the floor under a cloud of bed linen. Chambermaid was a loose title given how many extra duties Lizzie'd had foisted on her of late by Mrs Behan. She'd confided in Cecelia she wouldn't dare complain because her mam relied on the money she brought home with her on her afternoons off.

Lizzie swatted Cecelia away, untangling herself and making her own way up to her feet with a show of impatience. She smoothed her simple uniform and straightened her mob cap before looking down at her friend's muddy boots. Her lips tightened, and a muscle pulsed at the corner of her mouth.

'CeeCee! Haven't I got enough work to do without cleaning up after you too? I just saw Beatrice traipsing through to the drawing room in a sodden dress. She'll expect me to perform miracles and dry it along with fixing her ruined slippers somehow. Her ladyship's in foul humour this morning as it is. Now here you are charging at me through a door you've no business using, tracking mud in everywhere like a heathen.'

Her friend's choked distress as she flung the words out saw Cecelia hesitate. 'Sorry, Lizzie.'

'You don't think, CeeCee. You never think!'

Cecelia suspected this might be true. 'I'll make it up to you, I promise.' But she was already throwing her hip forward and haring toward the next set of stairs.

The raised voices of her parents drifted down the staircase before she'd pulled herself even halfway up, and when she heard her mother shout 'suitable suitor' and 'London', an icy trickle slithered its way down her spine. She continued slower, taking quiet strides up to the landing because whatever they were plotting for her future, it sounded far worse than she'd envisaged.

Cecelia lurked in the draughty hall outside her father's study. The door had been left open just a crack, enough for her to hear what her parents were tossing at one another.

'Alastair, look about you. Foxbourne House is crumbling around our ears! By the time Julian comes to inherit, there'll be nothing left for him but a pile of stones and a worthless title.'

Julian. It always came back to him where their mother was concerned.

'And where is the boy, Helen? Overseeing farm operations as I asked him to? No, he's not. I have it on good authority he's currently wagering on a cockfight on the outskirts of the town.'

'What can I say? The apple doesn't fall far. Julian is his father's son.' Lady Kildurran's retort was quick as lightning.

That was a low blow on her mother's part. The lady of the

house normally couldn't abide an ill word being said about her only son.

A low blow it may be, but it was also true. Her brother was already exhibiting signs of being as feckless when it came to money as her father was. He'd a penchant for skiving off, illegal betting on the horses and dogs, frequenting gentlemen's clubs and running up tabs they could ill afford. And now it seemed the barbaric sport of cockfighting could be added to that list. There was one strong point of difference between father and son, however. Lord Kildurran was passionate about Foxbourne. A gambler he might be, but he would gamble everything he had to hold on to his family's ancestral lands. He'd fight to the bitter end, whereas Julian was lazy. Her brother wanted the glory of a title but not the fight.

Lady Kildurran, a seasoned player when it came to managing her husband, changed tact and softened her delivery. 'Alastair, my love, it's imperative we secure a good marriage for Cecelia. You cannot argue that our way of life here at Foxbourne isn't in dire need of a financial injection if it is to survive.'

Cecelia's hands clenched into fists, her jaw tightening. She'd no intention of marrying anyone she didn't want to and certainly not for monetary gain for her family. The thought of being betrothed to a paunchy baron with wet lips and gout of her parents' choosing made her shudder. She replaced the distasteful image with that of Finian and how he'd looked like a proud Celtic king astride Raven on the banks of Lough Rae earlier.

Lord Kildurran's voice boomed back at his wife. 'What you're suggesting is pure lunacy. We can't afford to throw money away on frivolities like the London season! I've only just let Louis go, woman.'

'Throwing money away is not something you seem to mind doing when it comes to your horses.'

A sudden thump sounded, and Cecelia jumped, picturing her father having grown red-faced and banging his fist down on his expansive mahogany desk.

While he and his son were gambling men, his wife was not, although the odds of winning this argument were in her favour because what the Viscountess of Kildurran wanted, she inevitably got. Cecelia's mother was the power behind the throne, but still her father wasn't rolling over without a fight and had begun spluttering once again.

A flurry of movement out the corner of her eye saw Cecelia's attention drawn to the landing. She half expected to see Beatrice smirking there because there was no plunking practising of the major and minor scales to be heard drifting up from the drawing room. It wasn't Beatrice, however, but Lizzie gesticulating madly at her to come away from the door. Unlike her younger sister, Cecelia knew Lizzie had her best interests at heart. Nevertheless, she'd no intention of leaving her post until she'd heard the outcome of this spat, and she shook her head furiously. When next she glanced over to the landing, Lizzie had gone. Meanwhile, her father had moved on to the never-ending list of work required in the upkeep of a great house like Foxbourne.

'There's masonry work needing doing, and the roof over the principal wing needs attending to urgently if we're not to be eating our meals in a swimming pool come winter. Surely you can't be so blithely suggesting swanning off to your sister's in London for the season, squandering everything we have on the latest fashions, luncheons and parties for the sole purpose of Cecelia winning over some new-monied dandy!'

Lady Kildurran adopted a sneering inflection. 'New money or old, it's all money, and beggars can't afford to be choosers. A new-monied dandy, as you put it, will be drawn to the legitimacy that marrying into Irish aristocracy will give him in society's circles. And there was I thinking you as a gambling man would see the odds are in our favour, but only if we back the hand we've been dealt. Cecelia's beautiful, yes, I'll give you that, but it's not enough given her disability, and you must agree she'd benefit sorely from being packed off to a finishing school in Switzerland and having those rough edges of hers smoothed out. As that's not on the cards given our circumstances, we must act now before she gleans a reputation for being unamenable. The girl rides that horse of hers like a man for heaven's sake! And she doesn't listen to anybody. I've told her over and over it's unseemly.'

'She rides well, Helen.'

There was a derisive snort. 'And will that secure her a good marriage? I think not. Cecelia has two things to offer a man: her beauty and her family title. She must stand out from the crowd this season for the right reasons, and with a modest dowry, the proper grooming and etiquette lessons...'

Cecelia didn't hear the rest. All she could think of was that she was no more than a broken chattel to her mother, to be auctioned off under the guise of the London season to the highest bidder. Finian didn't see her as disabled, she was sure of it. There hadn't been an ounce of pity in his eyes when he looked at her, only interest. Or was she being fanciful?

'Cecelia is perfectly able to do whatever she sets her mind to.'

This was an argument she'd heard before, and Cecelia felt a fondness for her father – even if he was a hapless fool when it came to managing the estate – for standing up for her against his overbearing wife.

'Oh, you're not wrong there. She has a mind of her own all right, but what is it she sets that mind to? Horse riding, not even side-saddled? It's not seemly.'

Cecelia didn't know much about marriage but had enough of an inkling to understand a betrothal would mean change for her on so many levels it made her feel quite panicky. She tuned back into her father's argument, desperately wishing he'd continue to hold his ground on this occasion. She had to hope he would object strongly enough to put off the intentional husband-hunting her mother had planned for her in London.

'Our daughter marrying a showy young buck from across the water will only raise the ire of the tenants we have left, along with the locals. More so if she provides an heir to some *English* lord. There's an ill wind blowing, as you well know, and I'm already being made to feel like an unwelcome guest on my own land.'

'Do you think I enjoy being treated as though I'm a leper when I venture through the village? If we are to stand our ground and remain in residence at Foxbourne, then we will need the wherewithal do it. Besides, it's our daughter's duty to marry well and provide children. As I did,' Lady Kildurran retorted.

Cecelia hoped her indignant huffed breaths weren't audible in the study.

'Julian's certainly not showing any signs of settling down and providing me with a son to carry on the Altringham name.'

'Alastair, Julian has his career to focus on. Just listen to what I'm proposing.'

'I've heard enough.'

Cecelia took that to be a line drawn under the conversation, and she took a step away.

'No you haven't. I won't let my children's futures hinge on a horse.'

What future? Cecelia thought dully, immobile now. There was no sound other than footfall moving across creaking boards, which suggested her father was pacing.

'Not a horse, Helen. A *racehorse*.'

'Pfft. This will work just as well as your other schemes. We need to do more. Besides, I've called in the favour Octavia owes me for my having introduced her to Sir George all those years ago.'

The resentment dripped from her mother's words every time she said her sister's name.

Cecelia recalled an overheard conversation when her mother had gone into more detail about her fateful decision to marry for love and the lure of a title. She suspected Mother and Lady Clanebridge had been imbibing sherry and not tea, hence the loosening of her mother's tongue and her forgetting Cecelia had been playing behind the sofa. She'd made herself into a tiny ball as she'd listened to Lady Clanebridge tut in sympathy at her mother's predicament.

The Baron of Clanebridge looked like a fox with his gingery whiskers and pointy face and Cecelia couldn't imagine his wife had married for love.

'I should have followed my mother's advice, Sara, and married Sir George. He'd already made a fortune in shipping by then,' Lady Kildurran had lamented.

'Well, they do say mothers know best, dear,' Lady Clane-bridge had replied.

If I were Mother, I'd lob a piece of Mrs Nolan's barmbrack at you, Cecelia had thought.

Hidden from view, she'd pieced together enough of the story to work out that her mother had been courting her uncle, Sir George Cathcart, when she'd first laid eyes on her father and fallen heads over heels for what she'd seen then as roguish charms but now saw as annoying Irish idiosyncrasies. The young Helen had eased her rejection of Sir George by intro-ducing him to her sister Octavia, two years her senior, who had been eagerly waiting in the wings.

'It's a bitter pill to have swallowed, Sara,' she'd continued. 'Here I am mouldering away in a country that doesn't want me, living a hand-to-mouth existence, while Octavia and her chil-dren swan around London without a care in the world.'

Now, Lady Kildurran said, 'Octavia has generously agreed to sponsor Cecelia's coming out for the London season along with a small dowry. It's most generous of her and Sir George. That's not all either. Sir George has offered to take Julian under his wing and introduce him to businessmen and politicians who could be advantageous to his future prospects. I've had word from Miss Flemington, and she's returning to Foxbourne next week so Beatrice won't be disrupted. She can stay here and continue her lessons.'

Cecelia had heard enough and didn't hesitate in barging into the study.

The expressions on her parents' faces at her intrusion would have amused her if her blood wasn't boiling. Her father, his hair peppered with grey at the sides, was in head-to-toe tweed and standing with his hands clasped behind his back in front of the fireplace, while her mother, hair coiffed into marcel waves and a chignon was demure in her day dress as she squared off to him from the opposite end of the room.

'Mother, Father, I'm not a commodity to be bought and sold! I've no wish to marry anyone! I'll make my own way in the world from here on in.' Hot, unwelcome tears prickled because even as Cecelia flung this at them, she knew she was issuing an idle threat. Where would she go?

Worst of all was the malicious gleam in her mother's marble-blue eyes and her supercilious smirk. Her father – roaring about eavesdropping and impudence – pushed past her, declaring he'd had more than enough of the women in his family, leaving Cecelia and her mother alone. She sensed the slap coming, but still it took her breath away as her head snapped back.

'How dare you, Cecelia! And look at you cavorting about with your hair hanging loose like a wild woman.'

'What have I done to make you hate me so, Mother?' Cecelia whispered, clutching her burning cheek.

Lady Kildurran's pinches and slaps were reserved solely for her eldest daughter. It was as if she blamed her for the choices that had brought her here to Ireland. Cecelia fought tears, because she wouldn't give her the satisfaction of seeing her cry, even as she wondered what it would be like to know her mother's love. It was something she'd certainly never been given the chance to experience.

There was a swish of silk as Lady Kildurran moved to the door. 'You have one purpose and one purpose only, Cecelia – to marry well and provide an heir. You'd do well to remember that, and with that limp of yours, I'm afraid beggars can't be choosers.'

8

———————

ST PATRICK'S MOTHER AND BABY HOME, 1920

Cecelia couldn't shake the memory of the cold hands poking and prodding at her while a disapproving nun looked on before the doctor declared her fit and well. The check-up had forced her to think about the birth of the baby, and as she toiled in the kitchen, the memory of the cold looks in the doctor's and sister's eyes made her frightened over what was to come. Not that she knew what to expect exactly. It was all very murky because the closest thing she had to go on when it came to giving birth was the foal she'd witnessed being born in the stables at Foxbourne. The memory of the blood and gore that had been involved made her shudder, and after all the horse's pain and suffering, the poor animal had been stillborn.

The imagery that brought to mind turned her stomach, and she might have vomited. But she was practically empty. The hunger pangs were a constant ache, just like the apathetic cries from the babies in the nursery. She'd seen the older babies clutching the rails of the cots, crying for their mothers.

Why hadn't they been adopted and sent to homes filled with warmth and love? These were questions she'd have liked to ask the girls who'd been here longer than she had, but she didn't speak to anyone except when a response was required by one of the sisters. On those occasions, it would startle her to hear her own voice. Sometimes she'd wonder if it was possible to lose the ability to speak altogether if you remained silent too long.

The never-ending dishes in the kitchen had become Cecelia's permanent job, and her hands were red and cracked from constantly being in hot water and using the harsh carbolic soap. They pained her, and as she scrubbed the dishes clean, she'd recall times spent in the grounds of Foxbourne with Cyril the gardener.

Cyril's impromptu lessons on the medicinal uses of the herbs and plants he grew mostly for culinary purposes with their multiple uses had fascinated her. She'd listen as alert as a fox during the hunt to the gardener, ten or so years older than herself, tell stories of having foraged for them as a soldier when medical supplies were in short supply.

Cyril's herbs also used to help heal the marks left behind by her mother's vicious hands, and what he taught her had captured and held her interest far more than her wobbly-chinned old governess's droning lessons ever had. She'd been so pleased when she'd reached eighteen and no longer had to suffer through Miss Flemington's dull lessons.

Back then, Cecelia had been left in limbo, her time her own while her mother plotted her future. It was an arrangement that suited her perfectly well, but all good things came to an end. If only she'd known what the future held, Cecelia thought, plunging a bowl into the water, ignoring her burning hands. She wished Cyril had told her of a cure for a broken heart too, because love couldn't be turned off and on like a tap, not even when you'd been badly let down by someone you thought loved you back.

It hadn't taken long for word to spread amongst the other

girls of her soft hands and well-spoken manner when she acknowledged the sisters. Stories were whispered and giggled over amongst them in the dormitory at night as if she wasn't lying there in her cot hearing every word. She picked up on an undercurrent of glee in some of those giggles over how far the mighty had fallen. *If only they knew*, she'd think.

Cecelia refused to speak up and say who she was and where she'd come from, thus fuelling speculation, and Nessa had delighted in nicknaming her Lady Mags. The name rankled, but she rose above it, sticking to her plan of lying low and getting through the days. She had an end goal, and she would leave this hellhole as soon as she could to start a new life. It was a plan that thus far had helped her avoid Sister Agnes's beady eye.

It was a snippet of overheard conversation in the kitchen when the sister was out of earshot that upset the apple cart, however.

'You know she helps herself to anything of value,' the woman with the lank hair was saying, knife and carrot in hand.

'She never!' a pasty-faced younger girl gasped from the adjacent table used as a worktop that she was scrubbing down. She was wide-eyed at this revelation. 'The day my ma dragged me here, I wore a brooch my dear departed nan gave me.' The girl paused in her work to cross herself and look heavenward. 'It made me feel less frightened wearing it, and just knowing it wasn't far away, folded in my belongings, waiting for the day I can leave gave me strength. I don't know if it's worth much, but it means the world to me.'

'Well, don't expect to see it again,' the lank-haired woman said without much in the way of sympathy. 'Sister Agnes is a proper magpie. I know from the last time I was here.'

Cecelia tuned the rest of the chatter out as her mind whirred at the thought of the money tucked away inside her case being taken. She'd never worried about money before. That was something her mother did. But now it was a safety net she needed desperately, and the notion of Sister Agnes helping herself to money she'd done an unspeakable thing to earn would not leave her alone for the rest of the day or that night.

She couldn't face a second sleepless night, so once the kitchen was scrubbed down to Sister Agnes's satisfaction and the gas lamps turned off with a hiss, she decided she'd have to take action.

Having made her mind up, she went through the motions until she was lying on her back in her cot, willing the hours to pass while Molly sobbed herself to sleep. It was a sound that no longer distressed her, she'd heard it so often. Besides, Nessa was always on hand to comfort the young girl. Sometimes she'd feel a crack in her armour at the thought of having someone comfort her and vice versa, but still she stayed silent.

Gradually, the twilight seeping through the high windows deepened to darkness, and the breathing all around her evened out. There would be no safer time to sneak down to the storage room than now, and so she crept from the dorm, wraithlike in her thin nightgown and bare feet.

The corridor outside the dormitory stretched like a dark tunnel, and Cecelia slipped silently down it. She might limp, but she'd had plenty of practice sneaking about at night.

Peering over the bannister, she saw the ground floor was deserted, but she couldn't fully relax. There would be a nun on night duty who would either be in the office, or checking on the babies in the nursery or the poor unfortunate souls in the infirmary. It was rare for a sister to poke her head in the dormitory unless there was a ruckus of some sort, like a girl beginning to labour.

You're nearly there, CeeCee.

She pretended Lizzie was whispering in her ear, egging her

on. Although if Lizzie were here, she'd be telling her what she was about to do was madness.

Cecelia sat down on the top step and began sliding down the rest one by one. This was a technique she'd used before under cover of darkness at Foxbourne when silence was imperative, something her limp didn't allow for when it came to ascending or descending stairs. She made it to the entrance with barely a sound.

The main door was securely bolted, as was to be expected, and a sliver of yellow light was visible from the slightly ajar office door. A faint humming sounded from within, and it took Cecelia a second to register it was coming from the sister on night duty. If the nun were to decide to do her rounds right now, the first thing she would see upon opening that door further was Cecelia. She needed to hide and be quick about it.

There was nowhere that offered cover aside from the bench seat outside the Mother Superior's office though. Somehow, she'd have to squeeze under it and lie on her side. That or give up on the idea of putting her mind at rest and shuffle back upstairs. It wasn't too late.

But Cecelia had never been one to back down from a challenge, and she crossed the floor as stealthily as her leg would allow, pausing mid step as a door opened somewhere in the building and a cough echoed. She forced herself to continue the last few steps to the bench, where she dropped to her knees and wriggled like a worm between the legs of the seat until she'd slithered underneath it. It was exceedingly uncomfortable with her bottom hip digging into the flagstone floor, and all she could do now was wait and hope the night duty sister didn't shine the lamp in Cecelia's direction when she emerged from the office.

The sounds were magnified at night, Cecelia soon discovered, biting the inside of her bottom lip as she listened to a baby's cry, the plunk of something steadily dripping nearby and a scuttling noise. The anguished scream, however, ripped through the building and into her soul, making her want to squirm free of her hiding place and go to whomever was suffering. It had to have come from a labouring girl. The babies often decided to come at night, and she refused to dwell on the agony the poor girl must be in to make such a noise. Instead, she listened out for any sign the nuns would respond. After what seemed like an age, she heard the creak of a door opening, and yellow light pooled in the entrance.

All she could make out from where she lay was the nun's sensible shoes beneath her robe as she padded toward the corridor off to the right where the nursery and infirmary were. Alarm at the sudden tickle catching the back of her throat saw her eyes water as she swallowed, furiously willing the cough away. She felt sure someone, maybe even Him upstairs, was watching over her as the nun disappeared at the same time as the threatened cough did.

Now was her chance.

Cecelia squirmed out from under the bench and hurried into the dark and deserted office. Thank the Lord the storage space beyond was unlocked!

She stepped inside the musty room and scanned the shelves, trying to pick out her case. No easy task in the dark, windowless closet.

Hurry up, Cecelia, she urged herself, running her hand across the various items stored on the shelves until at last she felt smooth leather beneath her fingers. This had to be it!

She pulled the case free, relieved to have located it, and flipped the latches, holding her breath. Her skirt was still balled up inside it and the stocking tucked within its folds as she'd packed it. But the money was gone.

Cecelia wanted to sit back on her haunches and howl — there wasn't a single note left. Her anger at the theft would have to wait though. She needed to get back to her cot, while the nuns were distracted. She slipped the case back where she'd found it then backed out of the storage room into the office, which was still empty. As she made to exit it, however, a figure bathed in the glow of the lamp she was holding up blocked the doorway. And Cecelia's insides liquefied.

Sister Agnes was on duty.

9

Cecelia's pleading fell on deaf ears because you couldn't reason with someone as deranged as Sister Agnes. Her madness gave the nun an almost superhuman strength, and before Cecelia could react, she snatched a handful of her hair and began hauling her along behind her. Each time Cecelia tried to break free, the more her hair was pulled from the roots, causing her to cry out and the nun to hiss at her to be quiet. Her feet scrabbled on the flagstones as she was dragged head first from the main foyer.

'You're hurting me. Let me go. Please, I'm begging you, Sister!'

Cecelia was dimly aware they'd veered away from the entrance as a door was wrenched open and she was thrown inside a dark space. She knocked something over that made an almighty clattering then fell down on her hands and knees, emitting an, 'Oof,' as the air left her body. Before she could twist herself around to plead with Sister Agnes one last time, the door slammed shut. Instead of begging, Cecelia gasped into the inkiness, crying out, 'I know it was you who stole my money. I'll tell the Mother Superior you're a thief!'

The only response to this was a thunk as a bolt slid into place.

'That's where you'll stay until you learn humility.'

'Sister! No, don't leave me!' Cecelia screamed out futilely, hearing the fading tap-tap-tap of Sister Agnes's shoes.

Still on all fours, her eyes bored into the darkness, and panic steamrolled into her. She began panting in the fumy air, almost to the point of hyperventilating, but by some miracle, the voice of reason penetrated the fog. She recalled seeing Cyril drop to the ground in the gardens at Foxbourne and cover his ears with his hands upon hearing a loud, unexpected noise. He'd begin panting his fear out like a rabid dog. Now, just as she would Cyril, she ordered herself to breathe in through the nose and slowly out through the mouth until her breathing began to even out and her heart rate slowed. The horror at having found herself locked in a confined space remained, however.

Don't think about it, Cecelia. Imagine you're riding Camelot across the fields.

It was hard to do so, though, because when she closed her eyes to visualise her beloved horse, the memories were intertwined with Finian, and she refused to think about him. There was nothing for it but to shuffle about until she was sitting with her back pressed to the wall.

Patting around, she deduced it was a tin pail and cleaning supplies she'd sent flying. She righted them, and as she did so, her hand brushed the bristles of a broom leaning in the corner. Her brain began to process rationally that she was in the cleaning cupboard, and Sister Agnes would have no choice but to let her out in the morning. The thought comforted her because failing that, one of the girls would find her here when they came to fetch the bucket or broom.

To shout for help would only suck up oxygen in the cramped cupboard. Besides, given only Sister Agnes was about, it would be a waste of energy.

Cecelia pulled her knees up to her chest, wrapped her arms around her calves and rested her head on her knees. A scratching sounded somewhere in the darkness. Was it a rat or a mouse? She preferred to think it was a little mouse trapped like she was and put her fingers in her ears to zone the noise out, because where there was one mouse, there were more, and the same could be said for rats. *Focus, Cecelia, focus.*

It would be better to pretend she'd learned a lesson when the door was unlocked. She would promise not to mention the missing money. All she could do for now, though, was try and sleep. It was the only way to make the time pass quickly because in a few hours, when Sister Agnes returned to let her out, she'd find a cowed and contrite version of the girl she'd shoved in here. On the outside at least.

Only Sister Agnes didn't return in a few hours.

Time had lost all meaning as Cecelia alternated between standing to try and stretch her cramped limbs, bending at the waist so as not to bang her head on the slanted ceiling, and drifting in and out of a nightmare-peppered sleep. She dreamed she was riding Camelot and a horse was thundering up behind her. This time it wasn't Finian but Sister Agnes. Then she was beside the banks of Lough Rae, Camelot grazing nearby as she scanned the undulating waters, seeking something or someone, but the scenery changed, and then she was leaning over a deep, dark well. She could smell the water, taste the water, feel the push as someone shoved her, then she was falling, falling, falling and waking with a start. Her stomach was cramping with hunger pangs, and the thirst was unbearable.

Thuds would rouse her from her stupor every now and again, and she'd call out for help, having guessed the storage cupboard she was in was beneath stairs. Eventually, her calls grew weaker, her voice reduced to a useless croak, and instead she kicked at the door. Still no one came.

She was desperate to go to the toilet, but she held it because she'd not shame herself again by wetting herself. But the pain of a full bladder was making her nauseous.

Had she been forgotten? she wondered. Was Sister Agnes cruel enough to leave her here to die of thirst, lying in her own filth? Then her thoughts blackened. She would die, the baby with her. She wouldn't let that happen. Agnes would not win. Her tears were hot and salty, and her mind began to float away.

10

FOXBOURNE HOUSE, IRELAND, 1919

There was nowhere for Cecelia to run and nurse the swirl of fury, hurt and humiliation at her mother having struck her other than the stables. Her safe place. She didn't see Lizzie or Beatrice as she fled the study where her fate had been sealed by her parents, her tread on the stairs as heavy as her heart. Nor did she acknowledge Mrs Nolan, the cook, or Grainne upon passing though the kitchen and out the back door. Cyril raised a hand in greeting upon seeing her emerge from the servants' entrance, still toiling in the kitchen garden, though she couldn't bring herself to wave back. But when she saw Finian walking Raven about the yard, she hesitated. He was the last person she wanted to see when she was in such a state. All she wanted to do was cross the patch of loose stone between the back door and yard to the stables. In there, she could hide away with Camelot and shut the world out.

She'd made it halfway when Finian, not pausing in his walk with Raven, called over, 'How many colours are in a rainbow?'

Common sense told her to ignore him and go and hide, but curiosity won out as to where he'd dug that question from. 'Why are you asking me that?'

'Look up and see for yourself.'

Cecelia craned her neck and there, arcing over Foxbourne, was a glorious rainbow. Rainbows were a symbol of good fortune and blessings, both of which were in short supply where she was concerned. She wasn't prone to self-pity, but today Cecelia felt it was justified. Still, she was a glass-half-full girl, and rainbows were also a sign that a wish might be fulfilled. This was her chance! So, ignoring Finian's expectant gaze, she squeezed her eyes shut and silently stated, *I wish for the freedom to lead a different sort of life to the one I've been born to,* repeating it twice more just to be sure it was heard.

Finian and Raven were still circling her when she lowered her face from the sky, and she wondered if this was how a deer might feel being trapped by a wolf.

His creased brow and half-moon smile saw her don her aristocratic, aloof mask once more. 'Next you'll be asking me if I believe there's a pot of gold at the end of it.' For whatever reason, her feet felt as if they'd taken root.

'Do you?' Mirth danced in his black eyes.

Cecelia refused to smile. 'I might. The world would be a dull place if all the mysteries, lore and legends were dismissed simply because there was no hard evidence of their existence.'

'Like the Loch Ness Monster.'

'The *Mary Celeste,*' Cecelia bounced back. She'd been fascinated to read about the maritime mystery of the ghost ship.

'Or, closer to home, the selkies.' Finian's footsteps halted, and Cecelia read the challenge in his stance.

He presumed living removed from local life in the great house on the hill meant she wouldn't have learned of the mythical Irish creatures, seals in the water who would shed their skin on land and take on human form, but he was mistaken. The legend of the selkies was one of her favourites. Right at this moment, however, he was putting her in mind of the Pooka, the tricky faerie or spirit. Well, she'd show him.

'Yes, the half-seal, half-human selkie, although here in the countryside, it's the Pooka we need to be wary of.' Cecelia looked at Raven. 'They're known to take on the guise of goats, rabbits, even that of a large black horse. Or' – her eyes moved slowly across to him – 'a dark stranger.' She wouldn't give him the gratification of uttering the word 'handsome', as was most often slotted between the words.

The flash of surprise that whipped across his face momentarily swept her troubles away.

'I'm as Irish as you, Finian,' she said softly, watching his expression change. Had respect replaced his surprise?

'Yes, I think perhaps you are. And you haven't answered my question.'

'Seven – there are seven colours in a rainbow, of course.'

The weight of having to leave Foxbourne soon for London settled over her once more, and Cecelia resumed walking to the stables. She wondered where Tomas had got to and hoped he wouldn't drill her about the argument between her parents that had sent Beatrice charging out into the rain to alert her. To speak of what had been decided for her immediate future would only make it real.

'Wrong.'

Cecelia stopped and spun round, tired of his games. 'I'm not wrong. There are seven colours in a rainbow: red, orange, yellow, green, blue, indigo and violet.'

Finian shook his head, his hair so black it seemed almost blue under the wintery sun. The curl of his lips suggested he was enjoying himself as he squinted upward. 'That's what people think, but there's a whole range of colours up there the naked eye can't see. They blend and overlap one another. Spectral colours they're called.'

'And how would you know that?'

'I read about it.'

Cecelia frowned because if he was from Travelling stock, as

she'd assumed given his gift with horses, then it wasn't likely he'd be literate. Tomas had once told her the Travellers weren't educated because they were never in one place long enough for schooling, and Cecelia, who'd just suffered through the most tedious morning of lessons under Miss Flemington's tutelage, had resolved to run away with the Travellers the next time their wagons rumbled through Kildurran. Now she wished she had. A life on the road was far preferable to what lay ahead for her.

'What happened to your face?'

Her hand went to her cheek; it was hot and tender to her touch. 'Nothing.' She dropped her gaze, embarrassed, and continued to the stables. She'd fetch some comfrey from the garden later and make a poultice like Cyril had shown her how to do. That might prevent her cheek bruising.

'If you're looking for Tomas, he's gone to the blacksmith to pick up replacement shoes for Kildurran's horse,' Finian called.

'I wasn't.' She didn't look back.

The musky animal scents, underwritten by the bite of menthol liniment used for the rub down, had an instant calming effect on Cecelia as she stepped inside. Planting her feet on the earthen floor, she gulped in lungfuls of it.

The smell was a balm for the soul, far more appealing than the perfume her mother all but bathed in. She wished she could bottle the stable's scent, and the thought of dabbing it behind her ears and on her wrists before being forced to attend one of the ridiculous society balls almost raised a smile.

Camelot's soft nicker of acknowledgement that she was here moved her toward his stall, where his head had appeared, ears perked forward in anticipation of seeing her again in such a short space of time.

'Hello, boy.' She gently kissed his muzzle, as pleased to see him as he was her, then fondled behind his ears in the spot she knew he loved. The stable was quiet now. It was just him and her. Once, there'd been three stablehands employed to tend to the racehorses sheltered in here, but as their fortune dwindled, Father had let them go, selling the horses to the highest bidder to fund the purchase of Raven, a thoroughbred the likes of which he'd never seen before.

'At least you're still here, boy. I'd be lost without you,' Cecelia said, then she took a deep breath and told Camelot everything she'd overheard in her father's study, and how her interruption and refusal to play along with her mother's plan had culminated in her feeling the back of her hand.

Camelot was her trusted confidant because there was never revulsion in his glossy eyes. He didn't care that she was lame – or unlovable in the eyes of her mother. She'd only told him about her mother's harsh treatment because she was too ashamed to tell anybody else, even Lizzie. She knew her friend had seen the pinch marks and bruises, but she hadn't pressed her as to how she'd come by them. Lizzie was close enough to Cecelia to know she should leave it be. If she had wanted to talk about what went on behind closed doors, she would have, and she definitely did not.

How could Cecelia tell anyone she didn't stand up for herself against her mother, even though she was now a grown woman? To say she'd begun to believe she deserved the mistreatment would sound self-pitying. So Camelot bore the brunt as she whispered, 'The truth is, boy, I'm terrified of her.'

'And who is it you're terrified of? I'll sort them out for you.' Finian blocked the light. 'Is it the person who did that to your face?'

By the look on his own face, she believed he would do as he'd said, but still she opened her mouth to tell him it was none of his business. Instead, she burst into tears, furious with herself but at the same time unable to stop them. 'I'm sorry,' she sniffed both to Camelot, who was nuzzling her, and Finian.

'Don't be sorry. Sure, it's all women in my family. I'm well used to such carry-on.'

'You might be, but this' – she patted her pockets for an elusive hanky – 'is not how I behave.' Still, her subconscious hoarded the clue about his background. He was the only son wherever it was he came from.

'The ice maiden is only human after all.' Finian quirked a black eyebrow and thrust a hanky at her. 'It's not white as the driven snow anymore, but it is clean, and it'll do the trick.'

'Thank you.' She took it and wiped her eyes, reassuring Camelot she was all right. Then she passed back the damp hanky and rested her forehead against Camelot's, her hair a shield as it fell about her face.

Finian hadn't moved.

'I'm afraid I overstepped the mark just now with Mother and Father.'

'Your father doesn't strike me as the brutish type who'd strike a woman, but then I suppose you can never tell.'

'He's not, and he didn't.'

There was a moment's silence as Finian digested this.

'I'm a good listener, you know. My six sisters would tell you the same.'

'Six sisters! Your poor mother. I've only one, and she's one too many.'

Just as Cecelia wouldn't share her thoughts with him for a pound let alone a penny, she'd no intention of sharing more of what was, after all, family business with this man she barely knew. If she wanted to talk, she had Tomas or Lizzie, and Cyril too. He'd listen as he pulled weeds, but what could they say to her that she wasn't glaringly aware of. Nothing would change what had been decided, and short of running away in the dead of night, there was nothing she could do.

'Where's Raven?' she asked in an abrupt change of subject.

'Tomas is back. He's rubbing him down in the yard.'

Cecelia nodded, and for reasons she didn't understand – and despite her resolution not to share – she opened her mouth and said, 'I'm to go to London for the season and debut.'

'Like a prize filly being shown off at Ballinasloe Horse Fair?'

'Almost. Only, I'm the lame horse they're placing their bets on.' He'd put into words how she felt.

Finian ignore her comment. 'And you're not happy about being paraded about in all your finery trying to attract a buyer?' His eyebrow quirked again, but there was no glint of mirth in his eyes this time. 'Because I assume that the point of this London season is to find you a husband.'

'Of course I'm not happy, but I've little choice in the matter. Mother says it's a rich husband I've to find. Foxbourne's fate hangs on it.'

Finian stiffened. 'Sure, does your family not have enough already? And there's Raven, who's sure to bring in the big prize money.'

Cecelia felt the bitterness of his words like another slap. 'Foxbourne House is falling into disrepair. We only use half of it now because the west wing's roof is leaking and we no longer have the staff needed to run it. Father's fortune's been swallowed by land taxes.'

'A taste of his family's own medicine then. Are you different to them, Cecelia?' He reached out and gently stroked her tender red cheek with the back of his hand.

She should have stepped away, affronted by his audacity and disloyalty, but she didn't, and suddenly that was all she wanted. To be different from her family, to separate herself from what they stood for, but mostly she wanted to be loved. Cecelia was pinned under the intensity of that black-eyed gaze, and her lips parted slightly, certain he would kiss her.

'CeeCee, what's going on?' Tomas demanded as he led Raven into the stables.

'CeeCee?' Finian turned to Tomas and then looked back at Cecelia.

11

______

ST PATRICK'S MOTHER AND BABY HOME, 1920

The scrape of the bolt being slid free rang in Cecelia's ears. As the door opened, she stared at Sister Agnes through hollowed eyes like a fox startled in the light. She had no clue how long she'd been in the cupboard and had begun to think it was where she would die. That one day, one of the girls would be sent to fetch a bucket and mop only to find her skeletal remains.

'Out you come.'

She continued to sit there, sure she was dreaming, but the hand that reached in and dragged her out by the leg was real.

'Let that be a lesson to you, girl. God doesn't abide disobedience – it's a sin, and your soul is in peril.' Sister Agnes pointed down the corridor. 'Go and wash yourself – you stink, girl. Mop the floor in the cupboard and then get to your dormitory.'

It took Cecelia a few seconds to comprehend she'd been let out, and when she still didn't move, Sister Agnes clutched the sleeve of her nightgown, attempting to pull her to her feet. Terror at the thought of being put back in the cupboard rallied Cecelia enough to somehow stand up, and she stumbled, clutching the wall, not trusting her body to support her. A girl on her hands and knees scrubbing the floor glanced up and quickly looked away.

Cecelia's mind felt detached from her physical self as she pulled herself up the stairs, desperate for water. She cupped her hand beneath the tap in the washroom and slurped greedily, her tummy spasming as the cold water hit it. Then, she washed under her arms and her privates before forcing herself back down the stairs, where she mopped up the puddle of yellow there. Only then could she stagger toward her cot. She collapsed on it, and all she could smell as she lay there was Lysol and bleach from the cupboard. It was in her hair and on her skin, and she didn't think she'd ever be rid of the caustic stench.

It wasn't long before she became aware of someone approaching and opened her eyes. It was Nessa. Her brow was creased as she studied Cecelia, and this time the lively spark in her eyes had dimmed.

'I've been sent to fetch you. What happened?' she whispered. 'You were in bed when I went to sleep and gone when the bell rang in the morning. A whole day and a half's passed. I asked Sister Louise where you were, but she didn't know. She said she'd try and find out for me. Here.' She thrust a lump of bread at her. 'I'll bet you're starving.'

Cecelia didn't speak, but she took the bread and ate it quickly because for all she knew, Sister Agnes could be outside the dormitory, waiting to catch her out and throw her back in that dark hole of a cupboard.

Nessa gave her one last searching look then took her by the arm and steered her gently out of the dormitory to the dining hall. 'You'll feel better having something else to eat. Even if it is slop.'

Cecelia took her place on the empty bench seat in the dining room that Nessa led her to. She understood now that if she was to survive long enough to see her child born, then she'd need to draw on Nessa's strength and resourcefulness. Trust needed to be earned, though, and even then it could be broken in an instant. She didn't know if she had it in her to reach out, and she'd not given Nessa any reason to do so where she was concerned, but her kindness had seen her need, and she was reaching out anyway.

The only sound was the scrape of spoons on bowls, and she kept her eyes downcast, aware of curious, secret glances in her direction and the omnipresence of the nuns, watching their every move, waiting for them to sin.

12

FOXBOURNE HOUSE, IRELAND, 1919

All that existed was her and Camelot as they thundered over the ground toward her secret place. Tomas had sulked off. Let him, she'd thought as she'd stalked past him and Finian glaring at each other. She'd been so eager to make her escape, she'd led Camelot out and set off ahead of Finian, whom she'd been certain would follow her.

She'd been right, and he'd soon caught up with her, Finian egging on Raven with ease.

He was beside her as they emerged from the thicket to the lake.

'Hopefully we can finish our conversation without being interrupted this time.' A challenge flashed in his eyes, and their horses danced around one another, picking up on the tension between the pair.

'And where was that?' she asked, aware of exactly where they'd left off.

Finian's eyes crinkled, and she gripped the reins harder, convinced he could see into her soul, aware she was deliberately pretending forgetfulness.

'I asked you if you were different from your family, CeeCee?'

'Don't call me that.'

He was so close she could smell his scent – a mix of sweat, peat smoke and apple soap. Camelot and Raven had finished nudging and nipping one another now, and Raven was like a black dragon snorting smoke as he whickered softly. Camelot, meanwhile, contented himself with grazing the sparse offerings.

'I'm nothing like my family, not that it's any business of yours.'

'Do you believe in a free Ireland, Cecelia?'

The question surprised her, but her answer was easy. 'Yes, but Ireland doesn't believe in me anymore.' Now it was her turn to surprise him with a question of her own. 'Where do you come from, Finian Fahy?'

He eyed her speculatively. 'A smallholding on an estate much like Foxbourne. It wasn't an easy life – there were seven of us kids, and we all worked our fingers to the bone, but we got by. Da saw I had a way with our mare from the moment I was old enough to clamber on her back and made her my responsibility to care for. I loved auld Maggie. There was something about the way she trusted me...' His sharply drawn features softened.

'That's how I feel about Camelot.'

Their eyes locked in mutual understanding.

'I was drawn to the stables at the big house like a fly to honey. I couldn't keep away, and every chance I got, I'd head there to make a nuisance of myself, but I watched and learned until eventually I became useful.'

'The stables are my refuge,' Cecelia replied. 'It's where I feel most at home. There's no judgment there.'

Finian stared at her a moment and then nodded. 'My father was killed when I was twelve. His shirt caught in a threshing machine, and he was pulled in suddenly and crushed by the rotating belt.'

Cecelia's hand flew to her mouth, and she shuddered. 'I'm so sorry, Finian.' They were trite words for such a terrible accident, but what could she say? 'Were you there?'

The muscle at the corner of his mouth pulsed, and his jaw was rigid. 'I was. It was so quick. There was nothing we could do. It's not an image likely to be forgotten.'

'How do you survive that?' Cecelia pictured the scared young boy he must have been, and her hand let go of the rein. She half reached for him, wanting to reassure him with human touch, but she let her hand fall to her side.

Finian was talking once more – now he'd started his story, he wanted to finish it. 'You don't have a choice, but it was Maggie who helped me. She needed me, and I needed her. The routines of caring for her got me through each day. They're intuitive, horses – they understand what you're feeling.'

This was true, Cecelia thought, because how many times had she been comforted by caring for Camelot? Simply going through the motions of grooming him was soothing, and the rhythm of riding was an escape from what felt like a gilded cage.

'I was too young to take over running the farm though, and my mam couldn't manage with the little ones to care for too. Our crops failed, and without them we'd no way to pay the rent. Eventually we were evicted.'

Hot shame shot through Cecelia at the unjust treatment of a grieving family by an overseer like her father. 'Where did you go? And what happened to Maggie?'

'Maggie was sold before she could be taken off us for rent arrears,' Finian said bluntly.

A hard lump formed in Cecelia's throat as she imagined how the loss of his beloved friend, on top of what he'd already suffered, would have felt. She forced it down.

'My mam and sisters moved to Dublin. I stayed on at the estate, working in the stables as a way of paying off our debt.'

'I'm sorry for all your losses and suffering,' Cecelia said, wishing another word had been invented because she'd lost count of how many times she'd said 'sorry' in the last twenty-four hours. No doubt she'd soon be saying it to Tomas too, even if she didn't feel she should have to apologise to him. She hoped Finian, however, could hear how genuinely she meant her apology. 'I can't help what I was born into, but that doesn't mean I should be tarred with the same brush as my family.'

'You said you believe in a free Ireland.'

'I meant it too.'

'You've got a strength about you like Countess Markievicz.'

Cecelia's eyes widened. To be compared to the Irish suffragette and revolutionary was high praise.

'Dress suitably in short skirts and strong boots. Leave your jewels in the bank and buy a revolver,' she replied – the countess's famous phrase.

'Is that something you might be prepared to do for Ireland?'

Cecelia frowned. What was he asking of her?

'Will you come with me to a meeting in the village tomorrow night? There's someone speaking I think you should hear.'

Cecelia might be naive, but she was aware that if she agreed to go with Finian, she was stepping through a door into a murky world, a door that might not be easy to close and turn her back on if she decided she didn't want to follow him through it after all.

He retrieved a wedge of pamphlets from inside his coat pocket and pressed them on her. 'These might persuade you.'

She took the reading material and tucked it safely away on her own person. 'I don't need persuading.'

Countess Markievicz wouldn't have been frightened – she knew her own mind and was strong in her beliefs.

'I told you I'm as Irish as you are. I love my country, and I believe in a free Ireland.'

Cecelia could love him too if she let herself.

Tomas had moved on from his repairs and was engaged in an earnest discussion with Lord Kildurran – who cut a paunchy figure next to Tomas's lithe frame, ideal for jockeying – and a man she didn't recognise. Her eyes met Tomas's briefly in the hope of a clue as to what they were discussing. None was forthcoming, and her father didn't usher her over to be introduced either. Whatever the three of them were talking over was important, she deduced. That or her friend really was out of sorts with her. Either way, she didn't care, or so she told herself as she dismounted and led Camelot into the stables.

Cecelia found the house was quiet and still as she put her foot on the bottom step, eager to get to her room to read through what Finian had given her.

'Here's the lame duck.' Beatrice bobbed up on the landing.

'Go away, Bea.' Cecelia began hauling herself up with the bannister, but Beatrice was in the mood for goading her.

'It won't matter what fine dresses you wear, you know. No man will want to dance with a hop along like you. Your dance card will be empty, and you'll be the laughing stock of the season.'

Cecelia refused to rise to the bait. Besides, the last thing she wanted was a full dance card. 'I'd trade places with you in an instant if you were a few years older.'

Beatrice merely pulled a face and ran off, chanting childishly about 'quare-footed cripples' to look for trouble elsewhere.

Cecelia closed her bedroom door and turned the key in the lock. It wasn't something she usually did, but she didn't want Bea barging in on her.

Given the mood her sister was in, this was a distinct possibility, and she'd think all her Christmases had come at once if she were to catch her in possession of the subversive pamphlets. Cecelia could only imagine the pleasure she'd take in telling Mother and Father.

She sat down in the window seat where the light was best, took the band off the pamphlets and opened the first of them. It was by Michael Collins.

A changed young woman emerged from her bedroom upon hearing the dinner bell that evening. Cecelia's eyes had been opened by the passionate words of Michael Collins, Éamon de Valera and Arthur Griffith. She drifted through the meal of vegetable broth and brown bread, followed by reheated stew from the day before. There was nothing wrong with the food – Mrs Nolan was an excellent cook, but her mother's and sister's company at the table was to be endured rather than enjoyed. The slap still burned in Cecelia's memory as her mother spoke of nothing but London and the whirl of the high-society social scene. But she tuned her out, ignoring Bea's scowls and their father's absent-minded nodding along to what his wife was saying. He'd either come around to the idea of effectively selling his daughter off to the highest bidder and made peace with the expense of it, or, like Cecelia, he wasn't listening.

Cecelia couldn't stop mulling over Michael Collins' writing. It laid out the atrocities the Irish people had suffered at the hands of the British in blunt brushstrokes. She did not want to be tainted by the sins of her forefathers; she wanted to atone for them.

Her mind turned to the treatment meted out to Finian, his mother and sisters after the death of his father. The writings she'd devoured had been full of logic and emotion calling for action in a noble fight for freedom. It was as if something had sparked in her brain because she'd found something and someone to believe in, and she realised this was what she'd been looking for all along.

A sense of energy and unfamiliar purpose bubbled inside her, and she had no clue how she'd get through the rest of the evening and all the next day until the secret meeting commenced.

13

ST PATRICK'S MOTHER AND BABY HOME, 1920

Cecelia kept a tally of the time passing under her bed, etching a small line in the linoleum to signify each day with a knife stolen from the kitchen. This had been her only misdemeanour in the months since she'd discovered her money had been stolen. She kept the knife hidden in the bottom of her basket, using it to cover her markings each morning. It was the only way she could prove to herself she was still alive because she was dead inside. The other girls ignored the nightly scratching; everybody tried to get through their time here in their own way, and if it weren't for her countdown to when the baby would come and she could leave St Patrick's forever, she thought she'd surely go mad.

Some might say she already had if they were to eavesdrop on her hushed one-sided conversations with Lizzie late at night. Oh, she knew she wasn't here with her at St Patrick's right enough – that was a fate she wouldn't wish on anyone, let alone her dearest friend. It was just she missed her terribly. She missed the way her belly would ache with laughter at times when she was with Lizzie. Most of all, she missed the friend who'd accepted her for who she was in her heart, not blaming her for where that foolish heart had led her. She'd understood it was love that had led her down a tangled path of betrayal from Foxbourne to high society in London, then finally bringing her here to a place she was convinced was hell on earth. No one else would, and she couldn't share what she'd done with Nessa, not anyone. Her family's arm was long reaching, and so too was that of the IRA to whom she'd made a promise. And what of Finian, who'd promised to come for her?

Still, where the other girls were concerned, she felt a tinge of envy, especially when she heard Nessa and Molly sharing their secrets at night. Then she'd long to unburden herself and confess her own. Nessa had been so kind to her too.

Since the evening when she'd offered her the bread and she'd accepted, Cecelia sensed a curiosity in the younger girl to find out more about the soul she'd briefly glimpsed lurking beneath the icy veneer. She could never share her past with anyone in here, and so she'd put the shutters down around herself once more. Nessa would never believe that *Lady Mags* was a girl with a warm heart who could laugh like a drain or cry like a baby though, and she desperately wished she could show her that side of herself. A girl whose loyalty to those she loved knew no bounds but who also had it in her to betray her family and to spy for her country. So she kept Nessa's attempts at friendship at bay and her ear to the ground.

She needed to know what the future held and thus far had pieced together that some of the babies were adopted early in the piece. Their mothers, however, were expected to stay on for a year after the birth of their child to repay their debt to the sisters and do penance by working at the home. If the child wasn't fortunate enough to be adopted, then they might be farmed out for fostering before being sent to an industrial school. This was something she'd never heard of before, but she'd gleaned enough to know it was a type of orphanage that also took in abandoned or neglected children. The mothers who had nowhere to go outside of St Patrick's might be sent to work there or at the Magdalene Laundries to earn their keep.

She prayed her child would be adopted like the swaddled bundles she'd seen on rare occasions being whisked away from St Patrick's by well-turned-out couples who'd pull up in motor cars. On those fleetingly few times, she and the rest of the girls were kept out of sight. Now and again, however, they were paraded out to the front of the building and photographed. Babies died too, but no one spoke of that. To see their sunken-eyed, ghostly mothers as they left St Patrick's, however, was to know.

Cecelia's escape from the back-breaking days came at night when she couldn't sleep thanks to her baby's ferocious kicking, and with nothing more to tell Lizzie, she would revisit her old home. Despite wanting to leave it all behind, night after night she'd walk back down that twisting path that had brought her here to St Patrick's.

14

———

FOXBOURNE HOUSE, IRELAND, 1919

Cecelia opened her eyes to birdsong and the muffled sounds of the house coming to life for the day. The tap on her door sounded overly loud, and she jolted before clearing her throat, hoping it wasn't Bea come to gloat – or perhaps rail against the unfairness of not going to London too. She'd heard enough about that last night. 'Who is it?'

'Me, Lizzie. I've brought you some breakfast.'

Cecelia's shoulders relaxed.

The door creaked open, and Lizzie carried in a tray on which a cup of tea, a boiled egg and plate of toast sat. She set it down on the bedside table.

Lizzie perched at the end of the bed, and Cecelia pulled the tray onto her lap to begin tucking in. She could feel Lizzie studying her face and remembered her mother's slap. She'd all but forgotten about it with everything that had happened with Finian afterward.

'It's wrong her hitting you like so.'

She should have made that comfrey poultice, Cecelia thought as she gave a shrug more nonchalant than she felt. 'Sticks and stones and all that.'

'But I did try and stop you from listening in like so,' Lizzie added.

'I had to find out what they were arguing about.'

'And did you?'

Cecelia nodded. She'd found out so much more too, thanks to Finian, but she wouldn't speak of the meeting she was to attend with him tonight to Lizzie, despite Lizzie's brother having ties with the rebels.

'Will you tell me?'

'Eliza! Where are you?' Lady Kildurran's strident voice called before Cecelia could answer.

Lizzie rolled her eyes and stood up. 'I'll be back after I've seen what her ladyship wants with fresh sheets to put on your bed. You can tell me then.'

The food in Cecelia's belly had a galvanising effect. Once washed and dressed, she felt ready to face the day, but first she'd help Lizzie by stripping the bed.

Lizzie returned as she divested the pillows of their cases and eyed her friend suspiciously. 'And what is it you're after then?'

'It's my way of showing you how sorry I am for my thoughtlessness knocking you off your feet yesterday.'

'You're forgiven.' Lizzie beamed, depositing the fresh linen on the chair.

Cecelia picked up on a strange energy in the room and realised it was coming from Lizzie, who'd a daft smile on her face too.

'What did Mother want?'

Lizzie's eyes shone. 'I can hardly believe it, CeeCee. You and I, we're to go London! Has her ladyship told you I'm to serve as lady's maid to you and her while we're there for the season? Lord Rathlin is coming too.' She hugged herself, a dreamy expression on her face. 'London, me! Lizzie Murphy.

Can you imagine? I wonder if Big Ben is as big as I imagine it to be?'

Cecelia said nothing as she tucked her corner of the bed in, and Lizzie frowned again.

'Not like that, CeeCee. Sure, if you're to help me, it's got to do be done properly the way Mrs Behan showed me, or she'll have my guts for garters. Here – watch and learn.'

Cecelia barely paid attention as her friend folded and tucked the sheet under the mattress, pulling it tight before sweeping all the creases away with her hand. She was hurt that Lizzie should be so eager for the lure of the capital city across the sea, given what it meant for her. Nor would she ever understand her having eyes for her brother, Julian.

'Lizzie, you don't understand.' She picked up the top sheet. 'This isn't a holiday. We won't be admiring the sights. *I'm* to be one of the sights, shown off like a' – she remembered Finian's description – 'like a prize filly at Ballinasloe.' *With a limp*, she added silently, wondering what he saw when he looked at her.

Lizzie took the sheet from her, her eyebrow quirking. 'And where did you get a phrase like that? A certain racehorse trainer perhaps?'

So Tomas had mentioned having seen her talking with Finian in the stables yesterday. She was no longer in the mood to talk about that though. 'Never mind where. It's true – that's what matters. Mother wishes me to snare some new-monied dandy, given Foxbourne is collapsing around our ears and in desperate need of repairs for which, at present, there is no money in the coffers.' Cecelia didn't help her friend this time as she tackled the top sheet. 'What I want doesn't come into it.'

'You can be terribly childish, selfish and prideful too, CeeCee.' Lizzie straightened, her hand going to the small of her back. 'I'm not telling you that to be mean either but as your friend.'

Cecelia was stung. 'It doesn't feel like that.'

'Listen to me. It's survival of the fittest in these times we live in. Sure, my mammy has Seamus Foley lined up as a match for me because his family has a larger plot of land than we do. Do I love him? No, I do not. So why should you be different? Why should you get to choose whomever you want and to live the life you want?'

This was the first Cecelia had heard of her friend being married off. 'I didn't know. Why didn't you say something?'

'When should I have said something? Your head's too full of romantic notions – there's no room for anything else.' Her voice cracked. 'You never ask me how things are at home. I've lost my daddy and two brothers, and now I'm in the process of losing the only one I've got left—Frank—because of this place too. He resents me working here.' She waved her arm expansively. 'And he's going to get himself in bother with the authorities, given the men he's associating with. I don't want to lose him too.'

'I'm sorry, Lizzie. I didn't know how. I thought to speak of your losses would make it worse for you, and I'm sorry Frank's taking against you.'

Lizzie sank down on the bed, fighting tears, and Cecelia came to sit beside her. She took her hand in hers.

'And I'm sorry for you having to marry Seamus Foley.'

'Jesus wept, CeeCee, that's an awful lot of sorrys.'

'I meant each and every one of them.'

They sat in silence for a few moments, then Lizzie sniffed. 'There's Frank and others fighting for this glorious freedom for Ireland, but it won't bring freedom for the likes of us. What are we to do, eh? You're to marry a new-monied dandy from across the sea, and I'm to marry Seamus Foley when we return from London.'

They contemplated their fates, and Lizzie's tone was lighter as she said, 'And I don't mind telling you, CeeCee, Seamus Foley's a face on him that would drive rats from a barn.'

Cecelia's lips twitched. 'He can't be that bad.'

'Oh, he is.' Lizzie made paws of her hands and twitched her nose, giving a high-pitched squeak.

Cecelia began to giggle. 'You're to marry a rat and me a braying donkey.' She hee-hawed and did a lap of the room, then they both collapsed on the bed in fits.

She might have been born into a great house and Lizzie a small cottage, but they'd more in common than not, Cecelia thought, her stomach hurting.

The fire in the drawing room crackled as Cecelia coaxed it back to life with the poker as the simple meal of potato and roast duck settled in her stomach. The peat began to splutter, and she watched the turf smoke spiral up the chimney, aware that the silken fabric of her tea dress would go up like a tinderbox should a spark land on it. She took a step back. Her parents insisted the family adhere to the tradition of dressing for their evening meal, guests or no guests, with Lizzie roped in to help her mother with her toilette each evening. Lizzie had confessed to Cecelia that Lady Kildurran was a perfectionist and a hard taskmaster.

It was also the family's custom to venture through to this, her favourite room in the house. Cecelia enjoyed the drawing room not just because it was home to the baby grand whose keys Beatrice hammered at, though Cecelia loved to play as much as she loved Camelot. She loved the drawing room's graciousness. The room had a relaxed air lacking in so many of the formal rooms of Foxbourne where one perched instead of sat.

Ice chinked into a glass then, and the grandfather clock chimed nine.

There was now only two hours to go until she would sneak out to meet Finian. When he'd whispered in her ear outside the stables that he'd meet her by the coach house at 11.45 that night, she'd felt electric currents pulse through her veins. The day had stretched long, but she'd managed to while it away by avoiding Tomas and helping Cyril in the garden.

She was satisfied the fire would burn brightly now until it was dampened down for the night. As such, she sat on the sofa mirroring her mother and sister, hoping *Jane Eyre* would provide a distraction from their annoying chit-chat. The tea things and a plate of shortbread were on the low table between the sofas, and after helping herself to a piece, she picked up her well-thumbed book, intending to settle in.

Tonight, though, Jane, the strong-willed heroine she adored, couldn't hold her attention. Charlotte Brontë's words blended and blurred into one. Despite this, she kept her nose buried in the pages, peeking surreptitiously over the top and thinking that if a stranger were to burst in on them, all they'd see was a family at peace winding down from the day.

Her father was reclining in the high-backed armchair near the fire with the drinks tray close at hand. There was a rare air of contentment about him, as though he'd rubbed that whisky decanter until a genie had burst forth and granted him a wish – that all his financial woes and worries of being the last Altringham to inhabit Foxbourne had disappeared. He was nursing a whisky in one hand and a smouldering cigar in the other. What had he been discussing with Tomas and that strange man when she'd returned from her ride earlier? Cecelia wondered. Was that why he was in good spirits? She thought it must be to do with Raven.

His mood was particularly unusual given Julian – worse for wear with dark circles under his eyes and in need of a shave – had sauntered in just as they were seated in the dining room earlier. His tie had been askew and his suit crumpled, and poor Grainne had gone terribly red in the face when he'd addressed her directly to say there was no need to set him a place; he'd already eaten. To his parents, he'd merely stated he was in need of an early night before turning on his heel. Lord and Lady

Kildurran's demands to know where he'd been had fallen on deaf ears.

Her brother was a law unto himself, Cecelia had thought, unsure whether to be grateful that his behaviour had taken the focus off her, as Mother's previous good humour and twittering about London had ceased.

Beatrice, on the other hand, was playing the role of model daughter as she clacked her knitting needles, a skill taught to her by Mrs Flemington before she'd taken her leave of absence.

'I'm knitting you a scarf, dear Father.' She looked up, catching her sister's gaze. Beatrice's blue eyes gleamed slyly in the firelight. 'To keep your neck warm. You were complaining of a stiff neck the other evening, and I thought it might help you.'

Beatrice was all dimples and charm when it suited her, Cecelia thought, quick to glance away.

'Helen, aren't we blessed to have such a thoughtful child?'

Lady Kildurran bestowed a fond smile on her youngest daughter in agreement. Beatrice preened like a dog being petted.

'Cecelia, why don't you play for us? I'm in the mood for listening to something lively tonight.' Lord Kildurran was momentarily hidden behind a cloud of cigar smoke. He'd obviously forgotten his elder daughter's distemper at being sent to London against her wishes.

Perhaps it was wiser to pretend she'd accepted her impending debut in London society than it was to continue with her silent protest, Cecelia thought. 'Certainly, Father.'

Beatrice's clacking took on a furious quality, and Cecelia smiled inwardly because she could play the role of dutiful daughter just as well as her sister when it suited. Her obliging smile felt tight, but she kept it in place as she swept her skirt out from under her and sank onto the piano stool.

'Any requests?' Cecelia circled her wrists in a simple warm-up.

'"Pack Up Your Troubles in Your Old Kitbag." What say you, Helen?'

'If it pleases you, Alastair.'

Her mother could afford to be genial now she'd got her way about going to stay at her sister's, Cecelia thought, her fingers hovering briefly over the keys before she launched into the robust tune.

Father stamped his foot along, then set his drink and cigar aside and clapped heartily when she'd finished. 'Bravo. An encore, Cecelia!'

One more song turned into nearly her entire repertoire, and Cecelia's wrists were aching by the time her mother predictably announced it was getting late. She ventured upstairs to her room to get changed – not into her nightgown but into a more practical woollen day dress. It was nearly time to meet Finian.

The grandfather clocked chimed eleven. Cecelia, her coat buttoned to her chin, sat in the window seat watching the waning three-quarter moon disappear and reappear behind scudding clouds. Who would be at this meeting? she pondered, and would she recognise any of the villagers? A thrill ran up her spine as she stared out at the dark expanse of lawn. Her plan was to fetch her boots from the mudroom and slip them and her hat on once she'd let herself out of the house, and she was on tenterhooks now on the final countdown to the half hour.

At last, it rang out, and she rose from the seat and tiptoed to her door, opening it a crack and listening out. Aside from her father's rumbling snores, a result of the whisky he'd consumed, there was nothing. The house was asleep.

She crept from her room then stood stock-still in the

hallway as her eyes, enormous in her head, adjusted to the inkiness of the house's interior.

Cecelia cursed her leg, beginning to panic that Finian wouldn't wait for her, but it was too risky to have sneaked out any earlier. Her progress was slow because it was quieter to drag her leg rather than swing it, but as she was midway to the top of the stairs, the floor beneath her stockinged feet protested with a loud creak. She froze, holding her breath, relieved when the snores continued and no doors opened. The best option for the stairs, she decided, was to shuffle down on her bottom, as she'd done when the brace was still attached to her leg as a child. So, feeling faintly ridiculous, she did just that, bumping her way silently down to the entrance.

It was as she stood up and dusted the back of her coat off that she noted the lamplight. Someone was in the parlour!

15

———

What would she do if she were caught fully dressed wandering the house at this time of night? Cecelia cast about frantically for an excuse because she had nowhere to hide without making a run for it and waking the others upstairs.

Her shoulders stiffened at a rattling noise followed by the sliding sound of a drawer opening and closing. A throat cleared once, twice, and Cecelia's eyes widened then narrowed because she knew that sound. Julian had adopted a peculiar affectation of doing just this after his bout of bronchitis last year. It was her brother bumbling about in the parlour, but what on earth was he up to?

She risked a peek around the door.

'You might as well show yourself, Cecelia.' Her brother was holding up an oil lamp, which bathed him in an unholy glow and cast spectral shadows about his face, and he was staring straight at her. He was holding one of Mother's prize Dresden lace porcelain figurines in his other hand, and when her eyes swept to the cabinet where they were kept, she saw the shelf had been emptied. That wasn't all though. The writing desk with the drawer where the money set aside for household expenses was kept under lock and key was open, a scattering of papers spilled onto the floor.

'Why, Julian?' was the only thing Cecelia could think to ask.

'Debts, little sister, debts,' her brother said airily before rubbing at the stubble on his cheek. 'I thought I'd break a window and make it look like a burglary.'

'And do you expect me to remain silent while you stand by and rob your own family?'

Julian gestured to Cecelia's attire. 'You say nothing, I'll say nothing about your own nocturnal activities. Quid pro quo, as they say.'

Cecelia opened her mouth and then closed it. She had no choice and couldn't afford to waste any more time. Against her better judgment, she left Julian to finish his staged robbery and slipped silently from the house.

Finian was exactly where he'd said he'd be.

He dropped his cigarette upon seeing her, grinding it out with the toe of his boot before pushing off from the wall. 'I didn't think you were coming. I was about to go.' His voice was a low growl. 'They won't wait much longer.' He took a step away from the coach house.

'You shouldn't have doubted me.' She was aware of Tomas sleeping in the hayloft, and the thought of his disappointment in her if he were to catch her out almost made her change her mind. She forgot all about him, however, as Finian took her hand. A thrill bolted through her as they set off, and the walk across the lawns seemed interminable, but finally they reached the gates.

Cecelia emerged through them onto the lane beyond the estate. Finian dropped her hand and strode toward the horse and cart a short distance away. She caught hissed words drifting toward her and gleaned enough to know that she hadn't been expected and whoever was sitting on the bench seat, reins in their hands, was none too happy about her presence.

Finian must have convinced the driver she could be trusted because he clambered on the back of the cart, and she took his outstretched hand once more, quickly finding herself hauled up alongside him. They squeezed into a small space between crates down the back, and as an added precaution, he covered them both in burlap sacking. It reeked of onions, but Cecelia didn't care. All she was conscious of was she and Finian breathing as one beneath their covering, her shoulder, arm and thigh pressed up against his.

The cart rattled off into the night. Where they were going was a mystery soon to be revealed.

Cecelia felt as though every bone in her body had been shaken when the cart finally came to a halt. Finian tossed their coverings aside and helped her down, holding a finger to his mouth to signal the need for silence. She took a second to appraise where she was, but no clues were forthcoming. However, as she followed the two men over the rutted earth, trying not to stumble, she recognised the smell of animals. She had to be on a farm.

The moon chose to come out from behind the clouds just then, affording her a glance of her surroundings. Theirs wasn't the only horse and cart in the field, she saw. There was a cluster of motor cars too. Up ahead, she spied the lumpy, whitewashed walls and thatched roof of a farmhouse with a barn set back a little way from the house, both of which were in darkness. It was to the barn they were headed, she realised, as they veered past the house. A shiver of anticipation tempered with anxiety coursed through her as Finian rapped on the door.

'The moon is bright tonight,' he said softly, and the door creaked open.

An older man with a weathered face and wiry, white eyebrows encroaching on his eyes peered out at them, sizing them up before stepping aside to let them in. Cecelia blinked, not sure what to expect as the trio stepped inside what, from the exterior, appeared to be a deserted barn.

It was anything but.

The barn was lit by a single paraffin lamp, and for a moment, Cecelia felt choked by the air, which was thick with pipe smoke. The sweet tobacco smell mingled with dung, animal sweat and wet wool, and it was just as cold in here as it was outside, so she huddled into her coat, continuing her appraisal from under her hat. Well-used tools were stacked against rough stone walls, while a rickety ladder balanced precariously led to a hayloft. Overhead, through the slats, silvered moonlight sneaked in, illuminating the spiderwebs. Then her gaze spanned the sombre faces of the milling group, and she did her best not to linger or show surprise at how many she recognised. The voices filling the smoky space were hushed and urgent, but one cut through them all.

'Finian, Ruairidh, what's she doing here?'

Cecelia hunted out the source and locked eyes with Frank Murphy, Lizzie's brother. The hatred she could see blazing back at her for what he thought she represented made her shrink into her coat.

'She can be trusted, Frankie,' Finian replied.

Cecelia wanted to turn on her heel and run back out the barn door. She'd been stupid to come. Stupid for thinking she might belong here with these people, and when Finian left her side, crossing the straw-strewn boards to speak with Frank, she understood how vulnerable and precarious her position was. These were not ordinary times.

She took a step back but stumbled into a solid form and knew it was too late to leave. The choice was no longer hers to make. One woman against a roomful of men and women who had no reason to trust her and every reason to hate her Anglo-Irish blood would not let her leave without a fight.

Whatever Finian had said saw Frank glance at her once more, eyes narrowing, before he gave a curt nod. The shoulders of men around him relaxed. He was in charge then, Cecelia deduced, wondering if Lizzie was aware of her brother's illegal nocturnal activities.

Cecelia chose to remain near the back, having no wish to be too visible as Frank stepped up on a makeshift podium – an upturned crate. He wasn't a charismatic speaker, but he was deadly serious, his voice low and gruff as he went through the meeting's agenda. Cecelia'd had an inkling of what to expect this evening, but still, to hear things spoken of, like the planned raid of the nearby RIC barracks in a few nights, made it real. She tried to keep her expression neutral. Having heard Michael Collins' rallying cry within his written words, she understood that violence was a necessary measure in this war for independence.

As Frank stepped down, he sought her out and mimed zipping his lips closed. The two fingers he cocked at her like a pistol, a silent threat of what would happen should she talk, made her tremble, but she kept her head held high, determined not to show him fear. Her insides, however, had liquefied with terror at what she'd got herself into.

Now Frank had spoken, she assumed everyone would begin to disperse, but he wasn't the only speaker of the evening. A reverential silence fell over the barn as the crowd parted and a man who stood out from the ragtag small crowd for the fact he was well dressed stepped up in Frank's place. Perhaps she wasn't the odd one out after all, Cecelia mused.

She forgot her discomfort and to breathe as she listened to the man's impassioned speech. It was much like what she'd read in the pamphlets Finian had given her, and the atmosphere around her had become charged by his rallying call to action. She could feel his words inside her like a brand. She knew she'd never forget this evening, that it would be pivotal in her life and afterward.

When it was over and the man – who never gave his name – stepped down to be swept out the door into the night, flanked in the front and back by the sort of men you wouldn't want to cross, Finian turned to Cecelia. 'What would you do for a free Ireland, Cecelia? he asked.

'Whatever it takes,' she replied, meaning every word of it.

They barely made it inside the coach house, stumbling over one another in their haste to resume the hot kisses that had begun in the back of the cart on the return journey to Foxbourne. Cecelia had left the meeting fired up, a passion burning inside her that she hadn't known existed. It was a passion that needed an outlet. Finian had asked her earlier what she would do for a free Ireland, and she'd given him her answer. She knew too, as Finian slipped her coat from her shoulders, his eyes darkening as he began to unbutton her dress, she'd do whatever it took to have him too.

16

ST PATRICK'S MOTHER AND BABY HOME, 1920

The mound of potatoes dug from the gardens that morning appeared sky high to Cecelia. She was at the work table in the kitchen, steadily ploughing her way through them with the paring knife. There was no seat on which to perch while she worked, and her feet and legs ached with the extra weight she was carrying. The days seemed longer than ever because she was constantly weary. But Cecelia didn't complain. It had been drummed home to her she was no more special than any of the other girls and to do so would only bring a sharp rebuff. She'd already heard enough about suffering being penance to last the rest of her days.

It was as she paused to dig out the eye of the spud cupped in her hand that she felt a pop and then a warm gush between her legs. The knife dropped with a clatter, and she braced herself for Sister Agnes's wrath over her having wet herself.

'Clean that up, Margaret,' the nun barked with a note of disgust in her voice.

Feeling she'd got off lightly, Cecelia hurried off to fetch the cleaning things. She was eager to hide her mortification from the other girls at having wet herself without even having been aware she needed to go.

She hurriedly glugged disinfectant into a bucket and lumbered back to the kitchen with her smock clinging to her legs. As she got on with the business of mopping up her mess, a searing-hot poker of pain suddenly ripped through her, causing her to cry out in surprise and terror.

Wide eyes swung toward where she was hunched over on the floor.

'Hush, child. Don't make such a fuss. It's your time.' Then with a clap of the hands Sister Agnes ordered, 'Get back to work, girls, or there'll be no tea for any of you.'

Her waters had broken! She'd overheard whispered night-time conversations in the dormitory about this. That meant the baby was on its way.

Sister Agnes's eyes were flinty as she said, 'Once you've put the pail back where you found it, go and clean yourself. Someone will fetch you shortly from your dormitory.'

Cecelia was reluctant to leave the comfort of the other girls' presence, even if she'd barely spoken to any of them. She was terrified and didn't want to be alone but knew better than to argue. As the pains tore at her, her love for Finian turned to hatred for what was happening to her now.

It was a slow journey to the washroom, and every few steps, she was immobilised by the spasms ripping through her. To not call out took all her strength, and she clamped her jaw so hard she thought she'd surely crack her teeth.

Eventually, she made it to the basin, and once she'd cleaned herself, changed into fresh underwear and her nightgown, unsure what to do with her wet things, she lay on her cot. Cecelia curled on her side with her hands clasping her belly, moaning softly, and in between the pains, she sobbed with fear hoping what came next would be quick.

A bell rang in the distance. She wasn't aware of how long

she'd been lying there, but another bell had rung, and the shadows were beginning to lengthen on the floor. The poker was jabbing her faster and faster now, and through the haze of pain she saw an angel. Sister Louise was holding a hand out to her. She grasped hold of it, sobbing as she heard her say, 'God's with you, child. You'll have your baby soon.'

All Cecelia could remember after that was a sterile, cold room and lying on a cot with only a sheet covering it, a crucifix chastising her from the wall while a sister stood alongside the bed praying. There was the clack-clack-clack of rosary beads and another sister down the foot of the bed peering between her legs, saying, ''Tis the price of sin you're paying. Now bear down.' She also recalled kind brown button eyes and knew Sister Louise hadn't abandoned her. Her presence willed her on, and she used every ounce of her being to push the baby into the world. The mewling cry that suddenly filled the room both astounded and bewildered her. She'd done it.

'A girl,' the sister at the foot of the bed stated, swiftly wiping the newborn down and swaddling her.

Cecelia turned her head to one side to look at the wall as the newborn was whisked away, and she was told to bear down once more. A slithering sensation followed as a single tear trekked down her cheek. But she was to be given no peace or time to recover.

'Up you get.'

It wasn't Sister Louise's voice.

'Where's Sister Louise gone?' Cecelia sought reassurance from the kindly nun as she eased herself off the bed.

'She's been called away – not that it's any business of yours.' The older nun whipped the bloodied sheet off the bed, leaving it in a bundle near the door. 'Clean up, and put this on.' She picked up a smock from the shelf. 'When you're dressed, you can take that sheet to the laundry and return to your dormitory.'

Cecelia did as she was told, and when she reached her cot, it was a relief to sink down on it and release the torrent of tears. The emotion of birth was not something she'd expected. That there'd be pain, yes, but not these feelings that were too big to put into words and that she didn't understand.

Eventually, she must have drifted off because unexpectedly she was being shaken awake.

A girl she knew by sight but not name was standing beside her cot. 'You're to come to the nursery.'

Cecelia roused herself and padded after the girl, who didn't look back to see if she was following her.

As they neared the nursery, the wails of babies grew louder. Some were demanding, some apathetic – the latter a heartrending sound. Something primal stirred deep within Cecelia, spurring her on even though she was more tired than she'd been in her life. Her body felt raw, and she was still bleeding, while two wet patches had soaked through her smock, but she became oblivious to all of this in her sudden desperate need to reach her daughter.

Inside the nursery, the girl who'd been sent to fetch her hurried over to where a cluster of other girls were feeding their babies. She took her place amongst them on an empty stool, and a sister plucked a tiny baby from their cot, then held the little one out in front of her and ordered the girl to see to it.

Cecelia blanched at the barked order as she stood in the doorway, letting the odour of ammonia, sour milk and other things drift out to the corridor. A girl changing a fetid nappy glanced over and inclined her head. Cecelia took the hint and closed the door. She didn't want to look, but her eyes were drawn to a pasty tot who was standing up in his cot and clutching the rails, red faced and howling. Another poor little mite clutched a bottle and fed themself. Why was no one holding these babies and offering warmth?

She knew the answer, and it was one she didn't want to face. There was no point loving these babies because they'd either be adopted, fostered out or in another year or so sent to the industrial school. She felt numb at the realisation as she moved toward the other girls, pulled up a chair and gingerly sat down.

'Name?' The Sister fixed her gaze on Cecelia.

'Margaret.'

The nun marched over to a cot and fetched a small writhing bundle, which she placed in Cecelia's outstretched arms. She'd never held a baby in her life, and this hot, angry, swaddled child let her know she knew it too.

'Support baby's head, you fool girl.'

Cecelia carefully rejigged her.

'Not like that.' The Sister impatiently rearranged the baby girl. 'Now feed her and be done.'

How? Cecelia wanted to cry, and in desperation as the baby began to nudge at her breast, she unbuttoned her smock with one hand and tried to steer the tiny head with its downy covering of doe-brown hair toward her. The baby fussed, her little face furious, and Cecelia side-eyed the other girls, trying to see what she was doing wrong.

'What hope is there for you if you can't use the breast God gave you?' The Sister bustled toward her and yanked her breast, then jammed her baby's head onto it.

Cecelia felt her latch and begin to suck furiously. Tears marred her vision as she gazed down at the closed eyes and soft cheek of the baby she was nursing. Now she knew what those swarming big feelings were. Love. This babe in her arms was no longer 'the baby' she'd carried inside her for nine months. She was here and very real. This was her daughter, *her* baby. How could she give her up?

. . .

'You had a girl,' Nessa stated when Cecelia returned to the dormitory, thrusting a small pile of clothing at her. 'Here, I washed your things. What did you call her?'

'Thank you,' Cecelia said dully, taking the undergarments from her. Nessa deserved an answer in return for the small kindness. 'We're not supposed to name the babies. And I'll be in bother if I'm caught speaking to you.'

'That's true enough, but there's no big bonnet about to hear you, is there? And you must have a name for her.'

It all bubbled up inside Cecelia – the horror of the birth, the heartbreak of not being able to hold her baby afterward. Most of all, she wanted to tell her about the confusing rush of emotions, a love bigger than she could have ever imagined when her daughter had latched on to her breast and now the fear of not being able to keep her. But her reply was wooden. 'No, I don't, and nor will I.'

She got into bed and pulled the covers over her. She wouldn't name her child because doing so would make the inevitability of losing her harder. Since arriving here, she'd been determined her child would be adopted, leaving her free to leave St Patrick's and begin afresh, but holding her baby daughter in the nursery had changed everything. The bond was instant. Her throat had ached with the futility of her emotions because to keep the child safe, she needed to put distance between her and her family, but that would take money, and hers was gone. How could she look after herself, let alone her baby, outside St Patrick's four walls? And what sort of a mother would she be if she put her own want and need before the well-being of her child?

She explained none of this to Nessa, however, because it was too painful to put a voice to. Instead, she reached out her hand, desperate for comfort, and felt Nessa take hold of it.

17

FOXBOURNE HOUSE, IRELAND, 1919

It was raining heavily the following morning when Cecelia awoke. A smile played on her lips, and her fingers traced them gently. They felt tender and swollen. The pattering against the windowpane was almost hypnotic as she relived the moment Finian had pushed her gently down on his bed. He'd made her feel beautiful for the first time in her life. Not just that, he'd offered a different path for her to take to the one laid out by her parents – a worthy path too, putting what her father and his ancestors had done right – and she desperately wanted to take it.

She stretched and yawned in her bed. What would it be like to wake next to Finian? she wondered, curling her toes, aware she couldn't spend the day dreaming. Julian's staged burglary couldn't have been discovered yet, as the house was too quiet, and given the rain, she imagined poor Lizzie, the first to rise, frantically placing buckets under the worst of the leaks in the west wing. She'd be too busy to notice anything amiss in the parlour. Still, it was only a matter of time.

She'd no choice but to get up, so she reluctantly sat up and swung her legs over the side of her bed, allowing herself a moment to stretch and yawn. She'd only dozed for a few snatched hours, having lain her head down just as the birds were beginning to chatter. Her body had been tingling to its very tips and her mind too wired for deep sleep. Besides, she'd wanted to relive the evening and everything she'd heard, the swell of emotions stirred at the meeting, but most of all she'd wanted to replay the passion that had come later – the moment she'd given herself to Finian.

Cecelia knew she was forever changed and that all that had come to pass in the hours after midnight would stay with her forever.

The iciness of her bedroom meant she was dressed in record time, and as she made for the door, a scream ricocheted through the floorboards like a gunshot. The crime had been uncovered then, she thought, hearing pounding footsteps as she too hurried from her room.

Her leg ached by the time she reached the landing. It always throbbed when it rained heavily, and she paused partly to rest and partly to survey the scene in the entranceway below. Mother, her hands clasped in front of her as though praying, was leaning heavily against Julian, whose arm was clasped tightly around her shoulder, supporting her. If only she knew what a cuckoo in the nest he was, Cecelia thought.

Lizzie hovered nearby, wringing her hands, no doubt wishing Julian's arm was around her, while Bea was being told to stay away from the parlour by Mrs Behan, lest she cut herself on the broken glass. None of them saw her, so Cecelia nipped the inside of her bottom lip and prepared herself to give a convincing performance of bewilderment.

As she made her way down the stairs, the huddled group was alerted by the thudding of her bad leg as she dragged it down each step. 'What on earth's happened?' she asked without so much as a blink of the eye.

. . .

Breakfast was a fraught affair, the atmosphere teetering on the edge as enough tea was drunk to sink a ship. Lord Kildurran plunged his toast soldier into his soft-boiled egg as though it were a sword into a body. In between mouthfuls, he spat words like *audacity* and muttered about hanging not being good enough for those blackheart rebels who'd dare to bite the hand that fed them.

So the finger of blame for the burglary was being pointed at those whose loyalties didn't lie with the crown, Cecelia thought.

It was a relief when a loud rapping sounded, signalling the cavalry had arrived, and plates were pushed away and chairs scraped back.

The constable Tomas had been sent to fetch was a bean-pole of a man who assessed the crime scene while Julian hovered nearby. Cecelia wondered if she was the only one to notice her brother mopping his brow on several occasions while the constable took notes in between pacing slowly about the parlour. Tomas stood at the ready with a hammer and nails along with a stack of wooden planks to board up the gaping window. It was freezing in the cavernous hall at the best of times, let alone when an arctic wind was howling through it. The sooner he got to work, the better, Cecelia thought, shivering as she waited her turn to give her brief statement.

'I slept through the entire thing, Constable.'

Tomas, she sensed, was watching her, but when she offered him a smile, all she received in return was a look filled with a sadness she couldn't make sense of. Nor could she be bothered to, and she melted into the background, hoping nobody would notice her slipping away. They didn't, and soon she was splashing through freshly formed puddles in her haste to get to the stables. Her breath quickened as the familiar smells of horses and hay assailed her.

Finian was soothing Raven, who was pawing at the ground.

Wondering why the horse was agitated, Cecelia looked past him to see Camelot's stall door was open.

Not pausing to greet Finian, she made to push past him to the stall, but he stepped in front of her, blocking the way and grasping her by her upper arms. She could feel his fingers pressing into her flesh and wondered what was going on.

'I'm sorry, Cecelia.' Finian shook his dark head, but she shoved him away, determined to see in her beloved horse's stall for herself.

It was empty, and her questioning gaze raced to Finian once more. 'Where's Camelot?'

'Cecelia, I'm sorry.'

'Just tell me!'

'He's been sold. An agent brokered the deal with a contact your father had in England. He was picked up at first light and will be shipped from Dublin to England.'

Cecelia shook her head, feeling as though she'd fallen into the dark waters of Lough Rae because what Finian said couldn't possibly be true. Camelot couldn't be gone. He wasn't her father's to sell. He was *her* horse.

She spun round then upon hearing her name being shouted. Tomas was standing breathless in the entrance to the stables, his red hair plastered to his face.

'Cecelia.' His voice sounded urgent. 'This is the first chance I've had to talk to you.'

That was a lie – he could have forewarned her in the entrance earlier but was too much of a coward to do so.

'Why didn't you tell me?' Was that her shrieking? Her mind spun back to seeing her father, Tomas and a man she didn't recognise in conversation the other morning when she returned from her ride. She flew at him then, pummelling him with her fists. 'You knew. You knew, and you didn't say anything. I could have stopped it if I'd known. I'll never forgive you for not telling me, never!'

Tomas caught hold of her wrists and held her at bay. 'I couldn't stop him, Cecelia, and I didn't know how to tell you. I knew you'd be heartbroken, and I couldn't bear to see it. The last thing I'd ever want to do is hurt you.'

Finian prised her away and held her protectively to him. 'I think it's best you make yourself scarce for the time being,' he growled at Tomas.

Cecelia buried her face in his broad chest and sobbed. Her heart wasn't just broken, it was smashed so badly she doubted it could ever be mended.

Something had snapped deep inside her. Tomas, whom she'd loved dearly, had betrayed her. As for her father, he walked in his wife's shadow yes, but she'd thought he didn't possess her cruel streak, yet he'd done the cruellest thing imaginable to her.

The flickering firelight of rebellion that had been ignited in her last night had been fanned, and any last, lingering loyalty within her had vanished like Camelot. Her father was dead to her now.

18

That flame had burned brighter a few evenings later when Lord Kildurran had made everyone in the drawing room jump with his sudden slamming down of the newspaper before expressing outrage over the barracks on the outskirts of the village having been robbed. Weapons had been stolen, he'd thundered, and Cecelia had hidden her smile behind the pages of her book. This was what she'd heard being planned at the meeting. They meant business, Lizzie's brother, Finian and their comrades.

She'd relayed this to Finian as she lay with her head resting on his shoulder the next morning, having ridden on the back of Raven with her arms wrapped around his waist to the lake. This was where he'd spirit her most mornings. They'd make love then lie under a horse blanket, Cecelia in his arms, listening as he educated her about the ongoing injustices and efforts he and other like him were making, risking their very lives in fact, to right the wrongs of history. Little by little, hate began to consume her grief over losing Camelot, and it threatened to turn septic like an infected wound if she didn't find somewhere to put it.

Tomorrow, she'd leave for London. She had no choice in the

matter for now, so she sat up and drank in the vista. Raven was drinking water near the lake's edge, and Lough Rae looked even more mysterious than usual this morning, with pockets of low-lying mist hovering over its dark waters. The reeds were whispering too, or was it the faeries?

'What am I going to do? I don't want to leave you, Finian.' Cecelia wanted him to tell her he had a plan. To say they'd run away together and start afresh. She thought longingly of America, imagining a life where they could be whomever they wanted. If this was what he'd said they'd do, then she wouldn't have hesitated to pack her things and leave behind all this festering hatred, along with the only life she'd ever known, for a new beginning with him. She knew it was a foolish dream, though, because his love for his country ran too deep to abandon her in her time of need.

He cupped her face in his hands then, and what he did say wasn't what she desperately wanted to hear, but it set her heart pounding with fear and excitement nonetheless.

'Do you remember what you said, Cecelia, the night of the meeting in the barn, about doing anything for a free Ireland?'

'Of course I do. And I meant it.'

His eyes were even blacker than Lough Rae's water as they bore into hers. 'There's a way you can help.'

'How?'

He dropped his hands then and began to pace. 'You told me your uncle in London is heavily entrenched in politics. That's right, isn't it? Sir George Cathcart – he's in the War Office.'

Had she? She didn't recall doing so, but she must have. 'Yes. He is. Uncle George is a retired general.' Cecelia was curious where Finian was going with his questioning.

'And as such he has access to important information we could use to fight our side. Information as to planned military responses, coordinated attacks in retaliation to our activities here, like where the Black and Tans are to be deployed.'

It dawned on her what he wanted her to do. 'You want me to spy?'

'For Ireland, yes.'

Cecelia closed her eyes. What had her family ever done for her? Her father and his forefathers had stolen from this country they claimed to love. Her father had even stolen from her. She owed her family nothing, and this would give her an agenda of her own, as well as giving her time in London a purpose. It would carry her through her separation from Finian and make the farce of her participation in the season bearable.

She opened her eyes and asked, 'But how?'

'By listening – and looking. I hear your man's fond of entertaining and partial to a drop.'

'You know an awful lot about him, Finian.' Cecelia was taken aback. He knew more about Uncle George and her family across the water than she did.

'It's my business to, and I have my contacts.' His voice was a growl. 'Men talk when they've been drinking. Things slip that shouldn't.'

'Loose lips sink ships,' Cecelia murmured then.

'Never a truer word spoken. I want you to be our eyes and ears in that house, Cecelia. There'll be information in his study too. Confidential files he'll bring home for safekeeping.' There was an urgency in his tone.

'I understand what you're asking, but what do I do if I hear or find anything?' She wondered if he knew what an impossible task he was setting her.

As he began to speak of a contact in London – the Cathcarts' chauffeur no less – to whom she could pass on anything she uncovered, her eyes widened. It surprised her to learn that in this war for an independent Ireland, spies were everywhere, even in London, right under her uncle's nose. She remarked on this, and Finian's response was the Brits' arrogance would be their undoing in the end.

'Can I count on you?' he asked her. 'Will you do this for me?'

'But gentlemen linger after dinner to discuss their business while us women withdraw to the drawing room. Things are done a certain way.'

Finian snorted. 'And since when have you done things the expected way. You're a resourceful girl – you'll find a way.'

His trust in her incited her. 'I'll do it. For Ireland and for you.'

'Good girl, yourself. There're lives, my own included, depending on you.'

'What I won't do is marry some wealthy eejit I don't love.'

'You won't have to. I'll send for you before it comes to that. I love you, girl.'

She swooned inside on hearing this because she loved the very bones of him. He'd awakened her from what felt like a long sleep and imbued her with passion and purpose. She'd do anything for him. 'And I love you.'

When they broke apart from their kiss, Cecelia looked deep into his eyes. 'Promise me you'll send for me, Finian.'

'I promise.'

It was enough. It had to be.

19

———

ST PATRICK'S MOTHER AND BABY HOME, 1920

Cecelia's baby was two weeks old, and her efforts to feed her, along with the long days spent on her feet, meant she'd fallen into a deep sleep when something jerked her awake. Movement – an oil lamp was bobbing through the dormitory. A new girl was arriving and huddled into herself. She heard Sister Louise call her Theresa before she shone the lamp on the bed next to Nessa's, whispering instructions. She was fortunate it was Sister Louise who was on duty tonight, Cecelia thought, shuddering at the memory of her own arrival.

It was no surprise to hear Nessa whispering to the girl once Sister Louise had left. Not wishing the new arrival to get into bother, she called out, 'Shush, you'll get us in trouble.'

'Sister Louise turns a blind eye to talking, Lady Mags,' Nessa flung back at her. Their truce was forgotten now Cecelia's barriers were firmly back in place.

There were only so many times you could push a person away, Cecelia realised sadly, as fed up with the taunt, she protested feebly, 'Don't call me that. My name's Cecelia, and you know it.' She was not Lady Mags, or Margaret, as the Reverend Mother had decreed she should be called.

More than anything, she wished things were different and she could open up to Nessa, but to trust her, anyone, was to put herself and her baby at risk. Her mother would not forget, and she would certainly never forgive. Hogan, the Cathcarts' chauffeur who'd been her London contact too, had told her she should disappear. It was too risky to tell anyone who she was and why she'd come here.

'Yes, *Lady Cecelia*. Don't mind her. She's a fancy piece that one who thinks she's too good for the likes of us. But we're all sinners according to God, and that's why we're here,' Nessa whispered.

Cecelia said nothing. She was too tired to bite back, and she understood she'd hurt Nessa. What did it matter what this new girl thought of her?

Her eyes grew heavy and fluttered shut. Dark eyes and coal-black curls no longer taunted her. They'd been replaced by her daughter's tiny, sweet face, and she tuned out Nessa and the new girl she was befriending and drifted back to sleep.

Theresa, it turned out, had a glorious mane of red hair that glowed in the morning light, and there was something about her that made Cecelia feel their paths had crossed before. She couldn't put her finger on where though. Her red hair set her apart from the other girls, which wasn't a good thing in a place like this, Cecelia thought, as they shuffled in line for the washroom. She had stood out with her fine clothes and fancy ways, not to mention her limp, when she'd arrived, and Sister Agnes had been quick to slap her down. She wanted to tell this girl – whose real name she'd overheard her whisper to Nessa was Maudie – to keep her head down and not do anything to further draw attention to herself, but she stayed quiet.

When Nessa's whispered instructions as to what to expect morphed into a ghost story about the building having been a workhouse, however, she had to speak up. 'Stop filling her head with nonsense, Nessa,' she threw over her shoulder, being careful Sister Catherine didn't catch her talking.

Cecelia caught snatches of Nessa's retort, but she tried to pretend she couldn't hear her, especially when she said, 'No one likes her.'

Sister Catherine called out, 'No talking!'

Cecelia glanced down at her chest. She'd begun to leak. Catching Maudie staring, and still stinging from Nessa's remark, she hissed, 'One can always tell one's breeding by one's manners, and it's rude to stare, don't you know?' She turned away and shuffled forward in the line, feeling Maudie's eyes still on her. No doubt she was surprised by her limp. Well, Cecelia didn't care. Let her stare.

Days rolled over into weeks, and Cecelia watched on as Maudie and Nessa formed a tight bond, both girls protective of young Molly, who was now fit to burst. She watched and she listened, feeling terribly alone in the darkened dormitory.

One night, Cecelia, awake still, heard Nessa whispering and couldn't help but hear her telling Maudie about how she'd gone to work as a live-in housemaid for a factory owner and his family in Dublin. She'd only just turned fourteen and had let the man of the house have his way with her because he'd treated her kindly. Now, here she was at St Patrick's. Curious as to Maudie's journey, Cecelia's ears continued to burn and turned red hot upon hearing her confide in Nessa that she was from Rush. That was why she'd been familiar to her! She'd ridden Camelot through the town on many occasions. Maudie, she learned, had been informally engaged to an Irish rebel whom she'd given herself willingly to.

How she wished she could tell her about Finian! They had more in common than she could have imagined. When she spoke of being raped by a Tan, the pain in her voice at not knowing who her baby's father was, along with Nessa's naivety, nearly cracked Cecelia's icy veneer. Her heart ached for the torment Maudie was suffering.

Still, she said nothing, keeping her own story under lock and key. It was the way it had to be, even though she'd grown up a virtual neighbour of Maudie's.

Don't trust anyone, Cecelia, for your baby's sake, for Finian's sake and for your own. It had become her mantra. She'd known when she'd set off to London that someday there'd be a price to pay for what she intended to do. Well, that day had come when she'd arrived at St Patrick's. She'd never imagined her actions would come at a cost this high, though, because the loneliness that engulfed her days and nights was becoming unbearable.

20

———————

Just as Cecelia had feared, it wasn't long at all before Maudie caught Sister Agnes's eye, and while she was disgusted with herself over the relief she felt at no longer being under the nun's scrutiny, she worried for Maudie. She could sense Sister Agnes watching and waiting for a reason to strike as she had with her. The atmosphere in the kitchen was taut. It was like the nun was a rope being pulled tighter and tighter, and it was beginning to fray. Cecelia kept her own counsel, however, as she silently hoped Maudie would do nothing to make that rope snap.

But all of this disquiet was swept away and replaced with a more immediate concern when, in the darkened dormitory one night, Nessa began labouring. Her screams of agony echoed in all their ears long after she'd been dragged callously from the dormitory by Sister Agnes, who, as fate would have it, was on duty.

She didn't come back to the dormitory the next day or the day after that, and Cecelia held her daughter even tighter in the nursery. Nessa's disappearance without explanation only cemented the need to hold herself back from the others. No one could be trusted. She missed her though. She and Maudie were

the only two girls who'd offered the hand of friendship to her –
Maudie a kind soul who'd offered her pilfered bread which
she'd all but slapped away. She'd determinedly seen off
Maudie's efforts, just as she had Nessa's, because of the secrets
she carried inside her. Foreboding filled her as to what could
have happened to Nessa and her baby. She was terrified of what
it meant because if Nessa and her baby could vanish, then so
too could her own daughter.

The passing of time saw her baby girl introduced to soft mash,
and she was moved to a different wing, a nursery for weaning
babies. This was a space that should have been filled with
shouts and laughter as the children learned through play.
Instead, only their basic needs were seen to. For now, Cecelia
was allowed to take her baby's food to her as she supplemented
with her breast milk. But the dawning of each new day saw her
wake terrified that today would be the day she'd no longer be
allowed to do so.

Equally terrifying was how Nessa seemed to have been
forgotten by everyone except Molly, Maudie and herself, even if
she kept her own counsel about the girl she'd wanted so badly to
be friends with. It was as if Nessa had never been at St Patrick's
in the first place, and the only bright spot during the long
months since her disappearance was Molly bearing a bonnie
little boy. She called him Connor, and to see the young girl's joy
over her son was bittersweet because she didn't comprehend not
being allowed to keep him.

Cecelia had come to admire Maudie's loyalty. She was
determined not to let the disappearance of her friend go, but it
was costing her because she was wasting away.

You've got your baby to think of, Cecelia wanted to whisper
when Sister Agnes was out of earshot in the kitchen where they
worked alongside one another, but she doubted Maudie would

take kindly to advice from someone who'd never spoken more than a sentence to her.

One morning, however, as Sister Agnes herded Cecelia back inside the kitchen, reprimanding her for taking too long feeding the pigs, she fretted Maudie had gone too far. She'd used the sister's brief absence from the kitchen to slip away in order to press the Mother Superior for Nessa's whereabouts. Her stupidity or bravery got her nowhere, and her insolence had repercussions because Sister Agnes was raked over the coals for not watching her charges, and Cecelia knew it was only a matter of time until she made Maudie pay for going behind her back.

Then one evening, the rope holding Sister Agnes in check snapped.

It was the end of a long day and time for evening Mass. Cecelia and the other girls were shuffling out of the kitchen when Sister Agnes stepped in front of Maudie and accused her of stealing bread. Cecelia hung back to hear Maudie deny having done so while the others put their heads down and carried on their way. Her hands clenched into fists by her sides. She knew full well Maudie regularly pilfered what she could and gave the majority of her spoils to those who needed it most.

She watched helplessly, her jaw clenched, as the nun thrust her hand in Maudie's smock pocket then held a chunk of bread aloft triumphantly.

Maudie frantically denied all knowledge of how it had come to be there.

'Insolence!' the nun bellowed.

Cecelia jolted with fright, but she stood her ground, watching in horror as Sister Agnes pulled her arm back, and then the corridor echoed with the sound of her hand connecting with Maudie's face. All the times her mother had mistreated her overlapped with the present, and, without thinking, Cecelia launched forward.

'Leave her be!' she screamed as Sister Agnes's face melded into her mother's.

Too late. The rosary beads the nun held were whizzing through the air, and she heard a crack as they connected with her cheekbone before she slumped to the ground.

White dots of light danced in Cecelia's vision, and she pushed herself upright. It was no good – she couldn't do anything to help Maudie, not in this state, so she dragged herself to her feet and staggered off in search of help.

Sister Mary was exiting the laundry when Cecelia called out to her, and seeing her recoil, she touched her cheek. Her hand, when she pulled it away, was covered in blood. That didn't matter now though; what mattered was Maudie.

'Please, Sister, go to the kitchen and stop her. I'm afraid Sister Agnes will kill her.'

A shutter came down over the nun's plain features. 'Hush, child.' Then she took Cecelia firmly by the elbow and began hustling her toward the infirmary, closing her ears to Cecelia's pleas. 'I'll hear no more of that talk. It's your own fault for not drying the floor after you scrubbed it. How dare you speak ill of my fellow sister?'

'I don't understand, Sister. I didn't wash the floor. It's Sister Agnes. She's hurting Maudie. You have to make her stop!'

The infirmary nun stepped forward, relieving Sister Mary of her bloodied and protesting charge. She pressed a clean rag to the wound and told her to hold it there firmly while Sister Mary spoke up.

'Sister Agnes asked me to bring Margaret to you. I understand she fell in the kitchen. I suspect she cut her cheek on the work table. The girl didn't have the sense to dry the floor after washing it. 'Tis her only silly fault.'

Cecelia began to tremble uncontrollably upon hearing the lies. Shock was setting in, and the adrenaline began to seep from her body. Still she tried to make the sisters hear her.

'No! That's not what happened!' But her voice was feeble. 'Mau— I mean Theresa, she needs help. Sister Agnes is a brute. Why won't you listen?' Frustrated sobs began to heave from her as shock set in fully.

'Silence, child,' the infirmary nun snapped, bearing down on her with a rag soaked in boiling water, and when she was satisfied the cut was clean, she daubed on a solution that made Cecelia shout out with pain and sink into darkness.

The last remnants of Cecelia's icy veneer melted when she next saw Maudie. Her hair had been hacked into unsightly tufts, and she carried herself differently. The fight had been knocked out of her, just as it had been Cecelia. Sister Agnes had won again, having done her worst.

Cecelia lay in bed, her cheek throbbing, wondering why God wouldn't help them.

But there was worse to come.

Disbelief mingled with sorrow as Maudie sobbed out what had happened to Nessa and her baby. They were dead and buried. Sister Agnes had delivered the truth about their disappearance with delight as she'd meted out Maudie's punishment.

There was nothing Cecelia could do to change any of what had unfolded except to be kind to the apathetic Maudie. Her own heart was breaking for the young girl she wished she could have known better and her babe, gone before their time, but all she could do to honour their passing was to look out for Maudie.

It was what Nessa would have wanted.

She began pocketing rosemary and lavender from the kitchen garden at each opportunity and massaging the pungent rosemary leaves on Maudie's tender scalp where chunks of hair had been ripped from it. A sprig of lavender placed under her bed sheet would help her sleep too. She did the same for young Molly, who was distraught at the news of what had happened to her friend. But while Molly sobbed each night, releasing her pain, Maudie retreated deep within herself.

Cecelia wanted her to understand she wasn't alone in her grief because while she'd refused to open up to Nessa, she'd wanted to and had admired the younger girl's spark. How she regretted not being braver and breaking the rules of not speaking, and worrying over the secrets she carried being revealed. What did any of it matter when she was in here? Her mother wouldn't find her here. She'd kept her word to Hogan, who'd remained tight-lipped as to where Finian was, even when she'd threated to expose him if he didn't help her and Lizzie escape her uncle's house and run away.

She had done what he said and not breathed a word about anything she'd done for Ireland, and disappeared upon her return, but where had it got her? She was as trapped now as she'd ever been and had been left in the dark as to where Finian was by those whose cause she'd fought. She'd no knowledge as to whether he was even alive and, if he was, no way of telling him she'd borne his child. Even if she could get word to him, would he care? She still loved him despite everything.

It wasn't too late to reach out to Molly and Maudie though, and each night she crept from her bed and tended to Maudie and then comforted Molly. Poor Molly pined not just for her friend, who'd been more of a big sister figure to her, but for her mam and her home, despite what had happened to her there. She was desperate to take Connor and go home.

They might not know it, but Maudie and Molly had inadvertently snapped Cecelia out of her malaise and washed away her fears of her family somehow finding her at St Patrick's. Now it was her turn to try and do the same for them.

What she should name her daughter had become clear to her as she'd rocked her in her arms, stealing a moment while the sister on duty's attention was elsewhere. That night, when she returned to the dormitory, she told Maudie and Molly.

'I've named her, my little girl. She's to be called Vanessa. Nessa for short. She won't be forgotten.'

Molly momentarily forgot her tears as she hugged Cecelia, who was at first stiff in the embrace. She was unused to spontaneous acts of affection, but slowly her body untensed, and she raised her arms and wrapped them around the younger girl, returning the hug. It surprised her how the warmth of human touch could convey so much. This was why, even though Maudie had given no indication of having heard what she'd said, Cecelia took Maudie's hand once Molly had drifted off to sleep and held it until she heard her breathing settle into sleep.

Maudie's melancholy refused to lift, though, and Cecelia watched despairingly as she drifted like a soulless entity through each day until one evening after prayers, Cecelia saw Sister Louise taking her aside. When she returned to the dormitory later, she was a different girl, and after Sister Catherine had put the lights out and closed the dormitory door, it lifted her spirits to hear Maudie speak for the first time since the day she'd relayed what had become of Nessa and her baby.

Her voice was a croak at first, but it grew stronger as she held Molly's and Cecelia's hands in hers and relayed that Sister Louise had singled her out to confess she walked the fifty minutes to Glasnevin Cemetery whenever she could to visit the mothers and little ones buried there.

'She places flowers on their graves, Nessa and her baby's included.'

Cecelia could see Maudie's face in the moonlight bathing the dormitory in an unworldly glow. It was animated and alive. 'They're not forgotten after all,' she gushed, and it was as if a light had been switched on in her eyes once more.

The scar on Cecelia's cheek would always serve as a reminder of Sister Agnes's madness, but in lashing out, the nun had unwittingly brought Cecelia and Maudie together. Reacting on impulse, Cecelia did something then that she couldn't ever remember having done of her own accord before. She wasn't sure whether this was because she'd never had a reason to, or if she'd been frightened of making herself vulnerable. Now, though, her fear disappeared, and she opened her arms. Cecelia's heart cracked wide open as she pulled Maudie and Molly into a warm embrace, and the barriers she'd so carefully constructed around herself since childhood crumbled.

21

Three things happened soon after Sister Louise restored the girls' faith that they weren't simply being left to rot behind the walls of St Patrick's. Forgotten, fallen women.

The first was that Sister Agnes was taken off kitchen duties, which meant Cecelia and Maudie barely saw her. Molly, in the laundry, wasn't so lucky, but the nun left her alone so long as she worked hard. The second was that Maudie gave birth safely to a little girl she called Emer whom she fell head over heels in love with. And the third was Cecelia decided it was time to share her story with Molly and Maudie. She needed their friendship, and true friendship couldn't be one-sided. She knew their backgrounds and the secrets that had brought them to St Patrick's; now it was time for them to be part of hers. It was time for her to open up and put her trust in them.

'Maudie, Molly, are you awake?' Cecelia deemed it was safe to talk in the moonlit dormitory.

Both mumbled a drowsy yes.

'I want to tell you about my life before I came here.' Her voice was tentative, but she'd made up her mind.

The rustle of straw mattresses sounded, and then Cecelia saw Maudie had propped herself up on one elbow while Molly scrambled around on her cot so she was down the opposite end, chin resting in her upturned hands, her little face eager for a story.

'There's things I'm going to tell you that no one can ever know about, and there's good reasons for that,' Cecelia warned.

'You can trust us. Can't she, Maudie?' Molly was agog with excitement over what she might hear.

'Of course.'

Satisfied, Cecelia began at the beginning, telling them what it was like to grow up unloved, marked by a limp and cursed with a mother who took her rage and frustration at her life out on her. How she'd found joy and respite in spending time in the gardens and stables with her friends, Tomas and Cyril. She told them of the giggles and confidences she'd shared with Lizzie, how Finian had opened her eyes to the plight of her country-men, how she'd felt so betrayed when her father had stolen her beloved horse from her and how Finian had shown her a way forward. 'I fell in love with him and his words,' she said simply.

'I recognised you on my first day here,' Maudie interrupted softly.

Cecelia swallowed the lump in her throat. 'You were familiar to me, but I couldn't place you until I overheard you telling Nessa you were from Rush.'

''Tis strange to think our paths crossed there but that we could never have been friends in our old lives, even though we're on the same side of the fight.'

'And look where it's got us, this fight for Ireland's freedom.'

'Ronan will come for me,' Maudie said, and Cecelia envied her conviction because she didn't know if she'd ever hear from Finian again.

'I want to hear all about London and the fine dresses you must have worn there,' Molly urged.

'It's getting late, Mol.'

'Please,' Molly cajoled, and Maudie joined in.

'At least tell us a little more.'

So Cecelia continued. She was opening her heart to these girls, and she'd so much more to tell them.

22

LONDON, ENGLAND, 1919

The early March sky was oppressive with the promise of rain, yet Cecelia had never felt more alive the morning she, Mother, Julian and Lizzie were to leave for London. Her body was tingling with the memory of Finian's touch and the rebel role she would play in the fight for Ireland's freedom once she arrived in London. It dawned on her that this was the last time she'd step over Foxbourne's threshold for nearly five months, and while she wouldn't miss the house, she'd pine for Finian dreadfully. She sighed because she had no choice but to hold on to what he'd whispered to her last night when she'd told him she would miss him.

'It's a mere turn of the history pages because that's what you'll be doing, Cecelia. You'll be helping rewrite history.'

Tomas had brought the car around, a polished blue jewel in a murky morning. He was frantically strapping the family's luggage – a ridiculous amount in Cecelia's opinion – to the car's external luggage rack.

Lord Kildurran, Mrs Nolan, Grainne, Mrs Behan, Cyril and Finian were gathered on the steps outside the entrance, eager to wave them off, braving not just the cold but the early hour. There was no sign of Julian yet, and Cecelia whispered to Lizzie, 'Whatever the occasion, you can always count on my brother to be the last to arrive and the last to leave.'

But Lizzie was blind where Julian was concerned, and the remark fell on deaf ears. Beatrice was noticeably absent from the huddle too, having refused to come out of her bedroom.

Cecelia turned around, seeking Finian, and to her delight, she saw him blow her a kiss, undetected of course, but she held up her hand and caught it anyway. That kiss would have to sustain her between now and their return.

Her mother was a few steps ahead of her and Lizzie, dressed in a wide-brimmed hat and an eye-catching belted green wool coat. She was carrying a small travel case and tapping her well-heeled boot, impatient for Tomas to finish with the luggage and hold the passenger door open for her.

'Oh for goodness' sake,' Cecelia muttered. 'You've two hands.'

She moved around the woman she'd grudgingly returned to addressing as Mother for the sake of appearances and wrenched the door open herself. 'Come on, Lizzie – in you go. There's no point standing about freezing.'

She glared at her mother.

Lizzie cast a wary glance at Lady Kildurran but clambered in nonetheless.

'I don't see the point in employing staff if you're to do their job yourself, Cecelia,' Lady Kildurran sniffed.

Julian finally emerged and swept down the stairs, every inch the dapper eldest son of an Irish earl in his three-piece suit and coat. His white scarf streamed behind him, but the wind couldn't touch his side-parted and slicked-down hair.

Cecelia pulled a face, feeling the two women either side of her straighten at his appearance. Mother out of pride, Lizzie from misguided devotion.

'I can drive us if you like, Tomas?' Julian said.

'You'll do no such thing,' Lady Kildurran trilled.

Cecelia and Lizzie exchanged a relieved glance as, for once, Julian listened to his mother and sank into the front passenger seat. He twisting around in it to greet them, his eyes lingering a touch too long on Lizzie for Cecelia's liking.

'You only need crank the handle, old boy. I've seen to the throttle and choke, and the gears are in neutral,' Julian rattled off, leaving Tomas free to give the crank handle a sharp upward turn. He repeated it once more, and the car sputtered a few times before growling into life.

This was it, Cecelia thought. They were off.

It was early evening when the train from Holyhead chugged into Euston Station. The station's main hall was like a giant echoing cave, and if Cecelia had closed her eyes, she'd have known where she was by the screech of trains along with the smell of steel and coal. A uniformed porter pushed the brass trolley on which their luggage was stacked alongside them, and all around them, people hurried back and forth or lingered, anxiously looking at timetable booklets or the boards overhead.

Cecelia watched a man hanging off a small ladder with a long pole as he changed the timetable board and imagined the groans of travellers whose plans had just been upset as the word 'delayed' appeared. As she trailed after her mother and brother, she side-eyed Lizzie. Her mouth was hanging open. Her friend had never been out of County Fingal, and the station concourse was an assault on the senses.

The scene was a chaotic one, yet at the same time orderly and efficient. A solider limped toward them on crutches, and she instantly sensed a kindred spirit but swiftly saw his disability was the result of having lost one leg – to war, not polio. He had his tray thrust forth in the hope passers-by might spare him their loose change, and her heart went out to him, imagining how much he must have had to swallow his pride to beg like so. She could still feel something after all, she thought, catching Julian up and hissing at him to have some decency and help those less fortunate than himself. She all but stood over her brother, waiting while he dug around in his trouser pocket. Mother looked straight past the poor man, determined not to see him.

Julian retrieved a few coins then dropped them in the upturned hat, and the man's gratitude at such a small kindness saw Cecelia's tear ducts fill.

'That was very kind of Lord Kildurran,' Lizzie said as they continued toward the exit.

Cecelia shook her head and stared at her. She was completely blind when it came to Julian, so there was no point wasting her breath.

Julian had visited London every chance he got since coming of age, lured by the bright lights and loose living on offer. He was reliant on his mother's side of the family for their hospitality, and Cecelia suspected he must have successfully pulled the wool over their eyes as to his true nature. It was a skill her brother was adept at. He veered off to speak with a flower girl then returned to where they waited with a posy of handtied blooms.

'They're for Aunt Octavia. She adores violets.'

'Personally, I can't abide them,' Lady Kildurran sniffed.

If Lizzie dared say he was thoughtful, Cecelia thought she would scream.

They weaved through the foot traffic the short distance to the covered carriage entranceway. There, she saw a man in a dark uniform with a peaked cap standing next to a sleek motor car. He was holding a card with 'Altringham' plain to see on it. Julian picked up his pace, excitedly tossing back to the uncaring women that the vehicle was a Rolls-Royce Silver Ghost.

Upon having the chauffeur in her line of sight, Cecelia felt the fatigue that had been hovering after the last long leg of their train journey from Wales to London disappear. This was him. Her point of contact in London. Would he acknowledge her in any way to signal he knew what she planned to do come her first opportunity under the Cathcarts' roof? She would be the eyes and ears of the Irish rebels in a Belgravia town house.

'Ah, Hogan, good to see you,' Julian greeted the driver chummily as the porter began to unload their luggage.

'Yes, Lord Rathlin, and you.' Then the chauffeur said a formal, 'Good afternoon,' to the women before opening the back door of the Rolls-Royce for Lady Kildurran then helping her alight the step.

Cecelia sought eye contact in the split second before she followed behind her mother, but Hogan's piercing stone-coloured gaze gave nothing away. She did, however, catch his almost imperceptible nod, and it was all the confirmation she needed. This was the man to whom she would pass any confidential information she could gather while under Uncle George's roof.

From this moment forth, she was officially an Irish spy.

23

Soon, the motor car was purring slowly down a quiet London street filled with identical white terraced houses. All had bow windows, wrought-iron balconies and were as tall, narrow and elegant as the next. Like Julian, Cecelia had visited this pocket of the city before, but only the once, and that had been when she was still a child. If asked, she wouldn't have been able to point out which of the houses belonged to the Cathcart family; all she remembered from that time was feeling trapped and yearning to be back at Foxbourne.

Hogan deftly pulled the motor car over to the kerb, and he'd barely stilled the engine when the front door outside which they'd parked opened. A butler, illuminated momentarily by the warm glow inside, sailed forth and held his hand out to Lady Kildurran.

'Welcome back to Chester Street, Lady Kildurran. Lady Cathcart is expecting you.'

Julian greeted the butler in much the same manner he had Hogan, but if he found the familiarity vulgar, then he didn't let on.

'Franklin. At your service, Miss Cecelia,' he said when it was her turn.

Her lips arranged themselves into what she hoped was a smile fitting her station as he helped her from the motor car, and she tried not to stare at what was possibly the largest nose she'd ever seen. Meanwhile, a maid was hurrying up the steps leading to the basement servants' entrance. Lizzie plucked up her suitcase and was whisked down them, while Franklin ushered the threesome through the front door and into the gleaming marble foyer.

Her mother, who'd also made frequent trips back to London over the years, determined not to become too Irish, was in her element. Cecelia watched her draw herself up regally as she divested herself of her hat, gloves and coat and dropped them into Franklin's outstretched arms.

Cecelia shrugged off her own coat.

'If you would care to wait in here, my lady, Lord Rathlin and Miss Cecelia.'

A parlour maid had appeared seemingly from thin air as Franklin, barely able to see overtop the pile of coats, said he'd inform Lady Cathcart of their arrival.

They were swept through to the drawing room. Its windows overlooked the street, and it was every bit as grand as Cecelia had expected. She took a seat just as a refreshments tray rattled in.

A good fifteen minutes passed before Aunt Octavia swept into the room, full of warm greetings and apologies over keeping them waiting while she tended to 'terribly urgent' business.

Cecelia observed her mother rearrange her features, her fox-like smile never reaching her eyes as she simpered and fawned over her sister in return.

'The girls are terribly disappointed not to be home for the season and that they're to miss their dear cousin's coming out ball, Cecelia, but as I'm sure you're aware, they're enrolled at the Institut Villa Mont-Choisi in Lausanne for their final year, and it simply wasn't possible for them to be here.'

'I completely understand, Aunt Octavia, although it would have been delightful to see them both. I have such fond memories of them summering with us at Foxbourne.' A barefaced lie if ever there was. Her cousins were horrors. Good riddance to them over at their Swiss finishing school.

'George can't wait to see you all, but I'm afraid he won't be back until dinner as he's attending a sitting. We barely see him when Parliament is in session. Westminster is his mistress these days.' Aunt Octavia gave a tinkling laugh.

'I shall look forward to speaking with Uncle George,' Julian said, helping himself to another generous glass of sherry.

Another barefaced lie, Cecelia thought. All her brother was interested in was venturing out to the jazz clubs.

The conversation turned to Aunt Octavia's recent social engagements, all of which sounded terribly dull to Cecelia, but it was amusing watching her mother's face. Lady Kildurran rebutted her sister's stories of how important and necessary her husband was with one of her own regarding how full Lord Kildurran's days were, managing tenancies and acreage. She spoke of times more relevant to the past than the present, and Cecelia wondered why she was bothering. Aunt Octavia was well aware of the situation in Ireland and that the Kildurran peerage was a dying one.

The sisters moved on to more stable ground, chattering about the upcoming season and all the preparations that would be necessary to ensure Cecelia's coming out into society was a success.

'Isn't it wonderfully generous of your aunt and uncle, Cecelia?' Her mother's eyes narrowed, and Cecelia tried not to look baffled as to what she was talking about. She'd stopped listening a while back.

'To offer to host a grand ball here for you at their home,' Lady Kildurran prompted.

'Oh yes, very. Thank you, Aunt Octavia.'

'That's what family's for, dear.'

The sisters' conversation turned to dress fittings, and deportment and dance classes. Cecelia yawned. All of it bored her silly, so she asked to be excused.

'Of course, my dear.' Aunt Octavia shook a little bell, and another maid appeared. 'Anna, will you show Miss Cecelia to her room, please.'

'Yes, of course, my lady.' Anna curtsied, and Cecelia followed the lady's maid from the room.

Her aunt's voice carried after her. 'It's an awful shame, Helen. She's such a pretty girl. Still, between us we shall make every effort to distract the gentlemanly gaze from her unfortunate gait.'

The words never ceased to sting. Cecelia knew she should be well used to such remarks, but her face burned. Aunt Octavia, just like her sister, had a genteel exterior beneath which lurked a cold-hearted woman. It would be no hardship to betray either of them. In fact, it would be pleasure to do so.

'Anna, would you mind awfully giving me a quick guided tour of the house? I should like to get my bearings.' What she really wanted to know was where her uncle's study was.

'Not at all, Miss.'

'Where are you from?' The lady's maid appeared to be around her own age, Cecelia thought, trailing behind her. Her accent had a rolling 'R' she couldn't place.

'The West Country, Miss. Devon way. 'Tis beautiful there this time of the year. I'm hoping to be able to visit soon, as my mother's poorly. I don't like my chances though, not with the season around the corner.'

'I'm sorry to hear that.' Cecelia meant it – she liked the girl's friendliness and lack of guile.

No sooner had she thought this, though, than another maid hurried past and glared at her. Anna quietened down after that and only spoke to announce each of the rooms she flung open the door to. All except for one, which she merely gestured to. 'Sir George's study, Miss.'

Cecelia didn't care about the music room or drawing room and barely gave them a glance. Now she'd found out what she needed to, she was eager for the tour to be over.

'Oh dear, I'm feeling rather faint, I'm afraid.' She pretended to swoon. 'I think the journey has caught up on me and a rest before dinner's in order.'

'It's a long day's travelling you've had, Miss. It's not surprising you're done in. I'll show you to your room right away,' Anna said with a smile, not quite so formal now they were out of earshot from other staff once more.

'Thank you.'

Cecelia's leg throbbed as she climbed yet another flight of stairs, but she bit down on her bottom lip, moving past the pain as she limped after Anna down the hallway.

'This is your room, Miss. Lord Kildurran is next door, and Lady Kildurran's to stay in the guest suite down the end there.'

Cecelia peered past Anna to a room that was perfectly nice if you liked pastels. Her things had already been brought up in readiness for Lizzie to unpack them, and Anna, once she was sure everything was to her mistress's niece's satisfaction, pulled the door to, leaving her to rest and freshen up before dinner. But Cecelia had no intention of resting.

She splashed her face with water from the basin provided, then patted it dry and looked out the window, beyond which stretched a sea of chimney pots. How strange not to see rolling green fields, she thought, moving closer to the window.

The bedrooms overlooked a courtyard, and a man was standing in it, smoking. It was as if he felt her watching him because he turned then and looked up. A pair of stone-coloured eyes locked with hers, and Cecelia nodded. She knew what she had to do. In fact, she'd start this very minute by seeing if she couldn't slip inside Uncle George's study undetected. He wouldn't be back until later, Aunt Octavia had said, and there was no time like the present.

24
___

Cecelia's pulse jittered as she slipped into her uncle's study. Instead of closing the door, she pulled it to. If she was caught, she could say she'd wandered in accidentally, having lost her bearings. A weak excuse, but it was all she could think of. Her nose twitched at the strong odour of leather and cigars, and the brandy decanter glowed almost welcomingly. She made her way toward where it sat on the expansive desk.

The curtains were open, and the twilight evening outside gave her just enough light to see by. Unlike Lord Kildurran's cluttered accounting space, Sir George's was orderly with not so much as a speck of dust, so she'd have to be vigilant when it came to putting things back where she found them. Her fingers rifled through the pile of newspapers – this morning's copies of *The Times*, *The Daily Telegraph*, *The Morning Post* and *The Westminster Gazette* – then she moved her attention to the sheaves of paperwork.

There was nothing of interest, she soon deduced. She began to quietly slide open the desk's drawers – some stationery items in the top one, and in the second a stack of printed records of recent parliamentary debates but nothing worth passing on to

Hogan. However, the bottom drawer refused to budge. She rattled it gently. It was locked. This was the drawer she needed access to then. Where would the key be?

Cecelia patted about underneath the desk and then checked through the cigar box and any other likely spots before sighing, not sure what she'd expected. Her uncle held a powerful position – he was hardly likely to leave folders pertaining to the nation's security lying about. She didn't dare take much longer either, and so resolving to come back later when everybody slept, Cecelia padded to the door. She froze, her airways constricting when she heard footsteps, but they continued past the study. She counted slowly to one hundred before risking a peek down the hall.

It was only upon seeing the coast was clear that she began breathing again.

Uncle George had the posture of a military man and the red-veined cheeks of a drinker. He greeted his sister's family from across the sea warmly enough, but dinner turned out to be a tedious affair. Either her uncle forgot where the company he was dining with had journeyed from, or he was enjoying being belligerent.

Belligerence was a strong contender, Cecelia decided, given Mother had rejected him in favour of an Irish earl and the title of viscountess. She watched him knock back the wine, referencing the Irish situation with words such as 'barbarous' and 'ignorant'. It was hard not to blanch or answer back, but the thought of Finian saw her remain silent. To give away where her loyalties lay would not do.

Julian, however, didn't appear fazed by his uncle's blathering, given his birthright as heir of an Irish estate. He was concentrating on matching Sir George drink for drink. Cecelia thought her brother was a chameleon – Irish when it suited and

English when it didn't. Julian didn't do things for the greater good of anyone but himself, and if being English proved more advantageous, then so be it.

Cecelia kept one ear on Uncle George's rhetoric about the heathens across the water, but despite his imbibing, he didn't reveal anything of interest, and she grew tired of his insults, tuning him out by the time the main course was presented.

It was a relief to at last retire to the drawing room, where the men joined them for brandy and petit fours.

Cecelia was aware her task wasn't going to be an easy one. But nothing worth doing was, or so the saying went. Her eyes had been opened to injustice through Finian, however, and she wouldn't let him down.

It came as a surprise to see it was only just after 10 p.m. when her mother finally rose from her seat and announced she really must go to bed. Cecelia tried not to dwell on how many more interminable evenings like tonight's she'd endure between now and returning to Ireland.

'It would pay you both to get an early night,' Lady Cathcart directed at Cecelia, who didn't need telling twice. 'You've a full schedule of appointments tomorrow, dear.'

The two women climbed the stairs in silence, but when they reached the landing, Lady Kildurran grasped Cecelia by the wrists, her fingers digging in and her gaze chilly. 'Do not show me up tomorrow, or any day thereafter in this city, Cecelia. Take this as a warning.'

Cecelia shivered despite the stuffiness of the house. She would have loved to have answered back that she'd do as she pleased. Instead, she dug deep. 'I wouldn't dream of it, Mother.'

But Lady Kildurran was no fool, and her eyes glittered as she continued to squeeze Cecelia's wrists so hard her circulation must have been cut off.

In that moment, trapped in her stalactite stare, she recalled Lizzie's sentiment about the eyes being the window to the soul.

If that was true, then her mother didn't have a soul as far as she could see.

At last, the pressure eased and her wrists were released. Cecelia rubbed at them and hurried away, feeling her mother's distaste drilling into her back as she watched her limp to her room.

Freedom was her fight too now, so Cecelia bided her time until she was certain everyone had sunk into sleep.

The house felt even more foreign at night, and she recalled Uncle George's declaration, as he'd downed his brandy, that all Irish traitors to the crown should be rounded up and shot. It occurred to her as she reached the stairs that what she was about to do was treason, but she carried on regardless and found the study unlocked.

This time, she closed the door behind her, focusing on the shadowy furnishings. It was no good – she needed light, so she made her way to the desk, marvelling at the ease of pulling a cord instead of faffing with an oil lamp.

Yellow light pooled over the desktop, and she raked the room for potential clues, deciding to begin with the bookshelf. It didn't pay to think of the enormity of her task – opening each and every one of those enormous tomes in the hope one might reveal a hollow hiding place. She was about to move toward the shelf and begin in the middle when she heard something.

Cecelia went rigid, trying to place the sound. Was it footfall? Yes!

Panic rose as she swiftly turned the lamp off.

Her nerve endings were on high alert in the sudden darkness, and she knew she should hide, but where?

The steps, heavy enough to suggest a man was heading down the hallway, forced her to move, and deciding the desk was her best option, she hurried around it to pull the chair out. After dropping to her knees, Cecelia crawled into the space beneath the swathe of oak and dragged the chair back into place. Her breathing was too loud. Hunching like a tortoise with an enormous shell on her back, she concentrated on steadying it all the while silently praying, *Please God, let whoever is prowling about walk on by.*

The door slowly opening, however, meant her prayers were ignored.

The lamp Cecelia had extinguished only seconds ago lit the room once more, and she squeezed her eyes shut the way a small child does, as if being unable to see meant no one could see her.

Her scalp was prickling, and sweat chilled her body as her mind galloped ahead of itself. The worst outcome if she was caught by her uncle – whom she assumed it must be – would see her accused of treason. She had no reason to be in his study late at night other than spying, and things could go either way for her. She'd either be made an example of simply because she was family and used to show the Irish rebels that the British meant business, or she'd be sent home in disgrace, the matter dealt with discreetly by the family. Mother would make her life unbearable if that were to happen. Neither was a good outcome, but the thought of letting down Finian, the only person who believed she was capable of whatever she set her mind to, was her biggest fear.

Her heart was in her mouth as she anticipated Uncle George weaving around his desk, pulling his chair out and getting the fright of his life upon seeing his niece huddled where she had no business huddling. Why was he even in here? Had an urgent matter he'd forgotten to attend to earlier suddenly roused him from bed?

The pop of a stopper being released then a slosh of liquid suggested he'd decided to carry on his drinking here, in his study. She didn't dare feel relief when, instead of sitting at his desk, she heard a whoosh of air and realised he'd sunk down onto his leather armchair.

The seconds turned to minutes, Cecelia concentrating on

breathing as quietly as she could. Then there was a soft tap on the door.

'Come in.'

Things had gone from bad to worse, and Cecelia bit her bottom lip. She didn't move from her crouched position as she heard a giggle far too soft and feminine to be Aunt Octavia.

'You promise to speak to Mrs Grady about me having paid leave to go and see my mother first thing in the morning, Sir George?' the disembodied voice beguiled.

'If you please me.'

A glass clinked down, then a coquettish voice whispered, 'Does this please you?'

'Oh, it does.'

Jesus wept! Cecelia thought, in shock now she'd recognised the woman's distinctive lilt. It was Anna, the lady's maid.

The shock seeped out of her, and revulsion took its place at the flirty giggling, the swish of fabric and the muted thud as something landed on the floor. Under her oak canopy, Cecelia heard the rustle of papers and imagined the tidy pile she'd shuffled through earlier being roughly shoved aside, the ensuing rattle surely due to the stationery tin also being given short shrift. Then there was a light thump, as if someone had just sat upon the desk. Her insides clenched because there was no mistaking the animalistic grunts that followed, and she squeezed her eyes shut, thinking she might be sick.

This couldn't be happening, Cecelia told herself. It was a nightmare from which she'd wake. But she knew from the stiffness in her hands and knees that it was all too real, and the thought of her uncle and the young lady's maid doing what she'd done with Finian was abhorrent. What was worse was that, much like dinner earlier, it went on and on, grunt after grunt, moan after moan, until at last the entire desk shuddered and there was a final groan.

The panting breaths slowly calmed, and the rasping strike

of a match on flint broke the ensuing silence. Soon, the pungent aroma of cigar smoke filled the room. There was movement, and she supposed Anna was getting dressed and putting the desk to rights.

'You won't forget now, sir? My poor mother needs me.'

'Leave it with me,' Sir George growled.

Her uncle was gruff now.

The door opened and closed, and she blinked against the smoky waft making her eyes water and her throat tickle with a threatened cough. Her lame leg was beginning to scream too, protesting the position she'd folded herself into. She swallowed rapidly to keep the cough at bay, not knowing how much longer she could hold it in for. Then – a miracle! Her uncle switched the lamp off, and the floor protested as he too exited the room. Cecelia almost cried with the relief of not having been discovered. *Thank you*, she mouthed, rolling her eyes heavenward.

Still she didn't dare move, only allowing the cough to escape when she finally deemed it safe. When she emerged and unfolded herself, her joints cracked audibly, and she quickly massaged the top of her leg. The whole episode was too bizarre to have happened, but the smouldering cigar left to extinguish itself in the ashtray was proof enough that it had.

She'd had a lucky escape and shouldn't tempt fate further. If she'd any sense about her, she'd leave the study and go to bed. Common sense had never been Cecelia's strong point, however, and the thought of Anna and her uncle... well, it was like Beauty and the Beast. Her uncle deserved to get his comeuppance, using his power over a young woman like so. This and her steely determination to get what she'd come for saw her switch the lamp back on. That was when something gleaming caught her eyes – something she was certain hadn't been there earlier.

Her pulse began jittering when she realised what she was looking at.

25

Cecelia held Uncle George's fob watch in the palm of her hand. It must have fallen from his pocket when he'd tossed the smoking jacket he'd been wearing at dinner aside in his haste to get at Anna. She presumed he'd still been wearing it because she'd glimpsed the watch then but hadn't noticed the item attached to it. A key. She could have turned the study upside down and never found it, and yet thanks to Anna, albeit in a roundabout way, it had been handed to her on a plate. Well, the floor to be precise. There was no point wasting time – she knew it would slot in and turn the lock on the bottom drawer before she even tried it.

Cecelia wasn't disappointed. She eased the drawer open then she sat back on her haunches in readiness to begin sifting through the various files stacked within.

Bingo! she silently cried a second or so later, pulling a folder marked the 'The Irish Question' from the mix. She opened it eagerly and skimmed the various reports. When she scanned a typed list of names under the heading of 'Suspected Agitators', her mouth went dry. Amid all the faceless men's and women's names, one had jumped out at her.

Finian Fahy.

Cecelia's stomach turned to ice because all it would take was for Julian to mention Father's new racehorse trainer to Sir George and her uncle's memory might be jogged.

It was a risk to steal the paper, but one she had to take and hope her uncle had yet to peruse it properly for Finian's sake. She didn't hesitate, folding it into four and tucking it away in her dressing-gown pocket to pass to Hogan the first chance she got. At least the men and women on the list would be made aware they were being watched and wouldn't take any unnecessary risks. This was gold in itself, but there was more.

A handwritten note amidst the screeds of surveillance reports caught her attention. It contained several men's names and where in Ireland they resided. She studied the typed sheet attached to the note. It was filled with dates and times, and her hand shook as what she was holding hit her. The men whose names her uncle had recorded were informants! She didn't dare remove this permanently from the file and stood up, pulling a face at the memory of what had happened on top of the desk as she reached across it for the stationery box. Cecelia took out a fountain pen and pad of paper before leaning on the desk, but her hand was trembling too badly, and the ink blotted the page she'd pressed the nib to.

The knowledge had crashed over her as to what passing these men's names to Hogan would mean. She would be indirectly sentencing them to death.

Her eyes closed, and she saw a shadowy figure emerging from a darkened alleyway to step out in front of a man wandering home from the pub. Bang! Her eyes flew open. Then she thought of Finian, and Lizzie's brother, Frank. The Murphy family had already lost so much, and so had others like them. They were all good men fighting for a freedom that should never have been taken from them.

The last piece of information she jotted down was in a

report from Dublin Castle. She thought the information as to where extra RIC troops were being stationed might be of use, and once she'd copied down the basic facts, she slipped the report back into the file and placed the folder amongst the others where she'd found it before locking the drawer. It would pay to refill the fountain pen, she thought, and quickly did so. All that was left now was to place the watch and key back on the carpet where she'd found it and turn the light off.

Cecelia hesitated though, her mind whirring.

The key and the unlimited access it gave her to that bottom drawer was priceless to the cause. If she were to take it now, what would the consequences be? Uncle George had consumed a fair amount of drink tonight and would likely assume he'd misplaced his watch and retrace his steps tomorrow. When he couldn't lay his hands on it, his thoughts might turn to Anna, or he might assume there was a thief amongst the staff who'd seen an opportunity and taken it. But a search of the servants' quarters would reveal nothing, so she wouldn't be responsible for anyone's dismissal. He'd eventually conclude Anna was the culprit and had likely pawned it, but wouldn't accuse her publicly of stealing because that would reveal his own indiscretion. Cecelia assumed he'd rather continue their little arrangement than forfeit his fun for the sake of a watch he could replace. It surely wouldn't enter his head that Anna might pose a security threat either, therefore Uncle George would simply call a locksmith and get a new key made as soon as possible, thinking there was no need to bother changing the entire lock.

Cecelia felt a tiny thrill as she dropped the fob watch and key chain in her pocket, alongside the papers already folded and stashed in there. Then, after casting her eyes about the room and ensuring everything was as it had been, she turned off the lamp and crept from the study back to her bed as though she'd never left it in the first place.

· · ·

'Octavia, have you seen my fob watch?' Sir George shouted as he entered the breakfast room.

Cecelia's back stiffened, her toes curling to cramping point inside her shoes as she concentrated on maintaining a neutral expression.

'There's no need to shout. I'm not hard of hearing, and no I haven't. Shall we start again?' Octavia didn't wait for a reply. 'Good morning, George.'

'Yes, yes. Good morning, Octavia. Helen.' Sir George was impatient as he included Julian and Cecelia in the greeting. 'I hope you are all fully recovered from your journey. Julian, all set, my boy?' He strode toward his nephew and gave him a hearty slap on the back.

Cecelia expected the sliver of sausage her brother had popped in his mouth to come flying forth. He was probably looking forward to the dry, tedious day ahead of him at Westminster as much as she was the dress fitting and dance lesson her aunt had informed her were on the cards for her today.

'I am, Uncle.' Julian sounded enthusiastic. 'It's a grand opportunity for which I'm sincerely grateful, and one I intend to make the most of.'

'Glad to hear it.' Sir George crossed to the buffet, saying half to himself, 'I can't think where it's gone.'

'Are we back on the watch, George?'

'Yes, Octavia, we are. Things don't simply vanish.'

Lady Cathcart set her teacup down. 'You're quite right, dear. They don't, and it isn't like you to misplace it. Shall I have a word with Mrs Grady and ask her to enquire amongst the staff if they've come across it?'

'Yes. Thank you, my dear.' Sir George inspected the tureens. 'I'll have eggs, bacon, sausage, mushroom and tomato, Franklin.'

He was a man of big appetites, her uncle, Cecelia thought wryly, wondering if Aunt Octavia had any clue as to just how big. So far, the watch debacle had played out much as she'd thought it would.

'Oh, I haven't told you.' Lady Kildurran set her knife and fork down once Sir George was seated. 'We were robbed at Foxbourne not long ago.' Satisfied all eyes were on her, she weaved a tale of priceless figurines and murderous thugs.

Her story was more than a tad exaggerated in Cecelia's opinion, but then she knew who the 'murderous' thug was. Julian. Her brother just carried on tucking in, agreeing with their mother's dramatized version of events when she required it. Cecelia wondered if Julian had been born without a conscience. Then again, wasn't she sitting at the breakfast table with the uncle she'd stolen secret information from?

Mother had seemingly forgotten the rosy picture she'd painted of life at Foxbourne for her sister's benefit yesterday.

'Father has a horse and trainer he expects to do well this year at Curragh,' Julian said, changing the subject as he slathered his toast with butter.

Cecelia's teacup clattered into its saucer. She received a sharp glance from her mother but was more concerned as to whether Julian would name Finian – and her uncle's reaction if he did.

'Curragh?' Sir George asked. He'd polished off his breakfast in next to no time and was reaching for the newspapers that were waiting for him.

'Yes, it's akin to the Epsom Derby.'

'I'd hardly put the two in the same league,' Lady Cathcart jumped in. 'And I said it to you way back when, and I'll say it again now, Helen – gambling will be your husband's downfall. I don't know why you felt the need to sugar-coat how things have been for you this last while. I'm your sister, after all.'

Her mother didn't argue, and Cecelia wondered if Lord Kildurran's flutters on the gee-gees were worse than she'd been privy to. She supposed Julian had to have inherited his weakness from someone.

'I'm not a horse man myself,' George said, removing the first paper from the pile and thrusting it at Julian. 'It pays to be abreast of the goings-on locally and abroad before arriving at Westminster.'

He'd effectively cut off that line of conversation.

Cecelia sank back in her seat as Julian scanned the front page of *The Times*. Meanwhile, Sir George was flapping open *The Daily Telegraph*.

'Those blasted Irish are only boycotting our RIC officers now. They're refusing to serve them in the pubs and shops.' His disgust rang out from behind his newsprint shield.

'The situation's getting worse day by day,' Lady Kildurran declared, her hand on her chest. 'I can't sleep since the robbery.' She looked toward her sister. 'They're burning down houses like ours all across the country. You'll receive a telegram one of these days to tell you we've all perished.'

Cecelia was surprised by the anxiety in her mother's voice – surprised but unmoved. The lines had been drawn, and she knew whose side she was on.

'Darling Helen. Our home is your home. Isn't it, George?'

The newspaper was momentarily lowered as Sir George agreed.

'Alastair feels I'm being dramatic. He refuses to see how dire things really are, doesn't he, Julian?'

'Yes. I fear Father is the proverbial ostrich when it comes to his beloved Ireland,' Julian replied.

'Well, you simply must write to him and demand he send Beatrice over. Tell him none of you shall be returning until the state of unrest has resolved itself. What sort of a man puts his family in direct danger like so?'

'But that could be years, Mother,' Cecelia objected before she could stop herself.

A foot connected with her ankle beneath the table, and she tasted blood in her mouth as she bit the inside of her bottom lip to stop from crying out. It crystalized before her then, and she shook her head, not understanding how she could have been so stupid. Mother had no intention of returning to Ireland. She'd played her husband with all her talk of Foxbourne needing a cash injection and how the best way to ensure its survival was by securing Cecelia an advantageous marriage. She had it all worked out.

Her precious Julian would fare better here in London with a fresh start under her Sir George's wing, and Bea had been left behind so as not to arouse Lord Kildurran's suspicions that she wouldn't be returning at the end of the season. Bea was a casualty of their mother's selfishness and may or may not be sent for, but either way, the Viscountess of Kildurran would never set foot on Irish soil again.

She clearly had no qualms about leaving her youngest daughter and husband to moulder in their castle on the hill if it meant she got to re-enter London society, and Cecelia was to be her ticket to do so.

Cecelia followed her aunt and mother out the front door to where Hogan had brought the car around. The chauffeur swept the older women into the idling motor car and watched Cecelia. She was playing on her limp and making a meal of leaving the house. He stepped forward to offer her assistance, and Cecelia stumbled deliberately. As the chauffeur caught her, she whispered, 'Take them,' and pressed the papers she'd folded into a small square upon him. He made them disappear with a magician's sleight of hand, and she apologised for her clumsiness, loud enough for her mother and aunt to hear before climbing in alongside them.

'Our first appointment is at Eugène Limited. Your hair is

for the chop, young lady,' Aunt Octavia directed at her niece. 'I think Irene Carson's bob all the young ladies are emulating will suit you well.'

Cecelia had no interest in looking like the silent film star and wondered what would happen if she were to refuse to cut her hair off.

'I do hope this dance tutor I've engaged is as talented as I've heard,' Aunt Octavia murmured, half to herself. 'Madame Vacani's going to need to work miracles with Cecelia between now and the start of the season from what I've seen so far.'

Lady Kildurran said nothing as she ground her elbow into Cecelia's side.

26

ST PATRICK'S MOTHER AND BABY HOME, 1920

Cecelia's heart was thudding as she relived her clandestine night-time activities at Chester Street, and when she returned to the present, she was surprised to find herself not in a feather-soft bed in London's swanky Belgravia but on a straw mattress in a dormitory filled with slumbering girls.

'You can't finish there, Cecelia,' Mollie piped up. 'I want to hear more about Lizzie. Where is she now?'

'Back home in Kildurran with her mam. She could be married to Seamus Foley for all I know. And I'm tired, Mol.'

Darts of sadness over her friend's unknown fate were swept away by frustration at the lack of choices not just Lizzie but all of them faced, along with their babies. Babies who didn't deserve the grim circumstances they'd been born to.

'But I still don't understand how you came to be here.'

'That's a story for another night.' Cecelia was adamant.

'I had no choice but to come here,' Maudie muttered darkly. 'Now I've no choice but to wait for Ronan.'

'Me neither,' Molly said. 'My mam and da dragged me here, but I miss my mam something terrible all the same. She'll come and fetch me and Connor home soon.' She hummed for a moment as was her habit on the nights she didn't cry herself to sleep. Then her voice became slow and dreamy. 'I can't wait to show him the pigs, the hens and the sheep. He'll love collecting the hens' eggs when he's a little bigger.'

Cecelia's heart twisted at the other girl's naivety. Heartbreak like she'd never known in her short life was headed her way one day soon. Let her hold on to the belief that all would end well, she thought, because there was nothing to be gained in telling her otherwise.

The humming stopped. 'Does your family even know you're here?'

Cecelia's tone was sharp. 'No, and they mustn't, not ever.'

'We would never breathe a word of what you've told us tonight, would we, Mol?' Maudie stepped in, her voice reassuring.

'What about Finian?' Mol persisted.

'No, and I don't know where he is either.'

'But, Cecelia,' Molly persisted, 'you could leave here, just for a short while, and go to your da. Sure, he'd help you, and when you had yourself sorted, you could come back for Nessa. Then you could find Finian, live happily ever after.'

Molly was so childlike with her storybook endings, and she was also like a dog with a bone on the topic of her family, given she knew nothing about them. Cecelia spoke curtly. 'I can't go to him. My family won't help me. Like I said, they can't ever know I'm here. And I would never leave Nessa and risk her being gone when I returned for her.' Cecelia shook her head. 'No. I'll only leave St Patrick's if it's with her.'

Molly huffed again that she wanted to hear more, but Maudie urged her to let things be. 'Cecelia will tell us the rest of her story another night. Shush now, Mol. Leave it be. We need to get some sleep.'

'Well, I don't know how I'm supposed to do that when my

mind's all abuzz with high-society life in London and your shenanigans, Cecelia.'

'Well, if you don't go to sleep now, I won't tell you the rest of my story another night.'

That did the trick. Molly fell silent.

'Well, at least we're not alone. We're in this together, and we've got each other,' Maudie said while Molly yawned.

'I've not had many friends in my life, Maudie. Tomas, Cyril and Lizzie, they were it,' Cecelia whispered. She conjured their faces, missing them all, and wondered if Tomas would ever find it in himself to forgive the way she'd treated him. She hoped too that Lizzie was happy with her lot, and knew Cyril would be content so long as he was working outdoors, tending to his beloved plants.

'Well, now you've two more.'

Cecelia was heartened by this knowledge and whispered, 'Thank you.' Half of her wanted to spill out the rest of her story now and be done with it, but it was so late. She'd hidden so much of herself since leaving Foxbourne, blinded by her feelings for Finian, who'd gone to unimaginable lengths for what he believed in. He wasn't evil; he was simply driven by his belief in a free Ireland. She still believed in this too, but it hadn't bought her freedom. And Finian wasn't here to help, nor had he kept his promise.

The tender moment between herself and Maudie was interrupted by soft snores from Molly's bed, and teeth flashed in the moonlight.

'Maudie?'

'Yes?'

'Do you ever think about what you'd do if you woke up one morning and Emer was gone. I have nightmares about Nessa being stolen from me.'

She'd bolt awake, terrified for a few moments that it had happened. Her mother had come and spirited Nessa away. Not out of any love for her grandchild but to hurt Cecelia and to have something tangible to wave under Sir George's nose to ensure she was kept in the manner to which she was growing very used to. It was her worst fear for her daughter manifesting itself in her dreams.

'Well, you shouldn't. That won't happen.'

Maudie was wrong though, she thought as a shiver danced down her spine. Babies did disappear from St Patrick's. They disappeared all the time.

27

Something was amiss, Cecelia thought, stealing a glance around the girls gathered in the dining hall. They were spooning their stew in silence, but there was a restlessness to them. Some of the girls fidgeted in their seats, and their faces when they dared look up were fit to burst with a drama, especially Molly's – her enormous eyes were trying to convey something to Cecelia.

She scanned the length of the table, and then her spoon clattered into her bowl. Maudie was missing. Sister Mary, patrolling the length of the hall, was swift to reprimand her. What had happened for her to miss their meal? Fear culled her appetite at the thought of her friend having been locked in the cleaning supplies cupboard by Sister Agnes as she had once been, but she forced herself to eat the rest of the lumpy mess in front of her.

Evening prayers seemed to drone on forever, and in between kneeling and standing, Cecelia realised someone else was absent. Sister Agnes. Apprehension cloaked her then. It was too coincidental that both Maudie and Sister Agnes should have disappeared.

Her bottom lip was sore from nipping at it with worry as

they at last filed to the dormitory. Down the end of the gloomy bed-filled hall, she saw a mound in Maudie's bed and instinct made her want to run to her, but she held back, pinching the inside flesh of her arm to keep herself in check. The time between readying themselves for bed and the lights being extinguished was interminable, but at last Sister Catherine's padding steps grew fainter down the corridor.

Cecelia heard a rolling tide whisper through the dormitory but didn't wait for it to reach her ears. She was out of bed in a flash, aware of Molly hovering as she checked on Maudie. There was no moonlight to see her face by, but she was breathing steadily. 'I think she's all right,' Cecelia offered up.

Any relief she felt was short-lived, however, as Molly wrung her hands.

'Cecelia, it's awful, just awful. I was there in the nursery when it happened.' Her voice broke off into sniffles.

'Spit it out, Mol.'

'Maudie attacked Sister Agnes. She was like a madwoman, and Sister Joan tried to pull her off, but it was no good. She screamed for one of the girls to fetch the doctor, and he came and jabbed her with a big needle which made her slump to the ground like this.' Molly fell back onto her cot, and the straw mattress sighed.

Cecelia tried not to feel irritated with the younger girl's dramatics. 'What did Sister Agnes do to set her off like so?'

'She told her where Emer had gone.'

'I don't understand. Where has she gone?'

'We went to feed Emer and Connor like always, only Emer wasn't in her cot. Maudie began shouting, desperate to find out where she'd gone, and Sister Agnes came in to see what all the fuss was about. Sister Joan didn't want her to, but she told her anyway.'

'For goodness' sake, Molly. Told her what?'

'That an American couple had taken her home with them.'

'Oh dear God.' Cecelia swayed. No wonder poor Maudie had been pushed over the brink.

She kneeled beside Maudie's cot and smoothed her friend's hair back from her face. It was a blessing the doctor had put her out of her misery, for a short while at least. Her heartbreak would have been too much to bear.

A chill rode up her spine at the thought of being in Maudie's shoes. What if it had been Nessa? No! She couldn't allow herself to go there. All she could do was be here for Maudie when she woke.

'Sister's coming,' a voice hissed down the beds.

Cecelia slipped back into her bed and pulled the threadbare sheet over her, knowing she wouldn't sleep. How could any of them that had given birth under St Patrick's roof sleep knowing they could wake up tomorrow and find their baby gone? Eventually, exhaustion took over, and she began to drift.

'Maudie?'

Molly's voice tugged her back.

'It's all right, Mol. Shush now and go back to sleep. I'm only going to use the privy.'

Maudie was awake! Cecelia blinked into the darkness and saw a shadow moving through the gap between beds toward the door. She would be groggy from whatever the doctor had given her, so, worried for her, she murmured to Molly that she'd go and check on her.

By the time Cecelia stepped out into the corridor, a phantom-like shape was drifting closer to the stairs than the washroom. Maudie! She hurried after her as quietly as she could, not wanting to raise Sister Catherine, yet at the same time terrified she'd fall down the stairs.

Maudie spun round upon hearing her footfall, and fear saw Cecelia grab her wrists as she tried to coax her back to bed.

Maudie was determined, however. 'You still have Nessa. Mol has Connor. I have to find my girl.'

'Then Nessa and I will help you if you'll let us. It's only a matter of time until I lose her – you know that.' Cecelia meant ever word.

The pain of her loss radiated from Maudie, and when she thanked her for helping her stand up to Sister Agnes, and told her to go to Mol because she needed her now, Cecelia knew she'd lost.

'Don't forget us, will you?'

'Never. How could I? I'll come back for you one day, I promise.'

They both knew Mol would never leave here because she firmly believed one day she could return to her family farm with Connor and all would be right in her world.

'I believe you will.'

The two young women clung to one another for a moment, their friendship unlikely but cemented through circumstance.

Cecelia watched Maudie creep down the stairs and then hurried back to where she'd come from. There was nothing she could do now except ensure Nessa stayed safe and keep her promise to look after Mol.

When she returned to the dormitory, Molly was still sitting up. 'She's gone hasn't she?' Her voice was a tearful whisper.

'She has to go and find Emer. Put yourself in her shoes. What would you do for Connor?'

'Anything.'

Cecelia got into bed, hearing the echoes of a sentiment that felt as if it had been part of another lifetime now. *What would you do for a free Ireland, Cecelia?* And her reply. *Whatever it takes.*

'I don't want to think about Maudie's leaving. Will you tell me the rest of your story, Cecelia?'

28

LONDON, ENGLAND, 1919

March had long since given way to April, having passed by in a whirl of toile fittings for gowns Cecelia was to wear to her upcoming social events at the sought-after court dressmakers', Reville & Rossiter. These appointments were followed by dreary luncheons filled with gossipy small talk at popular society spots and, as the weather improved, garden parties. Cecelia was expected to be witty and charming as she twirled her parasol coquettishly. The evening might be spent at the theatre or the opera. All these occasions were opportunities for her to be seen, Aunt Octavia would stress, before putting her head together with her sister to discuss which young men appeared taken with Cecelia despite her disability. All the while the preparations for the coming-out ball here at Chester Street were being ticked off a never-ending list.

There were dance and deportment classes too, which Cecelia had been pleasantly surprised to find she enjoyed. The private tuition in the Cathcarts' ballroom provided a respite from the Ferris wheel of activities and being in her mother's and aunt's company.

Madame Vacani was indeed an excellent tutor who hadn't

concentrated on eliminating Cecelia's limp but rather on finding techniques she could use to adapt to the dance. She could hold her own on the ballroom floor now and enjoyed, for the first time in her life, feeling as though she were light on her feet. The deep swooping curtsy she was to perform for her presentation to the King and Queen had proved more challenging, however her weaker leg had strengthened sufficiently that she could now pull it off.

Cecelia had not once lost sight of her purpose for being in London, and she regularly made her way to her uncle's study, blanketed by night. Sir George hadn't changed the lock on the desk drawer, and she hoped the security information she was now adept at palming to Hogan as he took her hand to help her up onto the Rolls-Royce's stepping board was helping Ireland, helping Finian. The two were entwined in her mind and heart.

There weren't many things she'd felt good at in her life to date other than riding Camelot, but she'd taken to the business of spying rather well and was proud of her efforts. Although she could hardly crow about this newfound ability.

Lizzie had handed her three letters since their arrival in London – two from Finian and one from Tomas. She hadn't opened Tomas's, having no wish to read anything he had to say. Although she couldn't bring herself to throw it away either and had tucked it in her hiding place at the bottom of her underwear drawer. Finian's letters, however, she'd devoured and reread so many times she could have recited them. There was no mention of anything that would cast suspicion on either of them as the mail was being monitored these days, so he'd filled the page with almost poetic talk of spring at Foxbourne.

It made her long for Ireland. In his words, she could see the bluebells carpeting the woods and the cascade of purple wisteria climbing the house's south side, and if she held the paper to her nose, she fancied she could smell the blooming lily of the valley. She felt so far away from him here in this foreign world of London's high society, where she was an imposter and a traitor.

Easter had been and gone, and as the season began its gentle lead into May, something else had begun to occur too. Cecelia had what she could only describe as a bad-penny taste in her mouth, and that wasn't all. At certain periods during the day, she was being sick.

When she'd mentioned these symptoms to Lizzie, her friend had clapped her hand to her mouth. 'You don't think you're in the family way, do you? I remember me mam talking about the terrible sickness she was plagued with when she was expecting me.' Her eyes had grown saucer-like as they'd plunged to Cecelia's midriff.

'Don't be ridiculous,' Cecelia had replied, confident this couldn't be the case because Finian had said he'd been careful. 'I think I've picked something up.'

'I think it's fatigue you're suffering from then, and I'm not surprised the schedule you've been keeping. You've been burning the candle at both ends.' Lizzie had wagged a finger at her like a wise old lady.

'Hardly a schedule of my own making, but I suspect you're right,' Cecelia had replied, quashing the tiny seed Lizzie's initial statement had planted.

She hadn't mentioned being unwell again, somehow managing to keep the daily episodes of nausea under wraps, but she began to wonder. Could she be carrying Finian's child? The thought was frightening and at the same time exhilarating. She allowed it to grow, imagining Finian's reaction when she told him, picturing his joy at finding out he was to be a father. Of course, it was a foregone conclusion he would marry her.

The morning of Cecelia's coming out at Buckingham Palace, where she was to be presented to King George V and Queen

Mary, thus putting her officially on the market, finally dawned. It began with Lizzie waking her with a breakfast tray, and Cecelia propped herself up with pillows, listening as she ate while her friend gushed over the transformation the house was undergoing in readiness for this evening's ball.

'There's been endless food and flower deliveries, and downstairs has been a hive of activity since before dawn, CeeCee.'

Cecelia stifled a yawn, wondering how she would get through the day, let alone the night. It would be hard to hide the bouts of sickness from her mother, who had a hawkeye for anything being amiss. The nausea didn't stop her being ravenous of a morning though, and she dug enthusiastically into her egg.

The morning was a blur, but when the time came for Cecelia to get ready for her presentation at court, Lizzie hadn't come down from her excited high. She was lost in a daydream, humming as she held the white silk gown to her with one hand and theatrically waved the ostrich feathers Cecelia would carry with her throughout her presentation, pretending to curtsy.

'Your Royal Highnesses, it is I, your loyal subject, Eliza Murphy.' And she giggled, drunk with excitement.

Cecelia watched on from where she was sitting in her dressing gown on the edge of her bed, not sure whether she was amused or disgusted by Lizzie's carry-on.

'If your brother Frank knew you were so excited about my presentation at court, he'd disown you, Eliza Murphy, and you well know it.'

'I won't be telling him now, will I?' Lizzie flapped the ostrich feather at her and then froze.

It would have been comical if the colour hadn't drained from her face, Cecelia thought, as her head spun toward the door. Her blood trickled icily through her veins when she saw her mother standing there.

'What do you think you're doing?'

It was Lady Kildurran's calm tone that frightened Cecelia most, and poor Lizzie had dropped the dress so it lay in a heap at her feet. The feather, meanwhile, floated in a slow tease to the ground.

'There's no harm done, Mother.' Cecelia was swift to act, getting to her feet and scooping the dress and feather up.

'Oh, no harm done you say. Well, that's all right then.' Lady Kildurran's voice was chilly.

'Begging your forgiveness, my lady. I'm so sorry for my childish carry-on,' Lizzie finally managed.

'Disrespectful was what it was, Eliza.' Lady Kildurran made a clucking noise with her tongue. 'I've a good mind to send you back to Ireland. I should have known you couldn't be trusted. I wouldn't be surprised if it were you who stole Sir George's watch. I had my suspicions at the time but gave you the benefit of the doubt. It's never reappeared, you know.'

Cecelia felt sick.

Lizzie's bottom lip trembled, and fat tears sprang forth. 'Please, Lady Kildurran. I'd never steal. Never.'

'You know Lizzie wouldn't, Mother. Don't talk to her like that.' Cecelia gathered herself and stood between the pair.

'How dare you!' Lady Kildurran's voice raised a notch. 'You ungrateful little bitch. She's no more than an inbred Irish heathen.' She jabbed her finger in Lizzie's quivering direction. 'But you, Cecelia, you should know better.'

'I never asked for any of this.' The words flew from Cecelia's mouth as she held up the gown. 'This could feed an entire family on our estate for months, Mother. I don't believe in any of the pomp and ceremony, and I shall curtsy before the King and Queen with a traitor's heart.'

The slap saw Cecelia's head snap back and sent her reeling. Lizzie's hand covered her mouth as she let out a distressed moan.

Cecelia regained her footing, and her chin jutted forth.

'What would your king and queen think if I was to tell them how I got this mark on my face, Mother? Have you thought of that?'

Lady Kildurran was panting heavily and looked set to strike again but caught herself, turning on her heel and stalking from the room. The door echoed with a bang behind her.

'I'm so sorry, CeeCee.' Lizzie was snivelling as she clutched at her friend. 'I didn't mean to get you into trouble. You don't think she'll report me to Sir George, do you?'

Cecelia's tear ducts were prickling, but she wouldn't cry, she vowed, blinking fiercely and swallowing the pain radiating from her cheek. 'No. It would only make her look bad for bringing you with us in the first place. Besides, she knows you wouldn't steal. It was just words is all. So stop that now.'

She set the ridiculous feather down on her dressing table and laid the gown over the back of the chair before fetching a handkerchief from her top drawer. 'Here.'

Lizzie accepted the hanky gratefully, wiping her eyes and giving her nose a trumpeting.

'It's not your fault, Lizzie. It's mine. Mother will use any excuse to lash out where I'm concerned. Now, come on – I've got a presentation to be getting ready for.'

29

———————

The car had been inching along at a snail's pace since coming to a near standstill on Pall Mall, queuing behind fellow Rolls-Royces, Daimlers, Sunbeams and even the odd horse and carriage, all filled with debutantes groomed to within an inch of their lives, like Cecelia. Only, unlike Cecelia, most were peering anxiously out of windows while their sponsors were pillars of calm beside them. The sun had chosen to shine down on the cavalcade, but the atmosphere in the back seat of the Rolls reminded Cecelia of a deep winter's morning, when she'd open her curtains at Foxbourne to see a frozen-white landscape below.

Cecelia, extra powder pressed to her cheek to hide the red mark there, had not said one word to her mother, who was sitting regally alongside her, also dressed all in white in accordance with court dress requirements. The two women were still statue silent as Hogan inched onto the Mall and eventually in through Buckingham Palace's private entrance, the wheels turning slowly but surely toward the forecourt.

A royal footman in full court livery of scarlet and gold with white breeches opened the door of the Rolls and helped first

Cecelia and then Lady Kildurran descend. Mother and daughter entered through the palace's grand entrance, which Cecelia had barely taken stock of before they passed through to the robing room. She'd been coached through what to expect and was prepared for the hushed holding space where the only sounds were the rustle of silk and the odd sneeze.

Debutantes – all about Cecelia's age – adjusted their gloves or fluffed with their feathers while sponsors milled about adjusting trains. The fretfulness amongst the milling sea of white was contagious and tempered for one overwrought girl by a whiff of smelling salts. Cecelia watched as the girl's mother waved them under her nose. As Lady Kildurran straightened Cecelia's train, a voice whispered nearby, 'She never smiles, the Queen, so don't be alarmed.'

The culprit was swiftly shushed, and it was then Cecelia felt the queasiness set in, as if she'd partaken of a grease-laden breakfast. She recognised the warning of what was to come – aggressive spasms of her stomach which, once she'd emptied it, would pass just as an Irish sunshower would. She elbowed her way from the room and only just made it to the resting room. Bile scorched her throat because she hadn't eaten lunch in the hope that it would stave off the sickness, a plan that had clearly not worked.

'Miss, would you like a glass of water?' an attendant asked as Cecelia straightened and accepted the cloth she was passed to dab her mouth with.

'No. Thank you. I'm quite all right now.' She did, however, take the peppermint she was offered and sucked on it hard for a moment or two as she took stock of her reflection. There was no escaping the truth. She was with child and would need to get word to Finian, but now she needed to put her best foot forward and return to the fold.

The irony of the sentiment wasn't lost on her.

Lady Kildurran hadn't moved in her absence.

'Nerves, Mother,' Cecelia hissed. A lie. In her opinion, this pomp and ceremony was both outdated and ridiculous. When their turn came, however, the jitteriness radiated off her mother. And as they stepped into the haloed throne room, Cecelia felt like Judas.

'You asked me once why I detest you so, Cecelia,' Lady Kildurran said as Hogan drove them back to Chester Street.

It was true, she had, Cecelia thought, and she'd wanted an answer then, but now the moment of truth was here, she wasn't sure she did anymore. So she stayed mute, bracing for the poison dart the glittering malevolence in her mother's eyes told her was about to be fired at her.

'The answer's really very simple. I can't stand the sight of you because from the moment you were born, you became a constant reminder of an ill-spent summer. A summer when I comprehended the enormity of the mistake I'd made in marrying Alastair.'

'I don't understand.' Cecelia wished her voice hadn't quavered, but she could feel that something momentous was about to be slapped in her face, something there'd be no coming back from.

'Come on now, Cecelia – you're no fool.'

Cecelia shook her head, uncomprehending.

'I can see I shall have to spell it out for you then. You're not the Earl of Kildurran's child. It's amusing if you think about it because for all your sympathising with the Irish masses, you're as English as I am.'

'What are you saying?' Cecelia croaked as her mother fired her dart.

'Sir George isn't your uncle, Cecelia; he's your father. I married the wrong man.' Spittle gathered at the corners of her mouth. 'Octavia has the life that should have been mine.'

Cecelia swooned, feeling like an earthquake had struck, cracking open the ground on which she stood. The abyss below threatened to swallow her. She wanted to leap from the moving car and run as far away as she could, but her mother had seized hold of her arm. It was plain to see she was revelling in her shock, and Cecelia didn't want to give her further satisfaction, but the need to hear all of it now would be a scab she knew she wouldn't be able to stop picking at until she knew the truth.

'Does Father know?' It was the first time she'd referred to Lord Kildurran as her father since Camelot had been sold. The irony of it wasn't lost on her.

Her mother's lip curled. 'Your father— Oh dear, silly me. Force of habit I'm afraid. *Alastair*, I should say, does not.'

'And Sir George?'

'Has always known. Why else do you think he's footing the bill for your debut? And before you ask, Octavia is clueless. My fool of a sister thinks Sir George is just a generous, kind-hearted man with a deep purse when it comes to family.'

'You're blackmailing him?'

'I prefer to think of it as the ball being in my court.'

The ostrich feather dangled limply over Cecelia's lap as the vitriol of her mother's words seeped through her body. Everything she thought she'd known about herself was a lie. She resolved to get through the ball being held in her honour this evening, and then she would write to Finian. It was time to go home – wherever that may be because it certainly wasn't Foxbourne. But no matter what her mother said, she was Irish in her heart, and nothing could change that.

30

'Miss Cecelia Altringham, making her debut,' Franklin announced.

A smattering of applause and a ripple of approval came from the floor below as Cecelia, glorious in a floor-length ivory satin gown with pearl beading, began to make her way down the stairs. Mr Rossiter had excelled himself, and her gown shimmered and shone with each step. Fresh flowers had been woven into her softly waved hair, and she'd practised the gentle curve of her lips in the mirror earlier. She was every inch the debutante, and nobody in the gathering below would guess for a moment that she had a drumbeat going on inside her head.

Lizzie had declared that no gentleman would notice her limp because 'she was such a vision their eyes would never leave her face' as she'd made her way to the landing moments earlier to where Sir George, the man she'd thought was her uncle until this afternoon, waited to escort her downstairs.

Cecelia couldn't bring herself to look him in the eye as her gloved hand settled on his arm. All she felt for him was revulsion. But she morphed into an elegant ballerina, just as

Madame Vacani had taught her, as he helped her with the stairs, and the only face she focused on as she made her descent was her mother's. From her triumphant expression, she clearly thought she'd won – her daughter had finally been cowed and would obediently find a future husband amongst the eligible gentlemen in attendance this evening. Oh but she was wrong!

Lady Kildurran didn't know it yet, but Cecelia had two aces she'd yet to play. Her relationship with Finian and the fact she was carrying his baby.

The first thing she'd done upon their return to Chester Street was pen a letter to Finian. She'd kept the reason for the urgency with which it needed to be posted from Lizzie, ignoring her protests that it could wait given all there was to do in preparation for the ball. In the end, her friend had begrudgingly pocketed the letter and promised to drop it in the letter box that afternoon.

Finian would send her the fare to return to Ireland as soon as he read her news, and together they'd disappear. Mother, Aunt Octavia and the man she could never call Father would be left red-faced and smarting by the runaway debutante they'd invested so much in. People would talk, Cecelia thought, imagining the scandalous tittle-tattle amongst their set, and her mother's shame.

It was this image that would carry her through this evening with a beatific smile as she became the charming and delightful debutante. Let her mother think she'd won. It would make victory all the sweeter.

The Belgravia town house looked like a magic wand had been waved over it since that morning, the ground and first floors having been transformed into a floral wonderland lit by flickering candles in wall sconces and silk-shaded electric lights. Shiny young debutantes giggled together, dressed in all their finery as they looked out from under their lashes at the gentlemen come to mingle and hopefully, if the watchful eyes of their mothers had any say in the matter, marry one day soon.

Uncle George handed Cecelia to her brother, who steered her toward the ballroom where they were to dance the opening waltz and officially get the evening underway.

Her smile remained plastered to her face even as he whispered out the corner of his mouth, 'You've scrubbed up well, Cecelia, and you've rather caught the eye of one Jonathan Loxely. Well done, you. He's planning on asking Mother's permission to escort you to the Epsom Derby. The man has his own tent, and I'll be only too pleased to chaperone.'

Cecelia was aware of the man to whom her brother was referring and had overheard her mother and aunt discussing the fortune he'd made in construction when they'd agreed his name should be on tonight's guest list. She'd met Jonathan Loxely previously at a garden party and had instantly pegged him as a rogue seeking respectability who also happened to have a head on him shaped like misshapen potato. So far as her family was concerned, Cecelia knew, aesthetics didn't matter – it was the size of his bank balance that deemed him a worthy catch, and Jonathan Loxely was a big fish.

She momentarily forgot about her potential suitor as the orchestra of eight – a group who'd recently played at a party at the Ritz, Cecelia had overhead someone remark – launched into Johan Strauss's 'Roses from the South'. As Julian whirled her about the dance floor, she briefly allowed herself the joy of feeling almost airborne thanks to the hours upon hours of dance practice for this very moment.

Mr Jonathan Loxely was soon back on her mind, however, as he tapped her brother on the shoulder. It transpired his name was at the top of her full dance card.

'You dance very well,' her suitor stated as they began their circuit. He had streaks of grey at his temple, and the mole on his left cheek reminded her of an eye left in a potato.

'Are you surprised?' Cecelia asked, trying not to make her distaste at his anchovy-paste breath obvious. She didn't like the way his hand was pressing a touch too hard into the small of her back either. It felt proprietary, and she was already spoken for. If Finian were here now, he'd knock him to the floor.

'A little, if I'm honest. Polio was it?'

'Yes, and if I dance well it's only because I had a good teacher.' Cecelia could feel her mother's eyes on her.

She barely heard his ensuing compliments, all as oily as the fish paste he'd consumed, and was relieved when another man – who introduced himself as Sir Sebastian Riley – stepped in.

The waltzing gave way to polkas and the structured quadrilles. where Cecelia found herself partnered with a red-headed debutante and two gentlemen she vaguely recognised from the endless rounds of social events she'd been attending. She danced and danced, with one foppish man's face blending into the next while she imagined it was Finian's black eyes she was gazing into.

At last, the orchestra took a short intermission, and as she'd barely taken a breath since descending the stairs, Cecelia was eager to sit somewhere quiet in the fresh air for a while. She joined the small throng exiting the ballroom in search of refreshments, aware her mother had followed her. A glance over her shoulder saw her being waylaid by Aunt Octavia, who called her over to introduce her to a woman wearing an eye-catching tiara. Julian and Sir George were in the card room. No surprise there, she thought, helping herself to a glass of fruit punch from a passing tray and wandering through to the garden.

The cooler air was a welcome respite, and as she moved down the rectangular expanse of greenery toward the empty seat under the magnolia tree at the far end, she caught a snippet of conversation from a nearby cluster of guests.

'She's danced with Mr Stratton – he's an old Etonian in the business of textiles – twice. I've high hopes of a match.'

Cecelia pitied the poor girl whose mother, presumably, had high hopes. Personally, she hoped this Mr Stratton didn't also possess a potato head.

She heaved a blissful sigh as she sank onto the seat. It would be hours until she could climb into bed and put this awful, strange day behind her.

Braying laughter sounded, a champagne cork popped and glasses clinked, and she could smell the fragrance of the magnolia petals scattered about her feet. Overhead, the sky was a carpet of stars. Cecelia gazed up at them, wondering if Finian was looking up at the stars at Foxbourne too. Perhaps he could feel her thinking about him? Her hands had unconsciously settled around her middle.

A burst of tinkling laughter broke the serenity of the moment, and she glanced toward the sources. The red-headed debutante she'd been partnered with for the quadrilles and a brunette with their arms linked were backlit in the open French doors. The redhead's hair shone like copper, and she was swaying slightly, suggesting she should have stuck with non-alcoholic fruit punch. For a moment, Cecelia envied their easy camaraderie and wished Lizzie could come and sit here with her. She'd have liked to have told her about Mr Potato-Head Loxely. Wherever she was right now though, she'd be run off her feet, as all the servants would be this evening.

The redhead's voice floated toward her.

'It's pitiable really to see her making such a spectacle of herself.'

Cecelia stiffened. Was she talking about her?

'Yes, the baby elephant at London Zoo has more grace. And I heard the aunt spent a fortune on private dance lessons for her too.'

The redhead took a few limping steps, leaving Cecelia in no doubt it was her they were laughing about, then the two girls collapsed against one another in a fit of giggles.

Cecelia pressed her back into the seat, hoping to render herself invisible. Heat suffused her neck and face as their careless words sank in, but anger swiftly replaced the hot shame that she'd made a show of herself on the dance floor. They were just jealous, and what did their opinions matter to her anyway? Still, she waited until they'd melded into a gossiping group before quietly exiting the garden.

She tried not to replay what she'd overheard as she was once more swept away by a hee-hawing gentleman whose name was on her card. It was during the next dance that the opportunity presented itself to put the nasty remarks overheard in the garden to bed, and Cecelia seized it – or, rather, her foot slipped out when a certain redhead was partnered next to her once more.

'Oh dear!' Cecelia clapped her hand to her mouth as the girl – whose cheeks now clashed with her hair after one too many champagnes – went flying, landing in an untidy heap on the polished floor. A collective gasp sounded overtop of the music, and she was swiftly helped to her feet and marched from the ballroom by an older, sandy-haired woman dripping in diamonds.

I wouldn't want to be in her shoes, Cecelia thought with an internal smirk. It served her right. What did she expect dancing so close by such an ungainly creature as herself?

Supper was served at midnight, and the final few hours of the ball passed by with livelier foxtrots between the more traditional dances to ensure the partygoers stayed awake. Still, Cecelia had noticed one or two of the older women nodding off discreetly behind fans around the edges of the ballroom floor. Her attention was caught by Jonathan Loxely having a word with her mother, and sure enough, before the last waltz began to play, he made a beeline in her direction.

So, he was making his interest in her known, she thought, relieved her final dance partner wasn't to be Sir George. He could make all the arrangements he liked with Mother for future outings such as the one Julian had mentioned because it didn't matter. She wouldn't be attending. She'd be back where she belonged – with Finian.

'Might I request the last dance, Miss Altringham? It would be the perfect way to round off what has been a thoroughly enjoyable evening.'

Her mother gave a slight nod in her direction, leaving Cecelia little choice but to dip her head and accept. He placed his hand once more in the small of her back as the orchestra ended the evening as it had begun, with Strauss. This time, however, she sailed over the floor to 'The Blue Danube'.

It was a relief when the music ebbed away and Jonathan Loxely thanked her for a delightful evening. She tuned him out as he said he hoped to enjoy her company again soon but managed to drop what she hoped was a beguiling smile. One by one, the guests – some weary, some raring to move on to the next party – began to glide away from the Chester Street town house until it was empty, save for the family and the servants.

Cecelia was dead on her feet, and her leg was paining her so much that the stairs she was about to climb might as well have been Mt Everest. Her hand gripped the bannister as she ascended them slowly, pausing to look back to see if she could spy Lizzie milling about. She'd hoped to catch her eye at least once during the evening but hadn't seen her and was itching to tell her about the redheaded debutante before she collapsed into bed. Lizzie would love that story!

Thinking her friend might already be in the bedroom laying her things out for her, Cecelia managed the last few steps and ventured down the hall toward her room. But a pealing laugh from Julian's room saw her step falter, and she pulled a prudish face, wondering what foolish young debutante had managed to shake off her mother or chaperone to escape up here to her brother's room. She shook her head, her hand on her bedroom door handle, when a woman's voice cried out, 'No, my lord!'

It was Lizzie.

31

Cecelia pushed open the door to her brother's room, her previous fatigue forgotten when she saw Julian wrestling with his trousers with one hand and holding Lizzie down on the bed with the other. He was unaware of her presence as he spat ugly words like *tease* and *whore* at her. Lizzie's terror as she wriggled beneath him, trying to free herself, saw Cecelia spring forth like a predatory animal, hissing, 'Get your filthy hands off her!' Even in her shock at witnessing this ugly scene, she was aware that if she shouted and brought others running, it wouldn't be Julian who'd bear the blame for what he'd been about to do.

Anger made her strong, and she shoved her brother hard, sending him toppling over like a skittle so he landed with a thud on the floor. Lizzie sat up, pushing her uniform back down, and Cecelia held a hand out to her, helping her to her feet.

'Go to my room, Lizzie,' Cecelia ordered.

'Don't think badly of me. I didn't mean for any of this!' Her wild-eyed gaze sought Julian's. 'I thought he liked me.'

His only response was the curl of his top lip.

'This isn't your fault,' Cecelia told her. 'Go. Leave Julian to me.'

Cecelia glared at her brother, feeling nothing but loathing for the weak drunk grasping the edge of the bed as he tried to pull himself up.

The door clicked shut, and brother and sister were alone.

'You think your title allows you to take whatever you want. Well, your time's coming to an end, Julian. There's no room for you in the free Ireland. Your title, the estate, all of it will be gone. All that will be left is your bad debts.'

Julian lost his grip on the bed and slid back to the floor, almost in slow motion. His sneering laugh echoed about the room as he began to clap. When he spoke, his voice was a slur. 'Bravo, sister. Your passion for the peasants is truly entertaining to behold.'

'You're a spoiled little boy.' Cecelia couldn't stand to look at him a second longer and had half turned away, but her brother had other ideas.

'That little tart has been mooning after me for months. I was only going to give her what she wanted.'

Cecelia's hand twitched with the urge to smack the supercilious smirk off Julian's face, but if she hit him, then she'd truly be her mother's daughter.

'You're not so very different to Mother after all. I can see in your eyes that you want to hit me. Go on – do it.'

He was goading her, and she understood then it was out of guilt. So he did feel something other than what fitted his own selfish agenda.

'You never once stood up for me, Julian. You knew she hurt me, and you let her. An older brother is supposed to look out for his sister.'

'It's survival of the fittest in this world, dear sister.'

'Not everybody is disloyal, Julian.'

His sudden flaring at her words saw her take a step back.

'There she is, Miss High and Mighty, with her principles and misguided devotions.'

Julian had the same malicious glint in his eyes their mother had earlier, and Cecelia turned away. 'Sleep it off. And don't ever lay your hands on Lizzie again. She's too good for the likes of you.'

Julian managed to pull himself up then and lunged toward her, but Cecelia was quicker – her hand was already twisting the doorknob.

'I know all about you and that Traveller trainer of Father's.'

She let the handle click back and dropped her hand, knowing she shouldn't but rotating to face her brother anyway.

'I saw you with him down by Lough Rae. I wonder what Mother would say if she were to find out this year's reigning belle of the ball isn't whiter than white. The odds of securing a good match might not be in your favour if it became known you were hardly going to be the virgin bride.'

'Shut your mouth.' Cecelia was shaking, horrified by her brother sullying what was a precious memory.

But Julian was only just getting started. 'You'd do well to remember the things I know about you before you run your mouth off about tonight or any other night.'

She could smell the sweet but acrid champagne on his breath. His lips were fleshy and wet.

'I bet he told you he loves you, didn't he, your Traveller? That's what he is, you know. An itinerant with a talent for horses. Did he tell you that?' Cecelia's face must have given him the answer as he shook his head slowly. 'You stupid, stupid girl.'

Her instincts screamed, *Walk away, Cecelia, walk away now!* But she was immobilised by the door, needing to know what Julian had been sitting on, biding his time.

'I saw the way you cold-shouldered Tomas, blaming him for your horse being sold.'

She'd seen Tomas in cahoots with her father and the buyer with her own two eyes. 'It was – I saw him.'

'You're wrong. It wasn't Tomas who got in Father's ear over

selling your horse or introduced him to the buyer. It was your beloved Finian.'

'You're lying!' Cecelia stared at him for a moment as his face seemed to merge with her mother's, then she wrenched the door open and stumbled from his room.

Lizzie was huddled over in the armchair by the window, sobbing, and didn't look up when Cecelia closed her bedroom door and flopped back against it. Her breath came in short bursts, and her brother's words echoed in her ears. It was like being kicked over and over.

Tomas. His name dropped into her head. He'd written to her. Perhaps it was a confession and apology over his part in Camelot's sale. The proof that Julian had lied might be hidden in her drawer right now. She pushed off from the door, unearthed the envelope from beneath her underwear and tore it open.

Her hand shook as she held the single-page letter. Tomas was pleading with her to believe he'd never have done something knowingly that would hurt her like so. The proof of who had been involved in Camelot's sale lay in Finian's disappearance. He'd been there one day, gone the next without a word, leaving Lord Kildurran in the lurch for the upcoming race season he'd pinned such high hopes on.

Cecelia recalled the hurt in Tomas's eyes the last time she'd seen him. Finian hadn't written to tell her he'd be moving on, and she grasped frantically for reasons he'd disappear without getting word to her. Were the RIC closing in on him, or was he needed elsewhere by the rebels?

But it had already been weeks since Tomas had penned this letter to her, and there'd been nothing from Finian in the interim. He'd had ample time to get word to her if he'd gone into hiding. And she'd know if he was dead – that news would have trickled down to her via Hogan surely? She felt something twist inside her.

Was it possible? Could Finian be the one responsible for her anguish over losing Camelot? If he had been, then he'd also unwittingly betrayed his unborn child.

PART TWO

32

ST PATRICK'S MOTHER AND BABY HOME, 1922

Cecelia thought it was a small mercy they were a pair of hands short in the kitchen because at least *her* hands had been kept busy, even if her mind had a will of its own. If not for her little Nessa, she'd be terribly lonely now she was back where she'd been in the early days of her life at St Patrick's. The friends she'd let her barriers down for and reached out to were both gone now. Sometimes, she wondered about Finian now the war was all but over. Had he looked for her? She doubted she'd ever know.

Finian had been there one day at Foxbourne, gone the next, leaving no trace. Just like her friends at St Patrick's and so many others. Nessa and her baby had died, then Maudie had run away to find Emer, and finally Molly, whom she'd never thought would leave, had gone. Mol's mother had collected her, and the young girl's pleading and screams for her son as she'd been dragged from the home had continued to ring in Cecelia's ears for a long time afterward.

Sister Louise had told her quietly that Molly was needed to help on the family's farm. Connor, however, being another mouth to feed, was not. Cecelia suspected the little boy would also be a constant reminder to her mother of what Mol's father had done to her.

Molly's empty bed and the pain she would be in at being torn from Connor saw Cecelia resolve not to allow herself to get close to any of the other girls. It hurt too much to become part of their stories. She closed her heart to all around her except her daughter and poor Connor. The little boy sobbed whenever she came to feed Nessa, pining for the girl he'd never been allowed to call his mammy but instinctively knew was. All Cecelia could do was try to offer comfort, but even that was frowned on. And now, Connor was gone too without a word of explanation.

She presumed he'd been sent to the industrial school and that it was only a matter of time until Nessa joined him there. Why he'd gone before her daughter, she could only put down to his mother no longer being here. Cecelia knew this was Nessa's future, now she was of an age, because Sister Agnes had glibly informed her so.

Cruelty lurked around every corner of St Patrick's in the shape of that nun's habit, Cecelia had thought, knowing she'd spoken the truth. The gleam in her eyes had given away the pleasure she gleaned from hurting her like so.

Nessa wouldn't survive being away from her, and fear like she'd never known before gripped her. It was a lump in her throat and a boulder of ice in her stomach, and her eyes were bleary from staring into the dark each night, wondering whether Nessa would be gone in the morning. The hope that had sustained her after Maudie left, that her friend would somehow find a way to come back for her and Nessa, had been snuffed out. Why should Maudie revisit the pain and suffering of this place now she was making a new life for herself, hopefully with Emer? Cecelia wished her friend happiness, but despair at her own lot had her spiralling toward the bottom of a black pit.

Nessa was living proof of the passage of time, growing, yes, but not thriving, with a sallow pallor and eyes too large in her head. Her daughter took after her in every way except for her coal-black curls – they were the only evidence of Finian's part in her conception. At least her curls hadn't been cropped to within an inch of her head as had happened to some of the little ones, she thought, her hand unconsciously going to her own hair. She still wasn't used to it no longer being there – it had been hacked short when a lice epidemic swept the home. The smell of the paraffin her head had been doused in still haunted her.

It broke Cecelia's heart to hear the whoop that still wracked Nessa's little body all these months after whooping cough had swept through the room full of little ones too big for this place. What she needed was fresh, country air, and for a moment, Cecelia's step faltered as the length of dreary corridor was replaced with undulating fields. She raised her head, feeling cool droplets of mist on her face as she rode Camelot toward the woods, Foxbourne rising behind her through the mist, in search of elusive sunshine.

The sound of a door closing in the distance brought reality crashing back, and Cecelia carried on toward the kitchen because Nessa also needed a roof over her head, a bed and food, even if the latter barely passed muster.

The line between surviving and living had long since blurred, and the days crawled by slowly, full of tedious prayer and hard work, punctuated by pinpricks of joy when she was allowed to visit Nessa – yet at the same time they passed too quickly. Sometimes, she could scarcely believe she was still here, but while others came and went, her circumstances hadn't changed. She could not, *would not* leave without Nessa and had no means to survive outside St Patrick's.

Cecelia was worried too. The fear that Nessa would be spirited away to an industrial school was always there, niggling away at her. It was inevitable – she and her daughter were living here on borrowed time, having stayed at St Patrick's longer than most. She suspected Sister Louise had a hand in that somehow.

It was being one girl down to help with the daily cycle of chores in the kitchen that was responsible for Cecelia and the other girls she worked alongside running late to prayers at noon. She was last in the line hurrying down the corridor toward the chapel, an apology already on the tip of her tongue.

Then she froze.

Overtop of the clomping boots, an unseen voice straight from her nightmares drifted toward her. It echoed in the draughty corridor, or perhaps it was only reverberating inside Cecelia's head. Whatever the case, she stumbled over her own ill-fitted boots then righted herself. Her palms grew damp, her mouth dry, and her heart began pounding as an ice pick splintered her soul.

The past had finally caught up with her.

33

'There's no running in the corridors, child. Late or not. Now get inside.' Sister Mary blocked Cecelia's path then tugged at her arm to drag her into the chapel.

Cecelia yanked herself free, but the nun was having none of it. 'You're to get inside this minute!'

'No!'

'The insolence of it.' Sister Mary's chin's wobbled with indignation.

'Please, Sister, let me pass. I heard a voice.'

'Oh, God's was it? Telling you to run, was He? I think you're delusional, child. Do you have a temperature?' The nun reached out to press the back of her hand against Cecelia's forehead.

'I'm not sick.' Cecelia batted her hand away. 'I know what I heard.'

She drew on every inch of strength in her and shoved the sister aside. Tunnel vision drove her forward, her mind racing, and her chest felt like it was being squeezed by an iron band when, under the frozen gaze of the statue of Mary, she emerged gasping for air into the foyer.

The world tilted on its axis when she saw the overbearing outline of her mother, illuminated by the outside light streaming in through the main doors, her gloved hand gripping Nessa's like an alligator's jaw would its prey, and she cried out.

'Give her to me, Mother!'

'You were supposed to be at chapel,' the Mother Superior snapped. 'Go there this minute and be grateful your mother has graciously offered to give the child a home.'

Her mother turned, her chin raised as her chilly eyes grazed over Cecelia. The only glimmer of recognition was in the curl of her top lip and the glint of satisfaction in her eyes.

She turned to the Mother Superior. 'That girl's no longer a child of mine. She can rot in here for all I care. She's exactly where she deserves to be.'

The Mother Superior, unsure whether to herd Cecelia toward chapel or not, decided to see Lady Kildurran off first and pushed them through the door. 'I shall pray for the salvation of your souls.'

Cecelia didn't think, acting on maternal instinct as she charged for the door and sent the Mother Superior flying with a shove. She ran for her mother and Nessa, who was trotting alongside her toward an idling car. Her mother, hearing feet crunching over the gravel toward her, spun round, pushing Nessa, who cried out upon seeing Cecelia behind her. She drew herself upright, and momentarily Cecelia was transported back to being a little girl who lived in fear of her mother, but she wasn't her, not any more. She was a mother herself now, and she squared up to Lady Kildurran.

'Give her to me, Mother. Nessa stays here. She's not yours to take.'

Spittle flew from her mother's lipstick-stained mouth. 'And you're not fit to keep her. Oh, I know all your grubby secrets, Cecelia. Every last tawdry one of them. And if you come for this child at any time in the future, then I'll turn you in to the British authorities. You could hang for what you did.'

How did she know? Who'd betrayed her? Surely not Lizzie! Cecelia fell to her knees, grasping her mother's coat, aware she had only seconds until the sisters came running and dragged her back inside and she lost Nessa forever. 'Why are you doing this, Mother?'

Lady Kildurran prised her daughter's fingers from her coat, brushing the spot where they'd been as though Cecelia had left a stain behind. 'Why? Because you can't win, Cecelia. I won't allow it. You ruined everything by running away like you did. Julian and I were forced to return to Ireland with our tails between our legs. It seems Foxbourne is my destiny after all, and this place here' – she waved a hand at the building in front of her – 'is yours. As for your daughter, she'll ensure Sir George continues to play the game, especially when I tell him what you were up to in London right under his nose – and who the child's father is. Don't look so surprised, Cecelia. Julian told me all about your liaisons with our racehorse trainer – or should that be Irish rebel.'

'Finian?' Did she know where he was? Desperation seized hold of her because he'd not see her child – his child too – torn from her to be raised by his enemies.

'Oh, don't waste your tears on him. He's headed for the hills – America they think. It was a year or so back, I believe. The papers headlined it "fugitive on the run" due to his anti-treaty stance. Alastair was mortified when he realised he'd employed a high-ranking member of the IRA. Of course, he had a lot more to say when I told him what you'd done.'

Cecelia could hear a flurry of overexcited voices in the foyer and knew any second the sisters would rush forth to grab her.

'I don't understand how you found where I was.' She had to know for sure if it was Lizzie; the not knowing would eat her alive.

'A reward offered in the papers as to your whereabouts brought a little friend of yours crawling out of the woodwork – Molly her name was. She told me the rest of your sorry tale.'

As the nuns swooped on her, Cecelia's mother gave her one last triumphant look, but Cecelia, unable to absorb who had betrayed her, was looking past her to Nessa. She was desperate for one last glimpse of her daughter to sustain her through whatever came next. But Nessa was being helped into the car by a man, and when she cried out her child's name, he turned and fixed his stricken gaze on her.

'Tomas. No! Don't let her take her,' Cecelia sobbed as her boots scrabbled against the gravel. There were too many sisters for her to fight them off, and as the car began to slowly pull away, she saw Nessa, white-faced, staring out the window at her. Then she was gone and the door to St Patrick's had slammed shut, the key turning in the lock and the bolts sliding into place.

Cecelia would have collapsed if not for the nuns who had hold of her. Her sobs drowned out the approaching footsteps.

'I can't have her upsetting the other girls, and she's overwrought. Selfish girl that she is. A spell in the small room should calm her.'

Cecelia's vision was waterlogged, but she could just make out the Mother Superior, her face contorted with pain and her hand clutching her back, before she was dragged to a room beside the infirmary.

'Calm yourself in here, child, and think about the injury the Mother Superior has suffered at your hands,' a voice barked as Cecelia was pushed inside the small room.

There was a clunk as the key turned, locking her in.

The smell of Lysol and bleach, coupled with the scratching of rats, crippled her, even though the room was larger than a cupboard, with a window to let grey light in, and she could see it was devoid of rodents and cleaning supplies. Still, every muscle in her body was tensed, threatening to cramp, and breathing was difficult.

She would die in here, Cecelia thought, though she no longer cared if she did. Curling into herself, her mind retreated back to the beginning of the end...

34

LONDON, ENGLAND, 1919

Cecelia tried to cast Julian's spiteful revelation that Finian was behind Camelot's sale from her mind, though Tomas's letter, which she still held in her hand, only added fuel to the fire burning inside her. She wouldn't believe either of them! Her brother was spiteful and had said what he'd said to get back at her, while Tomas wore two faces. The friend she'd trusted was a liar. She tore up the letter and let it float to the ground, then, aware of Lizzie's sniffing, went and crouched beside her friend's chair and took her hands in hers. Lizzie's mob cap was skew-whiff, and Cecelia still wore her pearls, heels and ballgown, both girls hurting.

'It's all right, Lizzie. He can't touch you now.'

Her friend raised her head, eyes swollen and red as she began to burble. 'I only went into his room because he'd followed me upstairs with a bottle of champagne and offered me a glass.'

'Shush, it doesn't matter.' Cecelia pressed her hands gently between hers.

'But it does. I want you to understand. I don't want you to think badly of me.'

'I wouldn't, and I don't. I've got no blinkers on where my brother is concerned. Put it from your mind.'

Fatigue crashed into her, and all Cecelia wanted was her bed. She didn't want to think about Julian, her mother, her uncle, her father – none of it. Her head was thumping again, but she might as well have said nothing as Lizzie continued talking, determined to say her piece.

'I've never tried it, you see. Champagne. I wanted to pretend I was one of those well-born ladies, sipping from a fancy glass like them that were there tonight. I wanted to know what it felt like to be the sort of lady a gentleman could love, and I s'pose I thought he might try to steal a kiss.' Her baleful eyes fixed on Cecelia's, silently begging her to understand. 'And I can't deny I wanted him to. I'm an eejit though, not a lady, because a lady wouldn't venture into a gentleman's room like I did. I could see it in his eyes what he thought of me.'

'Oh, Lizzie, my brother's no gentleman. You've seen that for yourself now. You're worth ten of him.'

Lizzie shook her head, seemingly aware of her mob cap, which was now perched precariously, because she pulled her hand free from Cecelia's to pull it off and tossed it aside. 'Sure, it's my fault. I deserved it going into his room like I did.'

A fresh round of sobs erupted, and Lizzie bowed her head.

Cecelia suddenly felt old beyond her years and so very tired. 'Listen to me, Lizzie. You're not at fault. It wasn't you that behaved like a depraved animal just now, and you mustn't blame yourself.'

'But I do.' Her voice was muffled as she spoke into her chest. 'If I hadn't gone into his room—'

'Stop! That's enough.' Cecelia didn't mean to sound sharp, but she wouldn't have her friend assuming responsibility for her brother's disgusting behaviour. 'You've poor taste when it comes to choosing who to give your heart to, I'll give you that, but we can't help who we fall in love with.'

Something in her tone saw Lizzie raise her head. 'What is it?'

'Nothing.' Cecelia gave the hand she was still holding a squeeze and made to stand up, but Lizzie held on.

'CeeCee, I can see it's not nothing. It's plain as day on your face. You're disgusted with me, aren't you?' Her brow knitted together, and her bottom lip trembled.

'No. It's not you. Julian said something, but it wasn't true. He said it because he wanted to hurt me. I won't give him the satisfaction of repeating it.'

'It clearly upset you, whether it's true or not. You know yourself you'll feel better for telling me.'

Would she? Cecelia hesitated, unsure she wanted to verbalise Julian's accusation. Lizzie had warned her off Finian just as Tomas had. Her friend would hardly be impartial.

'CeeCee,' Lizzie urged. 'You can tell me anything.'

No, she couldn't. She had secrets from her friend, some she'd never share. 'You've already made your mind up about him. Telling you won't help.'

'Finian?'

She said nothing.

'What did your brother say?' Lizzie had a caginess about her.

'Do you promise not to agree with what Julian flung at me just because you don't like Finian?'

Lizzie shrugged uncertainly. 'I'll try, and in all honesty, CeeCee, I don't much like your brother anymore either.'

It would have to do. 'He accused Finian of being the one who went to my father and suggested the sale of Camelot.'

Lizzie bit her bottom lip and let go of Cecelia's hand, shifting in her seat. 'I'm sorry.'

'You said you'd at least try.'

'I can't lie to you.'

'I don't know why you'd go along with anything Julian says after what he just did to you.'

'I didn't say anything to you before because what was the point? You'd made your mind up it was Tomas who'd gone behind your back to your father, and you wouldn't hear a word against Finian.'

'You're just saying that. I think you should go.'

'Why would I try and turn you against Finian unless I had good reason. You're a sister to me, and I would never hurt you deliberately. So, no, I'm not going anywhere because I should have told you back then but...' She shrugged. 'I heard them, CeeCee. I heard Finian in your father's study. It was him who said selling your horse was the smart thing to do. Your father didn't have the funds for the second payment due to enter Raven in Curragh, and he couldn't afford the forfeit fee either. I'm telling you as a sister: Finian Fahy cannot be trusted, no matter how much you think you love him.'

'It doesn't make sense. Why? Why would he do that to me?' She might not understand his actions, but Lizzie's words held a ring of truth.

'I don't know,' Lizzie said miserably.

'I thought he loved me.' Cecelia stood up then and backed away until she connected with her bed. She sank down on the edge of it and kicked her shoes off.

Lizzie said nothing.

Cecelia rubbed her temples, wishing the little hammer banging in her head would stop. She'd risked so much for Finian since arriving in London. She'd done it for a free Ireland, but she'd also done it for him because she'd thought he would sweep in and rescue her from a life she didn't want.

Then, between the thrumming drumbeats, Cecelia had a moment of clarity and the answer – while it was one she didn't want to acknowledge – was right in front of her.

Finian understood the way to make her malleable to the

cause was to make her vulnerable and angry. So he'd talked her father into selling her horse – not because it made financial sense, as he'd said, but to turn Cecelia against her family. He'd counted on Lord Kildurran taking Camelot from her hardening her heart, not just against him but what he stood for.

He had played her because he'd been aware of who her uncle was all along and how valuable she could be to the rebels. While she, stupid girl that she was, had been like clay on a potter's wheel, allowing his hands to shape her into someone willing to betray her own family. What Finian didn't know was that he'd also betrayed his own family because the child she carried now would never know his or her father. There would be no ring on her finger ensuring her baby's legitimacy. Finian would not marry her. She doubted he'd ever even loved her, and he certainly wouldn't be sending for her. A sob escaped her lips.

'You just wanted to be loved,' Lizzie murmured.

It was true. She'd been so lost and she'd thought Finian would be the one to show her the way.

'I'm in trouble, Lizzie, and I don't have a clue what to do.' Her hands rested on her belly.

Lizzie stared hard at her, then a light of understanding gleamed in her eyes. 'The sickness, and you've been so tired. Ah Jesus, Mary and Joseph. You're to have a baby.'

Cecelia simply nodded.

35

'Marry someone,' Lizzie blurted out once the shock of Cecelia's predicament had worn off. 'Sure, you're the toast of the season, CeeCee. All the servants are saying so. Why can't you convince one of your lovesick suitors to put a ring on your finger sooner rather than later?' She slapped her hands down on her knees, her own distress shelved as she began to warm to her theme. 'You could tell him you can't abide the thought of a society wedding and that you'd rather elope. Sure, your lucky man will be so eager to have his way with you, he's bound to agree because the sooner you're wed, the sooner you and he can, well, you know.'

'Lizzie Murphy. You're the one who's delusional and talking nonsense.' Cecelia thought of the ugly comments of the redhead and her friend in the garden. She was hardly the belle of the ball. 'The only man who's expressed interest in me would soon work out something was amiss if I were to try and rush him to the altar. Anyway, it's my family title he's interested in, so he'd likely want an elaborate display. More importantly, I've no wish to marry him, no matter what my predicament.'

She didn't add that the thought of having to bed Jonathan

Loxely was completely repugnant, let alone committing to spending the rest of her life with him. Besides, despite what she'd learned about Finian, she still loved him, even if she was no longer sure he'd ever loved her.

Lizzie lapsed into silence.

'If Mother finds out about my condition, she'll flay me alive,' Cecelia said, half to herself, as the reality of her situation and lack of options began to sink in.

'You can't stay here.' It was Lizzie's way of acknowledging what Cecelia had said was true.

'Where would I go?' It hurt to say it out loud, but there was no point glossing over things. She couldn't keep the bitterness from her voice. 'Finian's left Foxbourne – Tomas wrote and said so. If he wanted me to know where he was going, he would have got word to me by now.'

'You could always go home, CeeCee. I'll come with you.' Lizzie's bloodshot gaze flitted to the wall separating Cecelia's bedroom from her brother's. 'Sure, I'm missing my mam something terrible, and I won't stay on here. Not after tonight. I'll take what little pride I have left and go home to Kildurran.'

Cecelia shook her head. 'I can't go back.'

'You could. Lord Kildurran's not hard like the viscountess. He wouldn't turn his own flesh and blood away. He...'

The way her voice lamely trailed off told Cecelia she didn't believe a word of what she was saying. They were both enlightened enough to understand that the Earl of Kildurran would be as scandalised by a baby born out of wedlock as his wife, especially if he stumbled on the truth. The father of Cecelia's child was an Irish rebel who'd convinced his daughter to spy for Ireland. Lizzie, too, would be shocked if she found out about Cecelia's night-time activities in Sir George's study, although with her brother Frank's leanings, she'd at least sympathise.

'That's the only difference between them. Lord Kildurran wouldn't beat me within an inch of my life, but I wouldn't be welcome under his roof, not in my condition.' She threaded and unthreaded her fingers. 'And I've no claim to Foxbourne any longer.'

'You've as much right to the estate as he does next door.' Lizzie jabbed her finger at the wall. 'It's hardly your fault Finian is a feckless liar. Why should you have to pay for what he's done, leaving you in the family way like so.' Defiance sparked as Lizzie got her second wind.

'For the same reason you feel you can't stay on here. And it isn't fair, but that's our lot, isn't it? There's more to it though, Lizzie.'

'Like what?'

'You said Lord Kildurran wouldn't turn away his flesh and blood, and that's the thing. I'm not. He isn't my father.'

Lizzie went slack-jawed hearing that and then clamped her lips together, hauled herself off the chair and marched toward Cecelia. 'Now it's you who's delusional and talking rubbish. Tonight's all been too much, CeeCee.' She pulled Cecelia's nightgown out from under the pillow and flapped it out before thrusting it at her. 'Here, put this on. I think you need some sleep.' She shook her head, muttering, '"He isn't my father." Why would you say something like that?'

'He's not,' Cecelia repeated, batting the gown away, impatient now. 'Mother took great delight in telling me so after my presentation.'

That stopped Lizzie in her tracks, and after staring at her friend for a long few seconds, she dropped her voice to a whisper as if the walls had ears. 'If Lady Kildurran spoke the truth, who is then?'

Boom, boom, boom went the drumbeat inside Cecelia's head. 'You wouldn't believe me if I told you, and it doesn't matter. All that matters is what do I do now? Where do I go, Lizzie?'

Lizzie's shoulders sagged, and she collapsed next to Cecelia. ''Tis a terrible pickle you're in, but there is a place you could go.'

For a moment, there was blessed silence, and the pressure in her temples abated as Cecelia felt a bud of hope unfurl. 'Where? Tell me.'

Lizzie appeared uncertain, and her mouth moved from side to side in contemplation. 'It's not a good place, CeeCee. You'd be made to suffer for your sins,' she said finally. 'But it would mean a roof over your head, and you could have your baby there safely. There's a home in Dublin run by the nuns where unwed mothers can go.'

'And how do you know about it?'

'My cousin Dervla – her mam took her there. Her beau was killed in the war before they could be wed, and she'd got herself in the family way. The nuns took care of her. My aunt told everyone Dervla had gone to help her poorly spinster aunt who lived all on her own across the water in Liverpool. She told Mam the truth of it though.'

'What happened to her baby?'

'She had a little boy. He stayed on in the nuns' care, and Dervla came home. It was like it never happened. Some of the babies are adopted though, Mam told me. I think she hoped Dervla's little lad would go to a good home.'

'And do you know the name of this home?'

'No. I just think of it as the Irish Adoption House.'

'That's where I'll go then. This Irish Adoption House.' It occurred to her then there was a rather obvious obstacle blocking this as a course of action. 'But I'm not Catholic, and you said it was run by the nuns.'

'Convert,' Lizzie replied with a shrug. 'Sure, if you can get your hands on some money, then I'm sure we can find ourselves a priest eager for a donation and to save a sinner's soul at the same time. A priest who'll deliver you there to the home himself for a price.'

Again, Cecelia wondered how Lizzie, who'd led as sheltered an existence as herself, knew such things. This time she didn't ask because she'd grasped hold of one word. 'We?'

'I'm leaving with you. My aunt will take us in until we can arrange everything for you.'

'Thank you.' Cecelia's voice was thick with the emotion of having such a loyal friend, a friend who was worth ten of her family. There was relief, too, at having found a way through the mess she was in.

'We'll need money though. We can't very well walk back to Ireland.'

'Yes.' Cecelia frowned.

'I've a little put by. It might be enough for our fares.'

'No. That's your hard-earned money, Lizzie, and you'll not be able to pick up where you left off at Foxbourne after leaving here abruptly either, so hold on to it for yours and your mam's sakes.' Cecelia had an idea of where she could get hold of their fares and more. 'I have some money owing to me. I'll call in that debt. You leave that side of things to me.'

36

———

Neither girl caught a wink of sleep, and Cecelia's eyes were pebbles in the snow by the time Lizzie tiptoed from her room needing to freshen up. Her day was about to start all over again because the servants in the Belgravia town house were hamsters on wheels. No matter they'd been up most of the night putting the house back in order so the family wasn't disturbed during the day, their routine would stay the same. The family, however, would get up at their leisure.

Cecelia was relieved when Julian, who hadn't once met her eye over a late breakfast, disappeared out at the first opportunity. Uncle George, too, was quick to retreat to his study, but there was to be no escape for Cecelia, who was herded from the dining room to the parlour by her mother and aunt. They expected her to relive the minutiae of the ball with them, and keen not to get off side with either of them when she was so close to getting away, she played along.

The evening had been a great success, Mother and Aunt Octavia clucked before picking over the finer details like a pair of mother hens would grain. Yesterday's spite seemed to have been forgotten on her mother's part. *Well, not on mine*, Cecelia thought as the sisters expressed delight over the evening having been mentioned in this morning's society pages. While they congratulated themselves, Cecelia attempted to read her book. She wanted to lose herself in that for a while, but it was impossible with their gossipy twittering.

A short while later, a knock sounded on the door, and all three women were presented with bouquets. It was the icing on the cake for the older women. There were pink and white roses for Cecelia, a posy of freesias for Mother and lilies for Aunt Octavia, along with equally flowery thank-you notes from Jonathan Loxely, exclaiming over a delightful evening. If the sisters were peacocks, then their feathers would have been on full display as they read the messages aloud to one another.

Their conversation carried on as if Cecelia wasn't even in the room, and if it weren't for her own plan to abscond with Lizzie the first chance they got, she'd have been alarmed by the rapid escalation of Jonathan Loxely's interest in her. He'd asked to have the pleasure of Cecelia's company at both an engagement party and eventual wedding, as well as the Epsom Derby. At last, however, Aunt Octavia yawned. It was contagious, and her mother followed suit. The sun was pouring into the parlour, bathing them in warmth, and the lack of sleep began to take its toll.

'It was closer to morning than midnight by the time we retired. I think a little rest might be in order, Helen dear.'

'I agree, Octavia.'

The two women rose, but Cecelia didn't look up from her book as she murmured, 'I shall stay here and read.'

For once, they left her be, and once their footfall up the stairs faded, Cecelia snapped the book shut. This was the chance she'd been waiting for.

She bided her time though, keeping her eye on the carriage clock, and when another five minutes had passed without either woman reappearing, she ventured upstairs herself – not to lie down but to visit her uncle in his study.

She tapped on the door of the room she was more familiar with than anyone in the house would ever know.

'Come in,' an impatient voice said.

She walked into a blue-grey haze of cigar smoke, behind which sat her uncle, a cup of tea by his side. He wasn't working then, just seeking respite from his wife and her sister's incessant rehashing of the ball. Cecelia could hardly blame him.

'Ah, Cecelia.' He appeared bemused by her presence. 'What can I do for you?'

She stood in the doorway. 'I'd like to have a word, Uncle George, if I may.'

'Certainly. Come in.'

Cecelia closed the door behind her and sought a seat, but there was only the chair behind his desk, and Sir George made no move to fetch it for her, so she was left with no option but to stand. She didn't mind because after she'd made herself clear, she was certain Sir George would be in greater need of a seat than she was. His actions, she surmised, were a deliberate ploy not to make her too comfortable. He wanted her to say whatever it was she'd come to say and leave him in peace. Well, she didn't plan on taking up much of his time and got straight to the point.

'Sir George, it's come to my attention that I am not Lord Kildurran's child as I've always thought but rather your illegitimate daughter.'

His eyes bulged, and his naturally ruddy colour deepened to maroon as he began to splutter. He was seized by a choking cough then, but Cecelia didn't offer to fetch a glass of water; she simply waited for him to regain control of himself. When he did, he set the cigar down in the ashtray and wheezed, 'I don't know where you got that poppycock from. And there was me thinking you a practical girl, not a fantasist.'

Cecelia wasn't perturbed, keeping her tone cool as she

stated, 'My mother kindly informed me yesterday I was the result of an illicit summer liaison with yourself.'

'Your mother?' He tapped the side of his head. 'The woman is touched in here. She doesn't know what she's saying half the time.'

She wondered how he got on in Parliament because despite his protests, his crossed arms, fidgeting feet and darting gaze that didn't quite meet hers gave him away. Hardly the poker face she'd have thought necessary for all the underhanded scheming that must go on at Westminster. 'Mother is many things, *Father*, including sharp as a tack. She was very clear in what she said. But don't fret. It's not a public acknowledgement of parentage I want from you. It's money.'

'Oh-ho. I see. You're your mother's daughter. There's no doubt about that,' Sir George growled, appearing more comfortable as he crossed his leg because money was a topic he understood. 'I won't be blackmailed, Cecelia.'

'I think it's too late for that. You already have been – by my mother.' Cecelia's actions weren't motivated by selfish gain like Lady Kildurran's, however. She was doing what she had to for the sake of her child and for Lizzie. Still, her mother's words came back to her, and she used them now. 'What I'm doing isn't blackmail but rather letting you know the ball is in my court.'

Sir George shook his head slowly, and over the top of it, a ribbon of smoke floated, trapped in the light with nowhere to escape to. 'There's been a small fortune spent on you already this season. How you have the gall—'

'I have the gall because I'm in the family way and I want to disappear. I have no wish to marry someone Mother and Aunt Octavia choose for me, and I'm sure whomever they set their sights on would have no wish to marry me when they become aware of my condition. If you give me what I'm asking for, then you'll avoid a scandal and you need never see me again.'

Sir George's eyes narrowed, and she could see he was beginning to see the sense in what she was saying. A scandal would do his political career no favours. Now, she just needed to get him over the line.

'If I'm not here in London, then my mother will no longer have any hold over you. Her words won't hold any credibility, even if she decides to tell Aunt Octavia about your tryst, the result of which is standing in front of you now.' Cecelia smiled sweetly. 'To be frank, I can't see her doing that, though, because Aunt Octavia wouldn't tolerate having her under the same roof if she were to find out her own sister had gone behind her back like so. That would leave Mother little choice but to return to Ireland, thus destroying Julian's future and her own. So you can see my way offers a more favourable outcome for all concerned. Oh, there's sure to be tittle-tattle over why I disappeared for a little while, but in your world, it won't be long until something more scintillating occupies people's mind. Before you know it, London will have forgotten I even existed in the first place.'

Sir George uncrossed his legs and sat forward. 'And what exactly are you asking for?'

'Only my due. Given you'll no longer need to put a dowry down, then three thousand pounds will suffice.'

'Three thousand pounds!' Sir George drew himself up, but Cecelia had been bullied by her mother her whole life, and she wouldn't tolerate it any longer.

'That's what I'm asking for.'

'I don't just have that sort of money lying around.'

'The bank will be open tomorrow. I'll give you until midday to come up with the sum. After that, I shan't hesitate to tell Octavia everything.'

That would give her time to speak with Hogan and twist his arm about driving her and Lizzie to Holyhead.

'And how do I know you won't turn up here with your brat, snivelling for more, in the future?'

'I can assure you, I have no wish to see you and Aunt

Octavia or my immediate family ever again. You'll have to take my word on that.'

If he refused to go along with her, Cecelia had one more card up her sleeve. Anna. She would threaten to tell Aunt Octavia about her as well as his affair were her mother. One accusation might be waved away as nonsense, but two? Well, that was one too many. The only reason she'd held back was because of the trickiness of explaining how she knew about his activities with his wife's lady's maid in the first place.

'I shall give you the money, Cecelia, but be clear there will be no more, and you will never be welcomed under this roof again.'

'Thank you, *Father dear*. You've made yourself quite clear, and believe me – once I leave, I've no wish to return.'

Cecelia turned to go. She'd done what she'd come to do, and while she wasn't cheering, she was relieved there was nothing stopping her and Lizzie from leaving now.

Sir George called after her. 'And, Cecelia?'

'Yes?'

'Leave a note. I don't want your mother or Octavia insisting we involve the police in your disappearance.'

'I will.'

There was nothing more to say, so Cecelia left the study to further put her plan in motion because when Mother realised she and Lizzie were gone, she'd know they were headed for Ireland and try to stop them. It would be best if they left during the night. They couldn't afford to wait around for the first train to Holyhead, so she'd get Hogan to drive them directly to the ferry in Wales. He'd do it if he didn't want his duplicitous role of chauffeur and rebel middleman revealed.

All she and Lizzie had to do was get through today, tomorrow and then neither of them would ever need step foot in London again.

. . .

Cecelia met Lizzie in the darkened foyer of the Belgravia town house at 1 a.m. as they'd arranged. She was clutching a suitcase with a few scant belongings and the money Uncle George had been forced to give her. The two girls didn't speak as Lizzie led Cecelia through the silent servants' quarters and out into the cold night air, where Hogan was waiting for them behind the wheel of the car.

37

ST PATRICK'S MOTHER AND BABY HOME, 1922

Cecelia was unsure how much time had passed since she'd been locked in the room. All she knew was that she'd never trust a living soul again. *Molly*. She shook her head, trying to make sense of it. It was Molly who'd gone to her mother. She'd sold her information in exchange for money. She hoped she'd done it for the right reasons, recalling how adamant the younger girl had been the night she'd told her she'd do 'anything' to get her son back. That at least she could understand, even if she couldn't forgive her because it had cost her Nessa. The irony in light of the lengths she'd gone to in order to procure money from Sir George for herself and her own child didn't escape her.

Tomas. She'd hoped one day, somehow, they'd be friends again. All of them – him, her, Lizzie and Cyril. She'd accepted it was Finian who'd gone behind her back to her father about Camelot, and had dearly wanted to tell Tomas how sorry she was for not believing him. She'd seen the horror on his face in the seconds before he'd driven away. Surely now he'd seen with his own eyes where she'd been and why, he would help her somehow?

A glow silenced the chattering monkeys in her head. It

provided heat that was seeping in through her boots and spreading gently through the rest of her body. It was like an embrace that reached into her very soul.

A voice like the wind rippling through the reeds of Lough Rae whispered all around her. 'Don't be afraid.' And Cecelia knew with certainty she was being watched over by an angel. The sensation of floating in a temperate sea and being loved saw her muscles release and her breath slow.

She wouldn't die in here. The Mother Superior was not Sister Agnes, and this time she would not be left to think she would rot away behind a locked door, a forgotten girl, until all that was left to say she'd ever been there was a pile of bones. Nor would anger and hatred consume her. She would not become her mother, and somehow she would be reunited with Nessa. That was the only thing that mattered. It was far too late for recriminations.

She felt it when the angel left. Her body grew cold once more, but now she was calm. She pulled herself onto all fours then crawled to the far wall to sit with her back pressed up against it. If she were to rage about being shut away, it would only serve to extend her time in here. Better to stay quiet, think and save her strength because she would need it to get Nessa back.

Her mother would not get the chance to hurt Nessa the same way she had her. Her daughter would not be a pawn to be used for revenge, and the second she was freed from this room, she would fetch her back.

This resolve burned until weariness took over and her head began to loll. It snapped up sharply, however, when she heard a sing-song voice drifting through the keyhole. There was nothing otherworldly about it, and Cecelia rubbed her arms when she noted the glee in it.

'You're all tarred with the same brush. Selfish, liars, bad girls the lot of you.'

Cecelia wanted to cry out for Sister Agnes to go away because surely she'd been punished enough? But she kept quiet, aware she'd be wasting her breath.

'Mother Superior didn't want to let the child go to a home where she wouldn't be raised in the one true faith, but Lady Kildurran is her grandmother, so she'd no choice. Your mother told us what a crock of lies your story was and how you were always a wayward, spoiled child who expected special treatment because of your limp. Now your girl's gone to a Protestant home, and her soul's in mortal danger, while Mother Superior decides whether to turf you out on the streets or send you to the laundries.'

Sister Louise opened the door to let Cecelia out a short while later, but she didn't move, and the nun entered the room, holding her hand out to her.

'It's all right, child,' she said gently, her brown eyes kind and reassuring. 'Come with me now and we'll find you something to eat. Sure, the world always seems brighter when you've a little food in your belly.'

'I couldn't stomach anything, Sister, and it's far from all right. My mother, Lady Kildurran, she's evil, you know.' Cecelia grasped hold of Sister Louise's hand but didn't budge, imploring her to listen. 'She only came for Nessa because she knows taking her will break my heart. She's exacting her revenge.'

'Revenge for what? I don't understand, child.'

'For running away.'

'Ah, come now. No mother willingly hurts their own child. You're understandably overwrought, Cecelia.'

It didn't escape Cecelia's attention that the sister had called her by her given name and not the one doled out to her upon her arrival at St Patrick's. She was grateful to her because she *was* Cecelia Altringham, the daughter of Lady Kildurran, not Margaret with no identity.

'She's the child's grandmother, and I'm sure she only wants what's best for her.'

'You're wrong, Sister.'

Sister Louise pressed her other hand overtop of Cecelia's. 'The Mother Superior is a wise woman. She'd not have let the little lamb go with her if she'd any doubt she wouldn't be well looked after. Sure, she'll want for nothing. It's for the best. In time, you'll come to see that for yourself. You might even find your way home to your family when you leave us.'

'I can't ever go home, Sister, and Nessa will want for nothing except love. She'll be reminded daily she's a bastard in the eyes of the Anglican and Catholic church by my mother, who'll take pleasure in telling her she was unwanted – unloved. I know this in here.' Cecelia placed a hand on her heart. 'Because it's what she did to me. And I also know what lengths a girl will go to in order to be loved. It's how I came to be here.' Cecelia's hand fell back down to her lap. 'You can't possibly understand the pain of being separated. It's like an open wound.'

Sister Louise continued to sandwich Cecelia's hand between hers. 'That's where you're wrong, child. I do understand.'

A note in Sister Louise's voice saw Cecelia's head snap up. A tear had pooled in the corner of the nun's eye, and Cecelia watched as it spilled over, tracking a path to the corner of her nose. The nun didn't seem to notice it though.

'I still bear the wound. It's why I gave myself to Christ.'

'You had a baby?' Cecelia couldn't keep the shock from her voice.

'I did.'

'But how?'

Sister Louise blinked the rest of her tears away. 'Oh come

now, Cecelia, I'm sure you've worked out the hows and whys of finding yourself with child. 'Twas only Mary who had the immaculate conception.'

'That's not what I meant.' Cecelia flushed, but Sister Louise's eyes had drifted elsewhere, and she seemed oblivious to how tightly she was squeezing Cecelia's hand.

'I'd an older cousin who helped my da on our farm. He took advantage of me one day in the barn, and afterward I ran crying into the house to tell my mam what he'd done to me. I'll never forget the way she looked at me, like I was a dirty girl, and she wouldn't hear a word about any of it. It was like it had never happened. Only it had because eventually my belly began to show the proof of what he'd done to me. I wasn't allowed to leave our farm or show my face to anyone who came calling. Then one night the pains came, and I screamed for my mam because I was certain I wouldn't see the morning. I bore a little boy and only caught a glimpse of him before Mam whisked him away. I remember he was crying, and then there was nothing but silence. Mam wouldn't tell me why his cries had stopped like so or where he'd gone, but I think I knew in my heart he was gone from this world before he'd barely drawn his first breath. His death was my punishment.'

Cecelia wanted to howl at the injustice of what this poor woman had suffered at the hands of her own family, what all the girls hidden away here at St Patrick's were suffering and for what her mother was making her suffer now.

'It was as if my little boy never existed. I was expected to slip back into my old life and carry on like nothing had happened, but I couldn't. I needed to acknowledge and atone for his life and his death. So I prayed, and I begged the Father for forgiveness, and he showed me the way. I could help those who couldn't help themselves as a bride of Christ.'

Cecelia wiped her own cheeks. 'I'm very sorry for all your troubles, Sister.'

''Tis the past now, Cecelia. It's the future we must look toward. Yourself included.'

'I don't have a future without Nessa, Sister Louise.'

Conflicting emotions flickered across the nun's face.

'You helped Maudie the night she left here to look for her daughter Emer, didn't you?'

Her silence was the only answer Cecelia needed.

38

'I don't like to speak ill of the Reverend Mother, but 'tis a strange thing that none of the other letters have been passed on to me until recently,' Sister Louise whispered in the flickering lights of the votive candles. She'd asked Cecelia to stay behind after morning Mass to help her trim and replace the candle wicks.

The Mother Superior had injured her back when Cecelia had pushed her over in her desperation to stop her mother leaving with Nessa and had been recuperating at a coastal convent ever since. Her absence, Cecelia suspected, was the only reason she hadn't been turfed out onto the streets after the way she'd manhandled her.

In some respects, facing life on Dublin's streets would be a relief because each day without her daughter here at St Patrick's was torture. To drive the knife in further, her request to be moved from the kitchen to the laundry in the hope of avoiding helping to feed the little ones their mash had been refused. The pain in her heart each time she entered the nursery Nessa had once occupied only to realise all over again her daughter was gone was like a physical assault. It would hit her harder than any slap her mother had ever wielded, and the questions would crowd in on her, shouting to be answered.

How was Nessa being treated? Was she crying for her mam?

Worst of all, though, was the niggling thought that burrowed like a worm into the dirt: Cecelia had never been allowed to show her daughter love, except during stolen moments when the nursery sister was distracted, so would Nessa even remember her?

She couldn't sleep with the questions tormenting her in the night. There were dark shadows under her eyes, and she was permanently light-headed with hunger but had no appetite to eat.

Cecelia had long since stopped believing in miracles, but now, as she listened to what Sister Louise was saying, she thought this surely had to be one.

'Please, Sister, I don't understand.'

'Dear Maudie O'Connor has been writing for some time to me wanting me to help her bring you and Nessa to her in America.'

'And will you help?' Cecelia held her breath, aware it was a lot to ask of the nun, the only person left at St Patrick's that she trusted. If she were to help her, it would mean going against a system she'd sworn to honour and obey.

'I answer to God, Cecelia, and I've prayed to the Heavenly Father to show me the way. It seems that He's watched over Maudie and helped her make a good life for herself and her daughter in America. God answered my prayer, and I'll help you too – willingly, with a clear conscience. That's why I've already written back to Maudie, and together we're putting things in place to ensure you can leave Ireland safely with Nessa.'

'Thank you.' Cecelia's hand was on her heart, her voice hoarse with unshed tears, and then panic rose that this wasn't real. She would wake soon to find it had been a cruel dream. She pinched at her flesh, seeking reassurance, but it wasn't enough. 'I don't believe it, Sister. I'm frightened to.'

'Don't be frightened, child. The Heavenly Father is watching over you, and perhaps it will become real to you when you read what Maudie has to say.'

'Yes, Sister.' Cecelia had barely had a chance to rejoice over Maudie keeping her word and the joy in knowing she and Nessa weren't forgotten when Sister Louise spoke up once more.

'That's not all.'

What more could there possibly be? Cecelia stared at her kindly face.

'Sister Agnes was all hot under the collar when I relieved her from night duty yesterday, talking about a man with red hair who'd called wanting to see you. He was most persistent, demanding to be let in, she said. Of course, she sent him on his way with a flea in his ear.'

Tomas! It had to have been. It wasn't just one miracle, but two!

'Sister, when he comes back – because he will, I know he will – you must get word to him somehow of what you and Maudie are planning. He'll help me get Nessa back from my mother.'

'I'll do my best, child, but listen to me now. You're to get yourself fit and well if you're to be any good to that little girl of yours, and that means eating what's put in front of you, or you'll collapse before you're even out those gates.'

'Yes, Sister.' Cecelia nodded, knowing she'd agree to anything. Her gaze was hungry as the nun's hands disappeared amongst the folds of her habit and produced a sheet of paper. *Maudie's letter!*

Sister Louise held it out to her. 'Here. Maudie wrote this for you. What she has planned will take time, and we'll have to be careful. Patience will be the order of the day, so hold your faith, Cecelia, and pray because God willing you'll be reunited with your daughter and your friend.'

The door to the chapel opened then, and Cecelia swiftly hid the letter in her pocket, turning her face from the girl standing there lest she see her excitement.

'Sister Catherine sent me to fetch Cecelia, Sister. She's needed in the kitchen.'

There would be no opportunity to read the letter burning a hole in her pocket unless Cecelia created one. So she set to peeling the vegetables with gusto. Her hands and wrists were cramped by the time she'd filled the slop bucket so high it was in danger of overflowing with potato, turnip and carrot skins.

'Sister, the bucket is in need of emptying,' she called over to Sister Catherine, whose nose was in a pot inspecting its contents.

A nod said she could venture out to the pigs and empty it, so she lugged the bucket out the kitchen door.

The chill was a shock after the smoky heat of the kitchen. The cold penetrated all the way to her bones but did nothing to quell her anticipation. If anything, she embraced the frigid air, knowing Sister Catherine suffered chilblains and couldn't abide the cold. She'd stay in the kitchen rather than step outside on such an afternoon.

The pigs were squealing, so she hurried to their pen and emptied the scraps in, then as they snuffled and snorted, she reached into her pocket. Her hands shook as she unfolded the paper, and her heart was battering her chest. The single sheaf was filled from top to bottom with small, neat handwriting and had been signed by Maudie.

Her hungry eyes devoured the words. Maudie was in a place called Savannah in the American South where she'd been reunited with Emer – not as her mother but through subterfuge as her nanny. The couple who'd adopted Emer from St Patrick's had called her Juniper, and Maudie had grown extremely fond of them both. They'd loved Juniper as much as she did and could give her everything she deserved in life, but sadly, they'd recently passed away. It was testament to the kind and generous people they were that they'd left guardianship of Juniper to her – having suspected all along who she was to the little girl – along with a generous allowance.

Cecelia's eyes welled as elation over her friend having made such a wonderful life for herself and her daughter crushed the harshness of her own circumstances, replacing it with hope. She squeezed the threatened tears away like she was wringing out the dishcloth, desperate to read the rest before Sister Catherine sent one of the girls out to see what was taking her so long.

Maudie, she read, had been writing to Sister Louise, whom she'd sensed had the kindness of heart to help them, ever since she'd let her go the night she'd run. Her letters had begged the nun to help her get Nessa and Cecelia to America, but she'd never had a response. Until, at last, somehow, a letter had bypassed the eagle eye of the Mother Superior. Sister Louise had been quick to write back, eager to help and fearful for Cecelia, who was wasting away. She'd given her the address of a girl who lived nearby whom she'd once helped and whom she visited regularly as part of her work in the community to use for future correspondence.

It's only a matter of time now, Cecelia. I have a middleman in New York who's arranging the paperwork you and Nessa will need to gain entry to America. A money order has been sent to Sister Louise, who will arrange your train tickets to Cobh and the sailing through a Dublin shipping agent from Cobh to New

York. You'll be given sufficient funds to get the train to Savannah upon your arrival to America, where I'll be waiting for you. Hold tight, dear friend. I promise it won't be long until we're reunited and you and Nessa are safe.

Cecelia hugged the letter to her chest. It felt like a third miracle.

39

The letter from Maudie was tucked away in amongst the straw
filling of her mattress. Cecelia was unable to bring herself to
toss it on the turf range in the kitchen when no one was looking,
and although she didn't dare retrieve it and read it again, just
knowing it was there reassured her that her torment at St
Patrick's would end soon.

Maudie's words had brushed aside the uncertainty of what
lay ahead for her and Nessa, and Tomas, as she'd known would
be the case, hadn't let her down. He'd come back to St Patrick's,
and this time Sister Louise had been on duty. A plan had then
been put in place, whispered to Cecelia in passing in the
corridor by the nun.

Once things were in place at Maudie's end, and Sister
Louise had everything Cecelia and Nessa would need to get far
away from Ireland to hand, she would get word to Tomas. The
timing of it all had to coincide with the White Star Line's
weekly sailings from Cobh to New York. Tomas would fetch
her and take her back to Foxbourne to collect Nessa then drive
through the night to Cobh. He'd asked the nun to convey that
Cecelia's little girl was well and had a keen interest in the

stables, just like her mammy. That had made Cecelia smile even as she'd tasted salt on her lips.

Together, she and Nessa would start a new life in America! The thought of a fresh beginning free from the prickles of her thorny past was tangible now. She could feel it, taste it, and oh how she'd embrace each day under those big skies she'd heard about. At night, she dreamed of Savannah, and in her slumber, the streets were paved with gold.

The shout of joy permanently bubbling in her throat during the day as she imagined how it would feel to run out those gates to meet Tomas and hold her daughter in her arms once more was only tempered by the haunted faces of the girls she was surrounded by. Girls who would never be as fortunate as she was. She vowed to always remember them and their babies in her prayers.

God singled Cecelia out once more when Sister Louise pulled her to one side. The other girls were trailing from chapel to begin their daily chores, but not one of them raised their heads, knowing it didn't do to poke your nose into the nuns' business.

'Margaret, you're to come with me.' Sister Louise spoke in a voice designed to carry and suggest a reprimand was headed her way.

Margaret. The name echoed in Cecelia's ears as she hurried after Sister Louise, who was setting a quick, foxtrot-like pace at odds with her usual lumber. Soon, she'd never have to answer to that name again.

Hitching up her habit so her chunky ankles were on show and with her rosary beads clicking, the nun climbed the stairs. Cecelia did her best to keep up, but lately her leg had been plaguing her.

'Margaret needs to be shown how to make a bed properly. Can you imagine after all this time?' Sister Louise said to a novice nun Cecelia hadn't seen before as she brushed past them, head bowed shyly.

The dormitory was deserted. Cecelia closed the door behind them and steepled her hands to her chin. 'Tell me.'

The nun's eyes danced, and her voice was giddy. 'Everything is in order. In two nights' time, I'm on night duty, and when it's safe for you to do so, you're to make your way to the office. I'll give you money, tickets, a passport, everything you'll need then. Your man Tomas will be waiting outside the gates for you. It'll be tight getting to Foxbourne then on to Cobh for the ship the next morning, but you can't afford to linger. I'm afraid once your mother realises you've taken the child, she'll send the Gardai after you. You must get on that ship.'

Cecelia's shoulders slumped, and she fell on the nun, sobbing with relief. 'Thank God, thank you. You're the kindest woman I've ever known, Sister. I won't forget you or the other girls.'

Seeing the nun's wistful smile and the way her eyes were tinged with sadness, she added, 'I wish things had been different for you and your baby, Sister Louise.'

'God bless you, child.'

There was no time for lingering goodbyes, and two nights later, as planned, Cecelia made her way undetected down to the office where Sister Louise was waiting. She'd retrieved the suitcase Sister Agnes had raided, and it waited for her on the desk. She swiftly discarded her nightgown and changed into the clothes she'd arrived at St Patrick's in, pulling her coat on overtop. She put her boots on and swiftly laced them up, not having time to think about how strange they felt on her feet. Then she pressed the latches on her case shut, picked it up and followed Sister Louise to the main door, which was unlocked.

Cecelia embraced the sister fiercely, looking over her

shoulder to the night outside. It was so still it was as if the air was holding its breath.

'I'll never forget you,' she whispered to the nun who, along with Maudie and Tomas, had saved her.

Sister Louise gave her a gentle push out the door. 'Go now, child – make a new life for yourself and your daughter. Don't look back, and be happy.'

Cecelia heard the door close behind her as she began to run over the crushed stones. She let herself out of the gate and spotted the outline of a waiting car on the quiet street. She hurried toward it and didn't once look back.

40

———

'CeeCee!'

Cecelia felt the nickname like an embrace as she reached the car Tomas was pacing alongside anxiously. He rushed toward her, and she fell into a clumsy hug, relief mingling with disbelief as she felt the solid strength of him. His scent was one she'd almost forgotten – wool and the mix of leather, hay and horses from the stables. She gulped it in because it had always had the power to make her feel everything would be all right. Still, she couldn't stop the sobs escaping.

'It's all right. You're safe now.'

'I'm so sorry for it all, Tomas.'

'None of that matters now. It's ancient history.' His breath was a gentle breeze ruffling her hair, but then he was pushing her away and urging her to get into the car. 'We can't afford to hang about here.'

Cecelia was eager to get away and did as she was told. Tomas cranked the handle then jumped in alongside her as the engine spluttered into life, and she drank in his profile. He hadn't changed – unlike herself. She was aware of her pasty skin, short hair and musty clothes, but most of all she knew it was what Tomas couldn't see that had changed. The scar from the night Sister Agnes had hit her with the rosary beads was a silver sliver on her face, having faded over time, but the scars she carried internally were still livid, and she could only hope they'd fade with time too.

There would be time for healing, she told herself, but not just yet. First, there were hurdles to overcome, and she didn't speak for fear of jinxing her escape.

Tomas seemingly understood her need for silence as the enormity of finally being free of St Patrick's sank in. The smell of the placed lingered in her hair and clothes, however – a reminder to be vigilant.

Cecelia only allowed herself to accept the nuns hadn't sent the Gardai after her once they were on the road to Rush. Their car's lights were the only ones steadily cutting through the darkness, with no other signs of life, not even a pony and trap given the time of night. With every turn of the wheels and passing mile drawing them further away from St Patrick's and closer to Foxbourne, her shoulders loosened, but her hands still clutched the seat.

Tomas, sensing her change in demeanour, cleared his throat. 'Your little Vanessa – she's all right, CeeCee. Grainne's been looking after her. She's a sombre little dote, never makes a sound, but I suppose that's understandable. The rest of the family, your mother included, has barely had a thing to do with her since Lady Kildurran collected her.'

He added so quietly that Cecelia barely heard him, 'That nearly broke me seeing you there.'

She could only think of Nessa now, though, and while it was a small mercy that Grainne, who didn't have a nasty bone in her, was caring for her, white-hot darts of jealousy still shot through Cecelia over the kitchen maid spending time that should have been hers with her daughter. She wasn't being fair, she told herself. Grainne was only doing as she was told. Nessa was unharmed and being looked after, and that was all that mattered.

'I call her Nessa,' she murmured.

'Nessa. I like that.'

Cecelia could hear the smile in his voice.

'Grainne brings Nessa to the stables sometimes, and she reminds me of you because it's the only time she becomes animated. Her eyes shine, and she claps when she sees the horse.'

Horse. Once there'd been many, then Camelot and Raven. The singular use of the word was a short, sharp reminder of why she'd turned against her father.

Put that behind you, Cecelia. It's the past.

Instead she smiled, recalling that Sister Louise had relayed this same snippet of information after Tomas had come to St Patrick's a second time. It had lifted her spirits. She swept feelings of resentment and hatred away – there was no longer room for those in her life – and pictured Nessa's delight over venturing into the stables where she'd always felt more at home than in the echoing rooms of Foxbourne.

'And what news of Lizzie?' She was almost afraid to hear the answer, hoping her friend wasn't trapped in a loveless marriage.

'Ah sure, Lizzie's grand. Worried about you, of course, especially because the rumours are flying about the little girl who's been brought to live at Foxbourne and your whereabouts. I've not told her about any of this.'

Cecelia knew he meant their plans to fetch Nessa and for Tomas to drive her to Cobh.

'The less people who know, the better. There'll be time for that when you're safely out to sea. Not that Lizzie would intentionally let what we were planning slip, but, well, wives and husbands do talk to one another, and it was too big of a risk.'

So it was as she'd feared. Lizzie was married to Seamus

Foley. Cecelia felt a surge of pity for her friend because she'd never know the sort of fierce passion that had flared briefly in her for Finian. They were feelings every woman should have the chance to experience once in her life, she thought, because despite everything, she wouldn't change what had happened between them. If she did, then she'd not have Nessa.

'He's a good man, Joe O'Carroll. Lizzie's made a good match, and she's a little boy who's the apple of his granny's eye. Mrs Murphy's a new lease of life since her grandson's arrival. It's good to see.'

Cecelia shook her head. 'Lizzie's mam had Seamus Foley in her sights as a match.'

The sideways glance Tomas flicked her was one of surprise as he shook his head. 'Sure, not at all. Seamus Foley is sweet on Grainne, and Grainne him. It won't be long before they announce they're getting wed.'

Each to their own, Cecelia thought, recalling Lizzie's remark about the man having a face that could chase rats from a barn with a smile. It gladdened her to know Lizzie had a child herself and was happy in her marriage. She deserved the very best sort of life. Then the smile faded because given everything Tomas was risking for her, after the way she'd treated him, she owed him an explanation as to how it had come to this. She licked her lips. They were dry at the thought of speaking up, but she knew she'd no choice but to get on with it.

'How much do you know, Tomas?'

He understood her meaning. 'Only what Beatrice told me. Lizzie was tight-lipped as to why she helped you run away from your family in London. She wouldn't speak of it or tell me where you were.'

God bless you, Lizzie, Cecelia said silently.

'Beatrice said you ran because you were expecting Finian's baby and somehow you wound up in that place.' A shudder ripped through him.

It was no surprise Beatrice had been the one to relay part of her sister's story. She'd have been in her applecart over the scandalous drama of her unwed sister being with child. Not just that but over who the father was. An Irish rebel no less.

'There's more to it than that.'

'I thought as much.' His expression was inscrutable as he focused on the road ahead and Cecelia laid it all bare. She skipped over nothing, and when she'd finished, she said, 'I did what I did for Ireland, but mostly it was for Finian, and if you no longer want to help me given what you know now, then I'll understand. I'm a bad person, Tomas. I've spied and I've blackmailed, but I'm also a mother, and if you ask me to get out of this car, here on the side of the road, it won't stop me. I'll still get Nessa back.'

'Hey now, calm down. I don't doubt it for a moment.' Tomas's fingers were gripping the steering wheel tightly. 'And do you still love him, Finian Fahy?'

This gave her pause, and Cecelia dug deep inside herself, examining her feelings for the man who was the father of her child.

'The truth is, I don't think I ever loved him. I've come to understand love is shown through one's actions, not just one's words. It was the danger Finian represented, the excitement, attention and chance to escape he gave me that I craved. Losing Camelot pushed me over the edge. I'd always felt in my family's eyes that I was less than them somehow, broken maybe, because of my limp, but he made me feel whole. I was a fool for him, but I can't ever regret that foolishness because now I have Nessa. So no, Tomas, I don't love him.'

'Then that's enough for me. You weren't a fool, Cecelia, and you're not bad a person. You're human.'

He held the car steady with one hand and reached for Cecelia's with the other.

She took it.

41

―――――

Tomas still had hold of her hand as they bumped along the lane leading to Foxbourne. The last time Cecelia had made this journey in the middle of the night had been with Finian after that fateful meeting in the barn. That journey had been the beginning of all that was to follow.

Tomas released her hand and steered the car off to the side of the lane, almost scraping the side of Lord Kildurran's precious motor along the hedgerow, and Cecelia peered out into the darkness. Just like that night, she would need to be furtive and keep her wits about her if she was to make it back to the car with Nessa. A ribbon of anxiety rippled through her, and she looked to Tomas for guidance.

'The gate's unlocked. I rolled the car partway down the drive earlier so as not to risk waking anyone.' He switched the headlights off. 'I think it's best you go alone from here, and I'll keep watch over the car in case anyone happens along.'

'What will you say if they do?' She wanted him to come with her because she was frightened now they were here, terrified of Foxbourne's inhabitants and what they would do if she were caught.

'I'll think of something. I'd go myself, but Nessa might not take kindly to my waking her in the dead of night, and if anyone does pass by, it will be easier for me to come up with a plausible story than you.'

He was right, and Cecelia steeled herself for what lay ahead, taking the spare set of house keys he was entrusted with.

'Go. Time isn't on our side. It'll take us the best part of the rest of the night to reach Cobh.'

He got out so she could climb over the driver's seat, and as she slipped through the gates, she heard a match striking flint as he lit a cigarette to ease his restless wait.

Cecelia cleared her mind, willing herself to stay calm as she focused on Foxbourne's foreboding dark outline. A three-quarter moon gave off an eerie glow to see by, and she didn't allow her aching leg to slow her, intent on her purpose.

She let herself in through the main doors silently and crept through the house as practised as any burglar, finding it unchanged in her absence save for a cloying scent of decay. Or perhaps that was her imagination.

The stairs proved a challenge but one she'd overcome before, though she winced when a protesting creak sounded beneath her foot. She waited like a bird with its head cocked poised for flight. The house continued to slumber, and satisfied it was safe to do so, she carried on.

Her heart stopped, overcome at the sight of Nessa asleep in the cot each of the Altringham children had once occupied in the nursery. Her black curls covered half her face, and she was curled into a ball, her fists clenched under her chin. Cecelia's chest constricted. Had she cried herself to sleep each night in the nursery, having never been on her own from the moment she was born? How alone she must have felt in this cavernous space. The tears that welled at what her daughter had gone through were swiped away, and she swooped her up into her arms.

The little girl startled awake with whimper.

'It's me, Nessa,' she whispered, holding the little girl close.

She must have recognised her mother's smell because her matchstick arms coiled around Cecelia's neck. A tsunami of emotion washed over her, but she couldn't afford to luxuriate in the moment.

'We're leaving now, Nessa. I've come to take you to our new home.'

She picked up a blanket and wrapped it around Nessa and then plucked her way back through the darkened house.

42

Cecelia kept checking over her shoulder to ensure Nessa was still there lying on the back seat, covered with blankets and sound asleep. She'd taken their moonlit flit in her stride, drifting back to sleep within minutes of them getting on the road.

'She's not going anywhere, CeeCee,' Tomas said, steering them round a bend.

Cecelia turned back in time to see a shape blocking the road ahead of them. 'What's that?' she asked, trying to keep her alarm at bay as she squinted into the distance, trying to make out what it was.

'I'm fairly sure it's a car,' Tomas replied, slowing but not stopping. 'Perhaps a checkpoint.'

'For what?'

'I don't know.'

His voice was calm, but Cecelia was anything but. She hadn't come this far to be stopped now. Something was wrong. She could feel it even as the voice of reason told her that her mother wasn't behind whatever this was because she wouldn't even know Nessa was gone yet. Word couldn't have reached her that she'd run from St Patrick's either. Still, a car parked in the middle of the road in the small hours did not bode well, and her palms grew sweaty as they crawled closer.

Her pulse began to skitter as a man got out of the car. He moved to stand in the full glare of their approaching headlights, his hand shielding his eyes from the light. He wasn't a Guard, she could see that much, so who was he, and what did he want with them?

'Tomas?' Cecelia's voice was thick with fear, and she twisted round in her seat once more, needing reassurance, but Nessa hadn't moved in the seconds since she'd last checked on her. If she had to, she'd snatch her up and run, taking her chances in the fields on either side of them.

Tomas had no choice but to brake and stop. And then as the man was bathed in the yellowy haze of their car lights, Cecelia gave a startled cry of recognition.

'It can't be!'

'Leave this with me to sort,' Tomas growled, half out the door already.

'No.' Cecelia laid her hand on his forearm. 'It's me he wants to talk to. Keep Nessa safe no matter what. Promise me, Tomas.'

He nodded, but she could see his reluctance to let her go in his deep frown. 'I'll be all right.'

She got out of the car leaving the door open as she approached him. He was thinner, more weathered, his hair cropped shorter, but it was him.

'Finian, what are you doing here? You're supposed to be in America.'

'Well, hello to you too, Cecelia. I must say I'd hoped for a warmer greeting than that after all that we were to one another, and unless I'm confused, I'm very much here in Ireland.'

'I don't understand.' She shook her head, trying to make sense of the impossible. 'Why are you here like this now? What do you want?' She wouldn't play games. It was pointless because he was too smart for that.

'You've my child in that car, Cecelia. You didn't think I'd let you take her away from her homeland now, did you? The homeland I've been fighting for all my life.'

A cold chill coursed through her. He meant to take Nessa. But how had he come to be here on this lonely stretch of road in the dead of night?

'You're wondering how I knew where to find youse?'

She wouldn't give him the satisfaction of saying she was because what did it matter? He was here now, and Hogan's words rang sharply in her ears. *You don't get to decide when to leave the army.*

'I know everything. I always have. I've eyes and ears everywhere, even in that godforsaken home you've spent the last few years hiding in.'

'Then why didn't you help me? Help my daughter for God's sake.' She would not say 'our' daughter and give him further ammunition. 'You must have known it was a hellhole.'

She already knew the answer.

'Ireland needed me. She still does.'

'You can have Ireland, but you'll not have my child.' She recognised any feelings she'd had for this man with the mad glint in his eyes for his country had long since died.

He was holding something out like a white flag, she realised. It was a letter.

'I'd have thought you smarter than to keep it, but you didn't burn it, did you? No, you tucked it away inside your mattress.'

Her mind recoiled as understanding dawned as to what she was looking at. It was Maudie's letter.

'It wasn't hard to come by. The promise of a few extra comforts and a word in the right ears was all it took. Everybody can be bought, Cecelia.'

'So you knew I was leaving tonight?' She was buying time, but time for what she didn't know because the situation was not going to change. She knew Finian well enough to know he would not back down from taking what he thought was rightly his.

'Yes, and I knew exactly where you'd go. It was easier to wait and let you bring the child to me than take her from Foxbourne myself.'

'Well, know this, Finian Fahy. I'll not be going with you, and neither will my daughter.'

His eyes glittered and his shadowed face was menacing as he advanced on her. 'Our daughter's Irish, Cecelia, and Ireland is where she'll stay. As for you, you can do what you like.'

Cecelia took a step backward, stumbling as he continued to bear down on her.

'Get back in your car and drive away now, Finian. I'm warning you. I will shoot.' Tomas stepped into the light, holding a rifle cocked, and aimed directly at Finian.

Cecelia seized the opportunity to run back to the car. She was just reaching for the back door, intending to grab Nessa, when a shot rang out, freezing her in time and place. It took a second for her to process what had happened, and when she moved around the car to where Tomas was standing, she found his hands still clutching the smoking rifle. Then her eyes tracked to where Finian lay unmoving in the road.

'I'd no choice, Cecelia. I gave him fair warning.' Tomas's jaw was set as he put the rifle back under the seat of the car.

She watched numbly as he went to Finian, reached around under his arms and hauled him up into the back of his car before he started it and steered it off the road. She stared, unable to tear her eyes away, as he took a bottle of spirits he'd found in the car, splashed them about and then lit the car on fire. It was to be Finian's funeral pyre.

'Come on. We have to go,' he urged as their own car rumbled into life and overtop of the engine she heard Nessa's cries.

She forced herself from her inertia and clambered in alongside Tomas. As he sped off, she reached into the back to soothe her daughter – woken no doubt by the rifle's rapport – back to sleep. Only when her thumb had found its way to her mouth and her breath was steady did Cecelia allow herself to think.

Tomas had shot a man.

She straightened, not saying anything, but Tomas broke the silence.

'I did it for you, and for her,' he said gruffly.

'I know.'

And this time it was Cecelia who reached for his hand.

43

Nessa was covered in pie-crust crumbs, with gravy from the steak-and-kidney filling smeared around her mouth. Tomas had had the foresight to pilfer Mrs Nolan's freshly baked pie from the larder in Foxbourne's kitchen earlier, and they'd all tucked in. It had served as a late breakfast, and Cecelia'd had to stop herself from gorging on the delicious meal, aware her stomach was unused to rich food after the blandness and inadequate portions at St Patrick's. She was relieved her little girl had woken seemingly unfazed to find herself in the back of a car or by the night's dramatic events. Then again, why would she be? Cecelia thought, given she'd already been snatched from St Patrick's, the only home she'd known, even if it was a miserable one, by her grandmother. She was likely used to the ground shifting beneath her, but Cecelia vowed when they got to America, she would provide a stable home for her.

They'd been on the road for the best part of ten hours with few stops, and her limbs were stiff. Poor Tomas's hands would be cramping too, she thought, throwing him a sympathetic glance. His finger drummed the wheel, gingery stubble had appeared on his jawline and his bloodshot eyes were focused on the road ahead. The height of the murky sun in the sky suggested it was past midday as they sped past a sign barely visible amongst the roadside greenery.

'We're nearly there, CeeCee.'

She squeezed his hand by way of reply.

Soon, through bleary eyes, Cecelia caught sight of the spires of a cathedral with seagulls soaring overhead. Cobh! They'd made it. She rubbed her eyes, chasing the cobwebs away in time to glimpse the White Star liner anchored in the calm harbour below them. Her and Nessa's ticket to freedom.

'There's our ship, Nessa!'

Nessa said nothing but clapped, having picked up on Cecelia's excitement, making her and Tomas smile.

'We made it, Tomas.' Though Cecelia knew she wouldn't breathe easy until the ship was out to sea and Ireland's shores were no longer visible. Only then would she stop looking over her shoulder, expecting to see her mother's cold glare.

'We did.'

They exchanged a glance that needed no words. In a little while, she'd be boarding that ship with her daughter. But time had an uncanny ability of crawling when you wanted it to speed by.

Sit tight, Cecelia; you're almost there.

It wasn't just herself and Nessa's imminent departure being thwarted at the last minute she was fretting over, however, and she voiced her new fear.

'What will you do, Tomas? You can't stay in Ireland, not now. My mother won't forget, and she certainly won't forgive you for helping me. Father will set the Gardai on to you for stealing the car. You know he will.' She didn't want to think about Finian and the possibility of his murder and fiery end being tied to Tomas as well. He'd hang for it if he were caught.

'You're not to worry about me. Sure, I'm like a cat with nine lives, so I am. I'll be grand. It's high time I made a fresh start somewhere else, and this is just the push I needed. Change is as good as a holiday – isn't that what they say?'

He was putting a jovial spin on his dire situation for her benefit, but she wouldn't be cheered and said nothing, looking out the window as the car began to putter down Cobh's steep, narrow streets. Tomas veered over to the side of the road which was lined with shops, pubs and boarding houses, the pavement teeming with colourful life. Then he reached into the breast pocket of his coat and thrust a handful of notes at Cecelia.

'Here, take this and get some things for Nessa. Sure, you can't be carting her on board that ship in her nightgown now, can you? Get what you need for yourself too. There's a sign for a draper's just a short way down there and a grocer's shop across the way for a few provisions.'

Cecelia looked toward the draper's. It was a valid point and one she'd been too tired to think of. She wasn't so tired, though, that she'd take even more from him than she already had, and she reached into the back for her case.

'I've money. Put yours away. I can never repay you as it is, Tomas.'

'I don't want repayment – that's not why I'm helping you. Save what you have, CeeCee. You'll need it when you reach America. Here – please take it. For me.'

Cecelia didn't argue further. Instead, she reached for the handle and turned to Nessa. 'I'll be back quick as a flash. Tomas will look after you.'

Her reward was her daughter's waving bye-bye.

'Don't take too long, CeeCee. That ship won't wait for you,' Tomas called after her.

Cecelia hurried away from the car, feeling exposed as she pushed past a cluster of sailors whom she could smell were already worse for wear. The local folk continued to go about their business around her as she hurried toward the draper's, with no one paying her much heed. This surprised her because she felt like her time at St Patrick's must have branded her.

When she pushed open the door of the shop, she was over-whelmed by the amount of clothes and fabrics on display. To stand inside a shop like so with money in her pocket belonged to another life.

'Good morning, Miss. May I help you?'

'Yes,' Cecelia said gratefully. 'I'm in need of clothes suitable for travelling for my niece – she's two but small for her age – and a few things for myself too.'

'Of course, Miss.'

Cecelia kept her word, relieved to see the car where she'd left it. She tossed the bags into the back, clambered in and soon had Nessa dressed in her new clothes.

'There. Don't you look a picture?' At least she would when she had the chance to wash her face, Cecelia thought. It was a peculiar thing, but she looked forward to the day her daughter wasn't compliant and was confident enough to shriek and cry like the tot she'd seen in the grocer's shop denied sweets. The little one had thrown herself on the ground in protest, much to her mother's embarrassment.

Nessa merely stared solemnly at her with those big, dark eyes of hers and did as she asked, although Cecelia's heart lifted when she sat next to Tomas once more and heard a baby voice exclaim, 'Gee-gee!'

A pony and trap rattled past. It was music to Cecelia's ears. It was the first time she'd heard her daughter speak, and her throat became claggy with emotion.

'Did you hear that?' She looked to Tomas, who was smiling.

'I told you she takes after you.' Tomas grinned blearily then got out to crank the engine.

The last leg of their journey, more fraught than she and

Tomas could ever have imagined, led them down the rest of the hill to the docks at the bottom. The quayside was thronging and made for a vibrant scene. Porters and sailors – Cecelia couldn't discern which – shouted to one another. There were stalls selling souvenirs and last-minute supplies people might need for their journey. Hawkers with food and sweets for sale mingled with priests offering blessings to those leaving Ireland's shores that day. Fleetingly, Cecelia thought of Father Brophy and her hasty conversion to his faith. She watched as mothers kept a close eye on their overexcited charges while fathers strode ahead, laden down like packhorses. There was a sense of sadness and excitement, of goodbyes and new beginnings on the dockside breeze as tenders loaded passengers to ferry them out to the waiting ship.

'This is where I'll leave you,' Tomas said, finding a spot to pull in.

Soon, Cecelia was standing with Nessa on her hip and her case in her hand, feeling the rush of people passing by them. She was torn. She didn't want to merge into the crowds and leave Tomas to whatever fate had in store for him.

'Stow away on the ship. Come with us, Tomas. Please.'

His smile was wistful and his eyes cloudy with emotion. 'Ah c'mon now, CeeCee. Sure, you know yourself what would happen if I were to do that. I'd be detained as soon as I tried to disembark in New York and sent straight back to Ireland. I'll figure something out. But you're not to be worrying your head about me now, do you hear me? Look forward with that girl of yours, all right?'

She didn't answer.

'CeeCee, you've Nessa to think about.'

'I hear you.'

He pulled her and Nessa to him and hugged them hard before pushing Cecelia gently into the tide of people. 'Go now and keep yourself to yourself until you reach America.'

He turned away but not before she'd seen him swallowing hard.

She moved in to join the wave of people leaving their homeland today, turning back as Tomas called her name. Had he changed his mind? Would he come with her? Her heart leaped.

He was standing cap in hand as he shouted through the midden, 'If I don't tell you this now, CeeCee, I might never get another chance to. I love you, girl. I always have.'

Then she lost sight of his face in the milling mob.

44

———

There had been a gut-wrenching moment when Cecelia had thought the game was up before she'd even been given her boarding passes for the ship. The clerk at the shipping office, which she'd made her way to after leaving Tomas, had looked up from the pile of documents she'd pushed toward him, eyeing her and then Nessa for a beat too long. Her stomach had plummeted all the way down to her boots. She'd been certain she was about to be pulled aside for questioning, and that either Maudie's documents or her silently rehearsed story would not stand up to closer inspection.

What if Mother got word to the authorities to keep a lookout for a young woman attempting to leave the country with a small child.

A cold sweat had broken out along her hairline and under her arms, but then to her relief, the clerk had picked up his stamp and banged it down on the necessary documents before pushing the passes toward her, his bored eyes already looking past her to the next passenger.

Now, she was curled up on the thin horsehair mattress

while Nessa sat behind her, playing with her mother's hair and watching the goings-on around them.

Her first impression of the steerage-class quarters the steward had directed her to was that they weren't dissimilar to the dormitory at St Patrick's. Just as the dormitory had been, this room, too, was stuffy, overcrowded and offered no privacy. Unlike at St Patrick's, however, men, women and children bunked in together.

How far she'd come, she thought fleetingly, remembering the girl who would once have travelled first class and who'd have been aghast at finding herself below decks like so. She was a different person now; motherhood had changed her and made her not just strong but whole.

The metal bunks were stacked three deep, and she and Nessa had walked in on a mad scramble to lay claim to them. Recalling her journey by boat from England to Ireland, Cecelia hadn't hesitated in swinging her bag up on a top bunk against the wall. There was a vent above where her head would lie that would let in fresh air should the seas get rough. She prayed this wouldn't be the case though, not knowing how she'd look after Nessa if she became sick as a dog, like she'd been on the Irish sea crossing.

Below her, families with overwrought children were sorting themselves out and deciding who'd sleep where. The din was cacophonous, with one child's wails particularly ear-splitting. But they were all here in the same boat, so to speak, and would surely look out for one another if need be. Though hopefully they were in for a calm crossing to America and it wouldn't come to that.

She remembered Tomas's words then. *Keep yourself to yourself.* He was right, she thought, the memory of Molly and what the lure of a reward had made her do still raw.

She'd lie here for just a minute longer and then go and wave farewell to Ireland with the rest of the ship on the upper deck. It was hard to comprehend that she was leaving the country she'd felt such a fiery love for, but the price she'd had to pay for that love had been too high, and her feelings for the Emerald Isle were now clouded.

Her eyes had drooped shut, but her mind was too busy for dozing, replaying the sound of last night's gunshot. She wondered if she'd ever rid herself of the sight of Finian's crumpled body. She'd made a murderer of Tomas. Kind gentle, Tomas who'd said he loved her. In that moment, she'd felt as though she were seeing him for the first time. It was as if she'd only just found him, and now she'd lost him.

Nessa tugged her hair, and Cecelia rolled over, reaching up to stroke her pale face. 'In ten days we'll be in America, Nessa. Imagine that.'

For the first time, Cecelia saw her daughter smile, and it was beautiful.

Cecelia did her best to keep a low profile throughout the sailing, but Nessa, well, she was another story. Within days of being at sea, the fresh salt-laden air had begun working wonders. It had put roses in her cheeks, while the three square meals in the dining room filled her belly. She was cradled at night and slipped off to sleep hearing her mother say, 'I love you.'

A sweet, shy smile had replaced her solemn frown, and with her halo of black curls, other passengers cooed and doted on her. It made Cecelia proud, but still she kept herself at a distance. The sea was mercifully calm and the weather clear during the day, and she didn't mind the nights as the ship swayed and groaned, while people grunted, passed wind and did all manner of things around them. The feel of her daughter's warm body curled into hers, a perfect fit, was enough. It would always be enough.

Each day at sea passed much the same at the last, and on the

tenth day, Cecelia was spotting seagulls with Nessa when a cry
went up.

'There she is – the Lady! The Lady!'

Cecelia held Nessa tightly in her arms against the crush of
people surging toward the railings and found a position in
amongst the throng. She craned her neck for her first glimpse at
the country that was to be hers and Nessa's home, her eyes
locking on the Statue of Liberty, tall and true, her torch held
high and lighting the way to freedom.

'God bless America,' another voice shouted out.

'God bless America, Nessa,' Cecelia echoed. 'We're here.'

45

───────

Cecelia and Nessa's paperwork stood up to inspection, and to Cecelia's immense relief, they passed the rigorous health examinations the immigration officials demanded. Cecelia had expected to feel jubilant as they disembarked from the tender at the Battery and she put her feet down on American soil properly, but instead she was wary, mindful of thieves thinking her an easy target travelling alone with a child. She kept a tight hold of her case and Nessa, and wasted no time finding a taxi to take them to Penn Station, where they'd board the train headed south.

For Cecelia, this last leg of their journey was one of wonder. As she sank back into the maroon upholstery of their compartment, she admired both the modern buildings and untamed beauty that unravelled beyond the window. There was also sadness at the loss of Finian. Once, she had believed herself in love with him, and he was, after all, her daughter's father. She'd come to understand that his fate had always been bound to violence. If not at Tomas's hand, then at another's. And Finian – she knew – would have chosen that end over a prison cell. Her thoughts strayed constantly to Tomas, praying he'd made it to a place of safety, wherever that might be. She'd been vigilant on the ship and was equally so on the train, but when the train finally chugged into Savannah's Union Station, the knots in her shoulders untied themselves and she finally felt safe.

Soon, they were in the milling crowd on the concourse with its marble floors and arched windows. Cecelia scanned the wooden seats for a glimpse of Maudie as people rose from them, waving or calling out to her fellow passengers. Already, a cloying heat was causing her hair to stick to her face, and she could taste coal smoke in the back of her throat. Porters in crisp uniforms were hurrying past, and a whistle sounded. A ship's foghorn sounded too, and although she didn't know much about Savannah, where she was to live, she did know it was a port city. That at least was familiar.

Then, pushing her way through the crowd, Cecelia glimpsed an elegantly dressed young woman who had a firm hold of a plump, sweetly pretty toddler. She looked away, and then her gaze travelled back. It couldn't be, could it?

Maudie and Emer were frozen in Cecelia's memory as they had been when last she'd seen them at St Patrick's. This woman looked so different, and Emer – *Juniper* she reminded herself – had been a small baby when she'd last seen her.

'Cecelia! Nessa!' The woman had seen her and was waving frantically while tugging the tot determinedly alongside her.

It was her. It was Maudie!

Cecelia set Nessa down as Maudie swooped, and they fell laughing into each other's arms.

'I don't believe it! I don't believe it!' Maudie was stuck on repeat before finally adding, 'You're here. It's really you. You made it.'

Cecelia burst into tears, overcome with emotion and exhaustion. When they took a step back from one another, examining each other's faces as if to make sure this was really happening, Maudie's eyes were brimming too.

Then they spoke overtop of one another. 'I've so much to tell you.' Which brought about a fresh round of laughter.

Cecelia was aware of Nessa peeping out from behind her skirt, and her attention flitted to Juniper, who was taking in the reunion between her mother and her friend with enormous blue eyes. She watched as Juniper reached up and tugged at her mother's hand.

'Oh yes, good girl for reminding me, Junebug,' Maudie said, rummaging in the bag she was carrying. 'I almost forgot. You've a gift you want to give Nessa.' She passed a wrapped rectangular-shaped box down to her daughter, who advanced confidently on Nessa and held it out to her with a smile.

Nessa didn't move, and Cecelia said, 'It's all right, Nessa. You can take it. It's for you.'

The little girl took the gift shyly and held it close to her as if frightened it would be snatched back. Maudie's mouth formed an 'O' of understanding before she said quietly, 'She doesn't realise she's to take the paper off. Juniper, won't you help Nessa open the present?'

Juniper didn't need any encouragement. 'I help.' She tore a corner of the pretty pink paper off, much to Nessa's shock. 'You.' She grinned at Nessa, who was still uncertain but eager to please so tore a little more.

Then Juniper ripped more of the paper, and this time Nessa flashed her sweet smile then pulled the rest of it off before showing it to her mother. Cecelia's eyes widened upon seeing a beautiful porcelain-faced doll in a box.

'Juniper picked it herself.'

Nessa looked from the doll to her mother.

'She's yours, Nessa.'

A lump formed in Cecelia's throat. This was the first present her child had ever received. The lump grew bigger, and she couldn't speak as she watched Juniper holding her hand out to Nessa. To her surprise and utter joy, Nessa passed the doll to her mother for safekeeping and clasped Juniper's offer of friendship.

Maudie smiled at the tableau and linked her arm through Cecelia's. 'Those two will be firm friends in no time. Now come on with you – let's get you home out of this heat. They say you get used to it, but you don't,' she chattered on brightly. 'You look like you could do with a nice, cool glass of iced tea and a slice of Winnie's Lane cake.'

'Iced tea?' Cecelia stared at her friend aghast as she led her through the station, the little girls a step ahead.

'Oh, I think you'll love it.' Maudie's laughter tinkled. 'I'll make a Southerner out of you in no time, just you wait, Cecelia Altringham.'

Together, the foursome walked out of the station and into the sunlight.

46

DUBLIN, IRELAND, 1985

It was just a building, and the ghosts were long gone. Cecelia had finally understood this as she stood alongside Maudie at the entrance to the now derelict mother and baby home. Juniper and Nessa had left them to wander the grounds. The friends, thick as thieves for most of their lives, had been rendered silent for once by the hushed, solemn atmosphere shrouding the institution where they'd been born.

Cecelia and Maudie didn't speak either. They didn't need to. They'd lived with what had happened here for most of their lives, and it was time to let it go. The monster this place had lived on as in Cecelia's head was slain. Bricks and mortar couldn't hurt her, and those that had hurt her while she'd been under their care were long gone. Soon, the home that stood here would be erased and shiny new buildings would spring up. That didn't mean it would be forgotten, however. It could never be forgotten, but it no longer held any power over her.

They hadn't stayed long. There wasn't any reason to, and the foursome had said their goodbyes for now. They'd meet up again in a few days. Maudie and Juniper were going to head back to their hotel, declaring themselves done in from the emotions of their day, while Nessa was determined hers and Cecelia's wasn't over just yet. She wanted to see Foxbourne.

'There's nothing to see. The fire would have destroyed most of it,' Cecelia tried to dissuade her, but her daughter was set on seeing the estate her mother had once called home.

Nessa knew the way, having studied the map before they drove away from St Patrick's, and Cecelia soon began to drift off in the passenger seat as they motored down the road.

'Momma, tell me about the day you saw daddy again?'

'Nessa Shanahan, how old are you?' Cecelia's head jerked up. Looking at the scenery whizzing past, she wondered when they'd veered off the main road and into the countryside. Nessa was driving a tad too fast for her liking too.

'A Southern belle never reveals her age – you know that, Momma.'

Cecelia smiled. Her eldest daughter might be in her sixties, her once black curls grey now, but she would always be her little girl, and as such she could still tell her what to do.

'Slow down. You're not used to these country lanes. What if a tractor were to come around that bend up ahead, or we meet a farmer herding his flock?'

'I'll drive like a snail if you tell me the story.'

'I'm too tired to give you the long version.'

'The short version then.' Nessa had already eased her foot off the accelerator.

Cecelia rested her head back against the seat. Truth be told, she never got sick of telling her children about the day Tomas had turned up in Savannah. That had been a colourful day on her patchwork quilt, and she cleared her throat then repeated the tale that had become family folklore.

'Your aunt Maudie had arranged for me to work for Aunt Annie, as we called her, at her boarding house. I was out the back hanging out the guests' laundered sheets six months or so after we first arrived in Savannah, when Aunt Annie ducked her head out the kitchen door and told me I'd a gentleman caller. Well, of course I looked at her like she was mad and told her I didn't know any gentlemen. Aunt Annie replied, "You must do, young lady, because there's one sitting in my kitchen. Not only that, he's sipping lemonade and eating pimento-and-cheese sandwiches."

'There was nothing else for it, so I pegged the last sheet to the line then followed her inside to the kitchen, and there he was. I thought I was dreaming, but it was him, your daddy, my Tomas, sitting at the table enjoying his afternoon refreshments.'

Cecelia closed her eyes briefly, smiling at the memory and remembering how she'd listened with her hands steepled to her lips as he'd told her of his perilous escape from Ireland to England. There he'd found work as an ordinary seaman with the Cunard Line, and had jumped ship in America. And there he was. She could still hear his voice as he'd said, 'I had to find you, CeeCee, because you never replied.'

'To what?' she'd asked.

'To what I called out to you before we parted ways at Cobh.'

'That you love me?'

Tomas had nodded.

'Well, as it happens, I love you, too, Tomas Shanahan.'

Cecelia opened her eyes and relayed Nessa's favourite part. 'I knew right then and there that if he didn't get down on bended knee and ask me to marry him that very minute, I'd have to do the honours.'

'And did you?' Nessa twinkled, already knowing the answer.

'I did. I dropped to one knee, and I said, "Tomas Shanahan, will you do me the honour of becoming my husband."'

'And he said yes.'

'He said yes.'

Nessa knew most of the backstory as to how Tomas had helped Cecelia and herself leave Ireland. She'd always known

Finian was her biological father too. No good would have come from keeping that secret, Cecelia had long ago decided. Things like that had a habit of jumping out of closets and destroying families. Still, in Nessa's eyes, Tomas was the only father she needed. He'd raised her as his own, no different from their other daughters, who'd come in quick succession after they were wed.

There was one secret that was between her and Tomas, however, one she'd never share with another soul. How Finian had died. It was something they'd never revisited through their married life. And Nessa had been told a romanticized version of events whereby Finian was a hero, the passionate Irishman killed fighting for his country's freedom. Cecelia liked to think he would want his daughter to remember him like so.

The landscape was becoming familiar, Cecelia thought, seeing the fields beyond the hedgerows. Then they rounded a bend and there they were. The gates leading to Foxbourne.

'We're here,' she informed Nessa, who slowed nearly to a stop in response.

'Can I drive up?'

The gates were wide open, covered in rust and barely clinging to their hinges as vines from the high hedges – no longer neatly trimmed – tried to swallow them.

'I don't see why not.'

The driveway was rutted and, like the entrance, overgrown. The lawn, which had been lodged in Cecelia's memory as looking like a bowling green, was no longer recognisable. There was no longer a house proudly overseeing the land either. Instead, all that was left were forlorn remains, like a fallen castle. The gardens Cyril had tended were tangled and had run wild. It was no longer the Foxbourne she knew. As for Cyril himself, she could only hope he'd found peace wherever his path had taken him from here.

'It's still beautiful,' Nessa breathed, stopping the car. Her hands remained on the steering wheel as she drank in the ruins of where her mother had been born. 'In a melancholic, mysterious way. Shall we take a walk, Momma?'

'If you like.' Cecelia allowed her daughter to help her from the car, taking her arm and leaning heavily on her as they made their way carefully toward what once had been a grand house.

'The stables were over there,' Cecelia said, fancying she could hear the thunder of Camelot's hooves in her ears.

'The only place you ever felt at home and where you first met daddy.'

Cecelia nodded, her mind thick with the past.

'It's strange to think my father and his men burned this place to the ground.'

'They had their reasons.'

Nessa came to a halt in what had been the kitchen, and Cecelia remembered Grainne and Mrs Nolan with their sleeves rolled up, working alongside one another. She thought of Lizzie too. She was gone now, but tomorrow she and Nessa would visit with her sons and their wives. She'd had a good life by all accounts.

'Thank God nobody was hurt,' Nessa said softly.

Cecelia's thoughts turned to her family, who, along with the staff, had escaped the fire unharmed. Her parents, along with Julian and Bea, had thrown themselves on the mercy of Aunt Octavia and Uncle George. She hadn't kept track of what had happened to them after that, never having cared to find out.

'Momma, can I tell you something?'

Cecelia twisted her head toward Nessa, waiting for her to say what was on her mind.

'Sometimes when I think about Foxbourne, I see flames. It's like I can see it burning. It frightens me.'

'You always had a vivid imagination,' Cecelia said softly.

'I think that's why I needed to come here and see it – well, what's left of it – for myself.'

'And now you have?'

'Now I know there's nothing here for me.'

Cecelia looked at her daughter, and then her eyes roamed over the land where she'd once ridden her beloved horse freely. She thought about what lay behind the trees she could see – the lough, where the faeries played on the banks and where her daughter had likely been conceived.

There was nothing here for her either, she thought, her arm firmly linked through her child's. Her quilt was complete.

EPILOGUE
FOXBOURNE, 1922

Cecelia hoped no one had happened down the lane outside Foxbourne's gates in her absence. It would take some explaining on Tomas's part as to what he was doing with Lord Altringham's motor car at this late hour. Nessa was cradled safely in her arms, and she was about to slip out of the dark, silent house into the night when she stopped shy of the front entrance. Cecelia understood then that she was her mother's daughter after all because, like her, she couldn't forgive, nor would she forget. She'd make sure her mother and the rest of her family never did either.

Her feet took on a life of their own, her limp forgotten as they carried her through to the front room. She paused to place Nessa gently down in the doorway. The room was lit with a thin beam of moonlight, and without hesitation, Cecelia crossed to the drinks table. She unstopped the sherry decanter and was hit by a sweet, alcohol-laden smell. It almost broke the spell, but not quite.

As though sleepwalking, Cecelia moved methodically about the room, splashing the sherry up the drapes, over the furnishings and across the worm-eaten floorboards. Then she fetched the matches from the mantle.

She lit one, the rasp loud in the stillness of the night, and stared at the flame that flickered to life – and then she dropped it at the foot of the drapes.

The tiny trail of fire flared as it caught hold of the drapes then whooshed into life. The fire soon spread. Cecelia could feel its heat as it snaked a path across the floor to creep up the sofa then closer to where she stood, statue-like.

Nessa's cough saw her blink, the sound pulling her from her trance, and she stared about her in disbelief at what she'd done. Then, turning away, Cecelia picked up her daughter and ran, never once looking back.

A LETTER FROM MICHELLE

Dear reader,

I want to say a huge thank you for choosing to read *Secrets at the Irish Adoption House*. If you did enjoy it, and want to keep up to date with all my latest releases, just sign up at the following link. Your email address will never be shared, and you can unsubscribe at any time.

www.bookouture.com/michelle-vernal

Ireland has such a multi-layered history – rich, beautiful but also heartbreaking. For so many of the women who suffered in the mother and baby institutions, their stories were ones without hope. And that's why, when I write, I give my characters – like Maudie and Cecelia – the hope and second chances those real women were too often denied.

I love writing these characters who find an inner strength they didn't know they had from motherhood. But the true heroines will always be the women who lived through those institutions.

Cecelia's story is fictional, but it is written from the heart and with deep compassion and respect for those who suffered in Ireland's mother and baby homes.

I feel so lucky to spend my days wandering the lanes and coastlines of Ireland in my imagination, creating places like Foxbourne and bringing to life characters I hope will feel like old friends by the time you turn the final page. Thank you from the bottom of my heart for giving me the opportunity to do so.

I hope you loved *Secrets at the Irish Adoption House,* and if you did, I would be very grateful if you could write a review. I'd love to hear what you think, and it makes such a difference helping new readers to discover one of my books for the first time.

I love hearing from my readers – you can get in touch on my Facebook page or my website.

Thanks,

Michelle Vernal

www.michellevernalbooks.com

 facebook.com/michellevernalnovelist

ACKNOWLEDGEMENTS

A huge thank you to my brilliant editor, Natalie, for her insight, patience and support in helping me shape *Secrets at the Irish Adoption House* into the very best version of Cecelia's story it could be, one I'm proud to share with my readers.

This business of writing is a solitary one, and it is wonderful to feel part of a team like Bookouture – not just that but a valued member of that team. All of you at Bookouture work tirelessly behind the scenes to ensure a fabulous book package is sent out into the world. A heartfelt thank you to each of you.

It's a privilege to be published by such a vibrant, forward-thinking publisher – and I'm always thrilled to see my stories brought to life under your banner.

And, of course, to Paul – none of this would happen without you.

PUBLISHING TEAM

Turning a manuscript into a book requires the efforts of many people. The publishing team at Bookouture would like to acknowledge everyone who contributed to this publication.

Audio
Alba Proko
Melissa Tran
Sinead O'Connor

Commercial
Lauren Morrissette
Hannah Richmond
Imogen Allport

Cover design
Eileen Carey

Data and analysis
Mark Alder
Mohamed Bussuri

Editorial
Natalie Edwards
Melissa Tran

Copyeditor
Laura Kincaid

Proofreader
Liz Hurst

Marketing
Alex Crow
Melanie Price
Occy Carr
Cíara Rosney
Martyna Młynarska

Operations and distribution
Marina Valles
Stephanie Straub
Joe Morris

Production
Hannah Snetsinger
Mandy Kullar
Nadia Michael
Charlotte Hegley

Publicity
Kim Nash
Noelle Holten
Jess Readett
Sarah Hardy

Rights and contracts
Peta Nightingale
Richard King
Saidah Graham

Dear Reader,

We'd love your attention for one more page to tell you about the crisis in children's reading, and what we can all do.

Studies have shown that reading for fun is the **single biggest predictor of a child's future life chances** – more than family circumstance, parents' educational background or income. It improves academic results, mental health, wealth, communication skills, ambition and happiness.

The number of children reading for fun is in rapid decline. Young people have a lot of competition for their time, and a worryingly high number do not have a single book at home.

Hachette works extensively with schools, libraries and literacy charities, but here are some ways we can all raise more readers:

- Reading to children for just 10 minutes a day makes a difference
- Don't give up if children aren't regular readers – there will be books for them!

- Visit bookshops and libraries to get
  recommendations
- Encourage them to listen to audiobooks
- Support school libraries
- Give books as gifts

There's a lot more information about how to encourage children to read on our websites: **www.RaisingReaders.co.uk** and **www.JoinRaisingReaders.com**.

Thank you for reading.